CULTIVATING SUNSHINE

J.S.R. Smith

Title: Cultivating Sunshine / J.S.R. Smith
Name(s): Smith, Jeremy
ISBN:978-0-9733667-3-0 (hardcover)
ISBN: 978-0-9733667-1-6 (paperback)
ISBN: 978-0-9733667-2-3 (ebook)

Printed and bound in the United States of America

Published by Smelbiney Publishing

This book may be purchased at a reduced cost for educational, business
or sales promotional use by emailing smelbineypublishing@gmail.com.

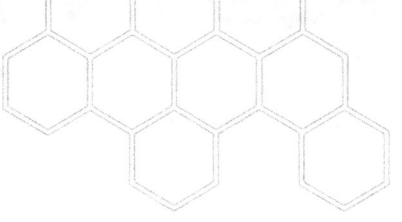

I WOULD LIKE TO THANK A GREAT DEAL OF
PEOPLE FOR THEIR LOVE AND SUPPORT:

Thank you to my parents for reading to me
every night of my childhood, recommending
books to me from when I started reading to today,
and always encouraging me to write.

Thank you to Cyra, my wife, for the writing dates,
faith in the story before it became a book, and for
helping with the characters' names.

Thank you to my friends (Steve, Erin, and Gill)
who were my first readers.

Thank you to Ashley for the vision, art,
understanding, and enthusiastic support.

Lastly, thank you to Macy for the best review a
first-time author could hope for from their target
audience ("*This is like a real book*"). That made me
feel like a real author for the first time.

CONTENTS

PROLOGUE

The teacher walks over to the board and taps it twice to bring up images of the world before and after the war.

"As you will recall," she says addressing the class of ten students. "We had been learning about the war, what led to it, its effects, and how the Government recovered afterward." She moves her hand along the bottom of the large white board. With each swipe images scroll across it from right to left showing a city bursting with people, overcrowded and dirty, then fire and rubble with skeletons of buildings left remaining after the shelling and bombing raids, finally men and women hard at work rebuilding amongst the rubble, all covered in grey dust.

"Can anyone tell me the population of the capital?" asks the teacher.

Multiple hands shoot up. The teacher points at one of the more promising students.

"Two million," says the boy. He pauses in thought for a moment. "Two million in the urban centre with another million and a half in the satellite communities.

"You're wrong," chimes in one of the girls. "The capital had a population of almost five million people before the war."

"The teacher asked for one of us to tell her the population of the capital, Stephanie," says the boy. He is named Nickolas, but all of the students call him Nick. "She didn't ask what the population of the capital was."

"Yes but …" Stephanie begins but the teacher holds up a hand to silence the class.

"You are both right," smiles the teacher. "And what's more, the confusion is my fault, I should have been more precise in my question. But since we have two of our best students engaged in this, I think it's a good opportunity to do a little recap of what we've learned about the before times and about the current state of affairs."

The other students shift excitedly in their seats. Each of them knows the importance of making a good impression on the teachers and other instructors. It will be fun to see who will come out on top in the little competition the teacher seems to be setting up.

"Here's how it will work," explains the teacher. "I'll ask a question of Nick and then one of Stephanie. Each must give a detailed answer. If they don't know the answer or get something wrong, the other can try to answer. If neither can answer, then someone else in the class can try. Understand?"

The students nod.

"Good, then let's begin. Nick, how did the war begin?"

"It began when what we now call the Eastern Bloc of countries unified and invaded one of our allies."

"They claimed that our government had annexed the land from them and installed a puppet government, but that's not true." Stephanie adds quickly.

"Very good both of you. But Stephanie, please wait your turn," replies the teacher. "But since you are eager, Stephanie, this one is for you: what do we call the nearly seventeen-year period of time just after the war ended?"

"That's easy," replies Stephanie. "It's the Recovery. The government put in place austerity measures to help us recover and to ensure there was enough food and resources for everyone."

"Some people say we are still in the Recovery," adds Nick. "There are still plenty of austerity measures."

"Like what?" asks the teacher.

"Well rationing for one," answers Nick.

"Well, it's true that there is still a need for some rationing. I bet we all wish we could have more chocolate," explains the teacher eliciting some giggles. "But we are well out of the severe austerity of the Recovery. I think you can all agree that since coming to this school, you haven't had to worry about food in your bellies or not having clean, hot water every morning."

The students smile. While the war happened long before they were born, they are all still too familiar with its aftershocks and most of them remember too well what it means to be hungry and cold.

"So, how did the war end?" asks the teacher.

It's Stephanie who is first to answer. "The Chancellor ended the war!" she says. "He was elected four years into the war. The previous government was failing and we were in danger of losing to the Eastern Bloc. But then the Chancellor came along and changed things. He installed a stronger senate and got rid of the bad generals who were losing ground. Within two years, we beat back the Eastern Bloc and they were forced to agree to a ceasefire."

"Excellent, Stephanie!" exclaims the teacher. "Now Nick, how long has the Chancellor been the leader of the government?"

"Since he was elected during the war," replies Nick. "He has been unanimously re-elected by the senate every term since then."

In the back of the class one of the students can't help but feel a little funny about this last answer. Her name is Mona and she thinks to herself that if Stephanie's answer was right and the Chancellor put a new senate in place, then wouldn't the people who re-elected him all those times be loyal to him? But Mona knows better than to try to question or correct the adults.

"Excellent work both of you," beams the teacher. "You are clearly our two top students."

Mona winces at this. She feels a little jealous that Stephanie with her pretty blond hair and the confident Nick are better than she is. She sits silently as the other students chatter and congratulate Nick and Stephanie for their performances. The teacher quiets the class and continues the lesson.

"Alright let's hear from someone else this time. What were some of the post-war challenges that the Chancellor had to deal with?"

The class is silent for a while before a student finally speaks up. "Weren't people mad at the Chancellor for doing bad things?" ventures one of the boys.

"What do you mean?" asks the teacher with a bit of an edge in her voice. She glances at the camera on the ceiling. "The Chancellor may have had opponents—all politicians do—but he is responsible for the prosperity we enjoy today."

"But don't they say that the Chancellor wasn't supposed to be the leader? That he cheated or something," attempts the boy.

"Leave it to Owen to give a made-up answer," says the teacher, eliciting laughter from the rest of the class. "Owen, not only is your answer wrong, but you are showing a severe lack of ability in your recollection." She continues addressing the entire class, "The purpose of this school is not only to educate you but to hone your memory so that you can remember things in accurate detail. You have all moved to the third pod for ten- and eleven-year-olds, which means you are supposed to be advanced in your training." She turns back to Owen, "I am going to have to have a word with your individual instructor about your progress. Maybe we have to put you with a younger pod so that you can redo some training."

The other students snicker as Owen flushes with embarrassment. Only Mona stays silent. She remembers some of the older kids in her orphanage talking about how their parents died after the war during protests outside the capitol building. But before she has time to say anything, a tone chimes three times and the students all rise from their seats and start filing toward the door. It is time for the real lessons of the day, the one-on-one sessions with their individual instructors.

CHAPTER ONE

Dots & Honey

"What's in the room?" Mona asks.

"You'll see when it's your time to go in," replies the instructor.

"You said the door wasn't locked, so why can't I go in now?" Mona fidgets impatiently in her seat. Her legs aren't quite long enough to touch the floor comfortably.

"When it's your time." It's the same response as always. Always a delay to some unspecified day. Mona lets out a huff and turns to face forward again. The room is the same as always: two doors and two chairs. The chairs sit facing each other. She came in through the door on her left. Behind that door is the library, the dormitory, the dining hall, the classrooms, everything she already knows. Behind the door on her right? Well, that's a mystery.

Mona assumes that the instructor knows what's behind the door on her right—adults always seem to know the answers to the test questions or what's hidden in the locked cupboards. There are no cupboards in this room, no whiteboard with test questions or mathematics problems, just four walls the same bland colour as the ceiling and the floor, and two hard-backed chairs: one for the instructor and one for her.

When her housemother first brought her to this room, Mona asked why it was so plain. Her housemother just smiled and gestured to the two chairs. While Mona sat and waited, she played one of the many memory games that they were taught in school. She shut her eyes tight and imagined herself looking down at a clean, white floor. This made her giggle because in this room she didn't even have to imagine. Still, she practised with her eyes shut—it was easier for the next bit.

She imagined holding small red balls in her hands, each no more than a centimetre in diameter. They were squishy and gave off the scent of raspberries (this wasn't part of the memory game, but she liked to add it in for fun). She imagined throwing the balls into the air and watching as they bounced around on the white floor, leaving behind round pink dots. The exercise started as she counted the dots, holding a clear image of the spotted floor in her mind.

Mona counted twenty-seven dots before the image became unclear. When she first started three years ago, she could only hold six or seven dots in her mind before the picture she'd imagined blurred and the dots moved around or disappeared.

"Mona," the instructor's voice snaps her back to the present. "You seemed far away. What were you thinking about?"

Mona is surprised that this was not a chastisement. Instead, the instructor seems genuinely curious.

"I was remembering the first time I was brought to this room. I played the dot game while I waited for you."

"You can remember that?" asks the instructor.

"Of course," replies Mona. "It was a big day for me."

"Can you remember how many dots you counted?" the instructor asks, leaning forward.

"I counted twenty-seven that day," says Mona proudly. She knows that twenty-seven is a good number. Most of her classmates are still only counting thirteen or fourteen.

"Twenty-seven is excellent." The instructor seems genuinely pleased and makes a note on her clipboard.

"I could count more today," says Mona with another hint of pride.

"If I recall the picture, I could count at least …" she shuts her eyes for a moment. "Thirty-four!" she says, letting out a deep breath.

The instructor looks surprised. "Did you just repeat the exercise?"

"Sort of. I remembered it and how everything got blurry after twenty-seven dots." Mona stops and thinks for a minute about how to explain what she did. It seems obvious to her, but the instructor always wants her to carefully explain anything to do with her memories. Mona continues, "Then I slowed it all down and thought about what the image of the floor looked like just before it got all mixed up. This time I was able to count to thirty-four."

"So, you were able to access an old memory and pull more stimuli from it?" The instructor is trying to stay calm, but there is definitely some excitement in her voice.

"You always say things like 'access' and 'stimuli,' but I can just remember more sometimes," Mona replies defensively.

"Mona, listen carefully, because this is very important," explains the instructor gravely. "I want you to be sure that you were thinking of an old memory and getting new information from it. It is okay if you were playing the memory game again, no one will be mad, thirty three is still an impressive number."

"Thirty-four," corrects Mona. "And I was remembering the old game, the one I played my first time in the room. I wasn't making up thirty-four dots. I was remembering the image and counting again."

The instructor smiles. She beams actually. Mona starts to feel uncomfortable. In all their time together, the instructor has rarely betrayed any emotion. She simply sits and asks Mona very specific questions about things that happened that day, or a week before, or sometimes a year or two ago. She makes careful notes. She asks Mona about how she accesses memories. Sometimes she tests Mona, asking her to recount whole conversations word-for-word. But she rarely smiles, and she certainly never looks as pleased as she does today. It is disconcerting.

"Why are you so excited?" asks Mona.

"Mona, you may not realize this, but you have just demonstrated an ability that I have never seen before. Whether it is the culmination of your training, your natural ability, or some combination, I don't know. What I do know is that you are the first student I have ever had who is able to glean additional information from a memory."

"Lots of people can do that," counters Mona.

"No. Most people remember specific details of an event. They hold onto those details due to their significance, or by replaying them in their head. Over time, an individual may remember more details, particularly if a stimulus prompts them. But more often, people forget details," the instructor explains.

"But I just remembered more. So, I must have had a stimulus, right?" asks Mona. She is beginning to worry that she's done something wrong.

"One of the purposes of this room is to limit the number of available stimuli. That's why we always meet here. It's why I am always wearing the same clothes." The instructor gestures to her simple grey dress and shoes. "The lack of external stimuli makes our lessons simpler. But more importantly, you weren't remembering additional detail from something that actually happened, you were remembering additional detail from a mental exercise. That's unheard of." She is smiling again.

"So, you can't do that?" asks Mona.

"No, I don't think many people can. You might be the only one."

"And it's a good thing?" Mona asks apprehensively.

"Oh yes," replies the instructor, not hiding any measure of happiness or pride. "It's a very good thing."

"Oh. Okay then." Mona still feels a little unnerved by the sudden display of emotion, but she is reassured to hear that she hasn't done something that would warrant a punishment of some kind.

"Mona," says the instructor. "With your permission, I'd like to try something different today."

"What kind of different?" asks Mona.

"Well, usually we practice memory exercises and I ask you questions about specific things, like the colour of objects, the number of people, the temperature …"

"The smell of a room," volunteers Mona, happy to be back in more familiar territory.

"Yes, exactly," responds the instructor. "But today I think I'd like to ask you some different sorts of questions. They may be more difficult, but they might also be more fun if you're up for it."

"What kind of questions?" asks Mona.

"Well, let's try one. What's your favourite food?"

"That's not hard!" Mona laughs. "My favourite food is honey or honey on toast."

"Did you have that for breakfast this morning?" asks the instructor.

"No, we're not allowed honey for breakfast. But I had some when I was in the kitchen for my rotation of chores." Mona blushes suddenly. She isn't supposed to snack while doing her chores—even though everyone who washes dishes or peels vegetables in the kitchen does. She hadn't meant to admit the minor trespass to an adult, but it just slipped out.

"It's okay, Mona," says the instructor. "I sometimes sneak a candy or two in between my sessions." She reaches into the small side pocket of her dress and reveals a caramel-coloured candy wrapped in cellophane. She gives Mona a quick conspiratorial wink.

Mona smiles. This is the first time an adult has ever admitted to a trespass in front of her. It is also definitely the first time that she was not punished for admitting to one herself.

"When I was putting away supplies," Mona continues. "I saw a great big jar of honey. It was in the back of the pantry. So later, when I was putting away dishes, I slipped a spoon in my pocket and made an excuse to rearrange the oatmeal on the shelves. Then when I was pretty sure no one was looking, I plopped the spoon into the honey and ate it." Mona smiles at the memory and unconsciously licks her lips. The instructor makes a quick note on her clipboard.

"Can you describe honey to me?" asks the instructor.

"It's a sweet, golden-coloured, viscous liquid," Mona begins. She makes no effort to betray the boredom in her voice. It seems that their brief foray into more interesting questions is over, and now they are back to detailed descriptions of items or events.

"What I meant to say was, can you describe what it is about honey you like?" explains the instructor. "Can you describe how it makes you feel?"

Mona closed her eyes. "It's sweet and sticky, but it kinda melts on my tongue. When I breathe in, the smell swirls past my nose. It's hard to explain, but it has a smell that feels warm somehow, like sunshine. It reminds me of the smell of flowers." Mona opened her eyes, "Can honey be a stimuli?"

"It can. In fact, tastes and smells are often very strong triggers for our memories," explains the instructor. "Mona, when you describe eating honey, you often lick your lips. Can you taste it?"

"No," Mona replies with a giggle. "Well, not exactly, but I can kind of remember the taste so strongly that it's almost like eating it. I don't know how to describe it. It's like a shadow or a ghost taste." Mona feels embarrassed at her inability to describe the memory. But the instructor is smiling again.

"Thank you, Mona," she says. "You can go early today. In fact, you should go to the kitchen and get a slice of toast with honey." She tears of a piece of paper and writes something on it before folding it and handing it to Mona. "Just give them this and you'll be allowed to have a treat."

Mona takes the note gingerly. This is unheard of. No one gets a special snack in the middle of the day. She smiles and excuses herself heading through the door on her left.

The instructor makes a few more notes and then leaves through the door on the right.

○ ○ ○

"So, what do you think? Is she ready?"

"She's the best student I have ever seen, and today's lesson shows her aptitude."

"It's more than just aptitude. I could almost taste the honey, just from her description."

"I'd like to keep testing her, maybe ramp things up a bit. I spoke with her instructor and she feels that more advanced exercises could further strengthen her abilities."

"But if she's ready, I don't see why we should wait. If we begin the process now, we can harvest one or two strong memories from her this year. She might even be able to produce more if the harvesting process doesn't prove too onerous for her. The fact that she can hold onto taste alone will make those memories highly valuable. Not to mention her capacity for detail—thirty-four dots in the memory game? That's more than impressive."

"I agree, but why not push her farther? With more training, we might get four or five strong memories out of her. And she said that it was only the shadow of a real taste. I'd like to see if we can get more from her, not just the impression but the actual sensation."

"Is that even possible?"

"I've heard other firms have tried it. Can you imagine how much we could charge for a memory of a delicious meal, if you could actually taste the food? Or for the memory of a song, where you can actually hear the music?"

"You're talking about implanting full experiences, not just memories. Can our technology even manage that?"

"Why not? The Selective Memory Extraction Procedure is designed to map and harvest the neural pathways connected to memories. Memories are often connected to our senses. For her, they seem to be so strongly connected that she is almost reliving specific memories. The only tricky part is training her brain to further strengthen those connections so that we have clear pathways for the extraction."

"And the implantation?"

"Selective Memory Implantation relies on the quality of the harvested memory. If the quality is good, the procedure should not be significantly challenging.

"You think it can be done."

"With time and training, yes. But the event will need to be significant in order to create a strong enough memory."

"We don't deal in insignificant memories."

"I mean the sensation will need to be compelling, something she really latches on to."

"All the better."

"Yes, only …"

"Only what?"

"Harvesting a memory like that will cause significant damage to her neural pathways. If we try to get two or three, the damage will likely be permanent and may affect other parts of her brain. Four or five …"

"Will kill her."

"Yes. Probably yes."

"We've lost others before her. Only a few, but the mortality rate has never been a major concern of yours."

"True. You've often shown more regret than I when we lose one."

"Is that so? Perhaps. But I can justify the loss if they yield memories that can be sold at a high profit. Yes, my only real concern is the loss of a revenue source."

"If you believe that, then so do I. If profit is your concern, then may I advise you that whatever events you plan for this student need to translate into the best possible memories. High-value memories. Make sure they are impactful and meaningful to her. We will only get one chance to harvest them. After that, even if she lives, we won't get anything of value from her."

"You're saying that we need to come up with solid gold memories, otherwise we're killing the goose."

"I'm saying she could give us years of good memories or four to five priceless ones."

"Priceless. I like the sound of that."

CHAPTER TWO

Plomp

M ona exits through the same door as always. The note is folded and
clutched in her hand. She smiles at the thought of eating honey
on toast.

Down the hallway to her right are six more doors like the one she just
stepped through. To her left there are three doors, then the hallway takes
a sharp ninety-degree turn, leading back to the dormitory and living
spaces. There are no windows.

Mona stands alone in the hall, scuffing her feet on the grey carpet. She
takes a moment to remember the session with the instructor. How long
was it? Was she the first out of the session or the last? Either way, she
should really make her way down the hall and head to the kitchen for her
snack, but instead she decides to linger to see if anyone else will come out
of one of the doors.

After four minutes and thirty-seven seconds—Mona is very precise
about measuring time when she doesn't have other distractions—the
doors open and her fellow students pour out into the hall.

"Did you finish early?" asks Stephanie.

"No," Mona replies. She doesn't feel like sharing the details of her
session or the fact that she got a special reward. "I just stepped out a
minute ago."

"Looks like you've been waiting," Stephanie presses. "Did you get kicked out? Did you do something wrong? Did you fail a test?" Stephanie's questions start to draw some attention from the others. Failing a test would be a mark against Mona, who consistently scores very highly on almost all assessments.

"You're fishing, Stephanie," snaps Mona. "You just worry about your own tests."

"Whoa, calm down Mona," says Stephanie, feigning innocence. "I was only asking because you're my friend."

Mona could almost laugh. Stephanie has never really been her friend. While Mona pushes herself to be one of the best students out of pride in her own abilities, she'd always thought that Stephanie tries to undermine the other top students to make herself stand out more. She already stands out as one of the tallest in the class, being one of the first to hit a major growth spurt. She's a head taller than Mona, with blonde hair and blue eyes that often make Mona feel cold.

"I wouldn't want you to be a plomp like Owen." Stephanie's voice is dripping with fake concern.

At the mention of Owen's name, the children all look down the hall. The light next to the second to last door is still on. Owen hasn't come out.

"Always the last to leave," remarks Nick. "Why do they keep him longer?"

"Because he's a plomp!" replies Stephanie. "He just plomps down and takes up space. I hear his instructor keeps him for remedial lessons."

Mona scoffs to herself. There is no way that Stephanie heard anything of the sort. Students see their instructors only at their sessions each day, just before lunch. They meet them in the examination rooms, each coming and leaving through their own door. The instructors don't visit the students in the dorms, they don't teach other classes, they don't eat in the kitchens, they just disappear behind their doors. It's like they don't exist beyond the instructors' exam rooms. Mona's never even seen anyone else's instructor. She knows from conversations that some are men and some are women, but she'd only ever had female instructors. Apart from that, she knows very little about the lives of the instructors.

"Whatever," says Nick, dismissing Stephanie's comment. "He's late and I'm not waiting. Let's go back to the dorms. It's nearly lunchtime." He moves past Stephanie and Mona with the casual confidence of someone who is used to others following his lead. As if on cue, the other students begin to file down the hall following Nick. Mona is the last one around the corner. She turns and looks back over her shoulder. Owen's door is still shut and the light is still on.

The first part of the hallway back to the dormitory is long and windowless. Then there is a set of stairs that climbs up to a second-floor walkway with big windows on either side. You can see almost the whole of the school from the walkway, but very little of the larger building to which it is connected. The walkway links directly to the dormitory, which is a square three-story building. The first floor is the common rooms; the second has a small study area and the boys' bathrooms; the third is divided into the girls' and boys' dorms and the girls' bathrooms.

Most of the students continue on, turning right past the study area and going into the second walkway that connects the dormitory to the kitchens. The second building is much bigger and houses the cafeteria, kitchens, and a larger common area. In turn, it is connected to the third building, which contains the classrooms, a small gymnasium, and the school's audio-visual library.

The students have free rein to go where they please in the time between their individual instruction sessions and lunch, but most head straight to the cafeteria. Mona lingers behind. She wants to stash her note in the dorm without being seen. It's not that she is worried about it being stolen by another student—it has her name on it, after all. It's just that she doesn't want to draw any unnecessary attention to herself, particularly from Stephanie.

So, she waits as most of the students head to the cafeteria building, pretending to read in the study area as the few stragglers stop off at the dorm or head to the bathroom. She flips the pages of her book and counts one by one as the other students leave for lunch. Once the other eight from her pod have left, she heads up to her dorm and places the note securely in the trunk at the foot of her bed.

Her bed is identical to the four others in the bedroom. Her pod, like the other pods in the school, has ten students: five girls and five boys. Each student has a single bed and a trunk containing their clothes and personal possessions. Most of the trunks only have clothes and perhaps a book or a single toy. The students don't tend to come with many personal belongings and almost no one has photographs or letters.

"Ten peas in a pod." Mona doesn't understand why the teachers all say that. Peas come in a can and there are certainly far more than ten to a can. She remembers one of her most recent shifts in the kitchens. Betty, the head cook, had Mona bring out all the cans for the meals that week. It was her task to open each of them. Mona had talked back to a teacher that day, so instead of the regular can opener, Betty had given her an old-fashioned one. Mona rubs her wrist remembering how she had to puncture each can and work the small blade around the edge with an up and down motion. It took ages to open all the cans Betty demanded. The punishment had worked. Mona was silent in her contrition and bit her lip the next time she wanted to correct a teacher.

How many peas were in the can? Mona could remember opening the can and seeing the mass of pale green peas, but she was too tired and frustrated from her punishment to think about counting them. Looking back now, she could count at least 248.

Still thinking about peas, Mona leaves the dorm and heads down the stairs to join the rest of her pod for lunch. Turning the corner at the bottom of the stairs, she bumps right into Owen, who is heading up to the boys' dorm.

"Hi Mona," says Owen, smiling. "You heading to lunch?"

"Yup," replies Mona, moving past him.

He stops on the stairs and looks back at her. "I don't suppose you'd wait for me? It's only I'm often the last to be let out and that means I usually walk to lunch on my own. When I get to the cafeteria everyone is already sitting and eating. I usually sit by myself or with another pod."

Mona has certainly noticed that Owen often sits by himself. Even when he is with other students in their pod, he doesn't take part in many conversations. Sometimes students in other pods let him join them, but the older ones ignore him and the younger ones get him in trouble by asking him to tell stories. It's not that the students aren't allowed to tell stories; it's just that Owen gets so animated that he often ends up raising his voice or standing and moving around as he acts out what his characters are doing.

Mona giggles as she remembers a particularly funny story she overheard him telling some of the younger pods. It was about a dog that was purple because it only ate grape-flavoured gelatin. Owen stood up and, waving a banana above his head, he exclaimed that it was only after the dog ate a whole bunch of bananas that its fur changed colour. "Sure, the dog is yellow now," he said. "But he's basically gone bananas."

How did he come up with those stories? Dogs don't eat bananas, and the colour of food doesn't change the colour of their fur. Still, it made the little kids laugh and even some of her own pod giggled. The teachers gave Owen three extra rounds of dish duty for causing a commotion.

"Why did the dog only eat gelatin?" asks Mona, breaking the silence.

"It's the only food I could think of that was purple," replies Owen, smiling that Mona remembered the story. "Why are you thinking of my story?"

"It was funny," says Mona smiling back. "Where did you hear it?"

"I didn't hear it, I made it up. The younger pods like funny stories and I like to make them laugh."

"How do you make up that kind of story?"

"I dunno. I just do, I guess."

"You're good at it."

Owen blushes a little. "Thanks. I'm not too good at the regular schoolwork, and my instructor used to get mad when I made up stories. Now he ..."

"You're not supposed to make up things that didn't happen in the one-on-one sessions," Mona interrupts. She is shocked that Owen would recount false details to his instructor.

"I know, just sometimes I can't help it." He looks up the stairs and then back at Mona. "So you'll wait for me?"

"Only if you have another funny story to tell me on the way to lunch," she says with a smile.

"I'll see what I can dream up."

o o o

"Why is she talking to that boy?"

"They're in the same pod. All the students interact with their pod-mates on a daily basis."

"I know, it just worries me. He is not a strong student."

"Perhaps she will be a good influence on him?"

"More likely he will be a bad influence on her. We should move him to another pod. Or better yet scrub him from the program."

"You're overreacting. Let me remind you of the considerable investment it takes to train a student to this age and level. Even if he is a poor student, he may still yield a moderate product. The investment could still pay off. Scrubbing him this late in the game would only result in a loss."

"True enough, but it concerns me that he fabricates stories and, worse, he pollutes his one-on-one sessions with his own fantasies."

"That is a valid concern. We may have to have a talk with his instructor."

"Or give him a new instructor. The girl's instructor is very strong, perhaps she could get him back on the right path if you still feel he is worth the investment of more time and resources ..."

"He is. They all are. Once they've reached this age, we cannot afford the loss of one student, weak or strong."

"Then shift the instructors."

"The boy's instructor is very promising. He's worked with us for some time. We stole him from a rival firm; they did not appreciate his aptitude or his ability to use the equipment to pinpoint the exact memory to harvest. He's as good as any of our technicians at the process. Better perhaps. I'm interested in seeing how this will help harvest memories from the students when they are ready."

"Fine. If you have faith in the instructor, let him stay. But we should see if we can separate the girl from the boy. I don't want him influencing her. She shows too much promise."

"On that, we are definitely agreed. We have to protect our investments."

CHAPTER THREE

Misspoke

Harriet closes the door behind her and immediately kicks off the flat grey shoes. The room is dark and quiet. She waves her hands in front of her and the lights flicker to life. The pleasant cozy darkness is replaced by harsh lighting with a greenish tinge accompanied by an electric insect noise.

Harriet places the shoes in a cubby-hole and pulls the drab dress off over her head. The grey stockings go in a small bin by the wall of cubby-holes. There will be a new pair in her cubby tomorrow, along with, as always, the same shoes and neatly folded dress.

She places the dress on top of the shoes and touches her thumbs to the sensor next to her cubby-hole number. A sliding door shuts and locks and her ID card pops out next to the thumb scanner. She stands for a moment in her undergarments before unlocking the next door.

Finally, she is back in a world of colour, even if the lockers of the changeroom are only a pale yellow. She unlocks her locker with her ID and changes into her normal clothes: purple leggings, black boots with a slight heel, and a blue dress. She smooths the dress down, enjoying the feel of the fabric—soft compared to the coarse, sterile material of the uniform.

Harriet understands why the uniform is so plain. But just once it would be nice to wear some colour, or at least something more comfortable. Mona would like that. Harriet smiles and pictures how Mona would react if she entered the exam room wearing something bright orange or yellow.

Harriet picks up her bag and, still smiling, walks out into the hallway. Sam steps right in front of her, so quickly that she can't help but bump into him.

"Gotcha," says Sam.

"Every time," replies Harriet. "You think I'd be expecting it by now."

"Lunch?" suggests Sam. "If you've got the time."

"Sounds good. I have to do a write up about today's session, but it can probably wait until the afternoon."

"One of your superstars this morning?" asks Sam, as they walk down the corridor toward the cafeteria.

"Yes," replies Harriet. "Only ..."

"Only what? They either show promise or they don't right? I've got this one boy who started off strong, but he's just too flighty. Daydreams, you know. He can't help but insert things. It's like he's trying to tell stories, not recount events." Sam's brow wrinkles. "I can't get him to concentrate without raising my voice or threatening punishments."

"How does he respond?" asks Harriet.

"Technically, fairly well," explains Sam. "You know, his descriptions improve and he stops playing make-believe, so that's good. But I can tell he's afraid or upset. He focuses more on technical details than on the impression."

"So it's just information then," replies Harriet, beginning to understand the problem.

"Exactly! His descriptions lose all the excitement and enjoyment. He becomes a camera or a tape recorder." Sam looks down, a little defeated. "Can I tell you a secret?"

"Of course," Harriet replies. She draws closer to him as they enter the busy cafeteria.

"Sometimes, after we work through some of the exercises, I ask him about what he dreamt the night before."

Harriet is blown away. No instructor she knows of has ever thought to ask about a dream. Dreams aren't real. The events in them can't be verified. They are important, sure, but mostly as a way to help the mind process daily thoughts. In terms of memories, they are almost useless. How long do the details last after you wake up? Within minutes, you're left with only a vague sense of the events and images in the dream. You might hold onto an overall emotional impression but how long does that even last?

"I know what you're thinking," says Sam, interrupting Harriet's train of thought. "I can't remember the details of a dream very long after I'm awake either. Not unless something significant happens, like falling or being surprised by something. I think I only remember those things because they wake me up." Harriet is surprised that Sam seems so in tune with her own thoughts. She can remember a dream she had about him a few nights ago, but she blushes when she thinks about it. She would certainly never tell anyone about that dream, least of all Sam.

"I think children have different sorts of dreams, though," continues Sam. "First of all, they have fewer fears and less complicated emotions."

"I don't think that's entirely true," replies Harriet.

"Fair enough. More honest fears and emotions then." They smile at one another in agreement. Sam goes on. "If they have a happy dream, it's really happy—intensely happy. If they have a scary dream, it's all their fears played out at once."

"So they wake up crying or eager to share a good story. So what?" Harriet picks up her sandwich, feigning a lack of interest. She's curious about where he's going, but she's worked with him long enough to know that it's better not to jump on board with one of his ideas too soon. He needs a skeptical audience to help him refine his thoughts.

"So they're left with a very strong impression! Maybe not all the details we usually like to have but thinking about the dream can easily bring about an immediate sense of joy or dread," Sam is still talking quietly, but he's beginning to become more and more animated.

"All the things that your student is lacking when you insist that he only recount the facts," Harriet realizes.

"Exactly," says Sam. "The only trouble is, I can't always tell where his impressions are coming from."

"Maybe you could …" Harriet stops suddenly as Miller joins them at the table.

"Good afternoon Sam, Harriet," says Miller, nodding her head at each of them. "What are you two talking about?"

"Nothing really," replies Sam.

"Oh come on Sam, you were practically bouncing in your seat!" replies Miller. "What is it? Do you have a promising student?"

"I guess," says Sam apprehensively. "I mean, he could be."

"Go on," encourages Miller.

As Sam explains, Harriet watches Miller's face. She can see that Miller is listening intently, but notices that her eyebrows go up a bit when Sam mentions dreams.

Sam notices too and starts to stammer. It's not surprising. Miller is one of the most respected instructors. She has trained dozens of excellent students and made the Company buckets of money. She is also rumored to be next in line for promotion to director.

"Through his dreams, he's latching on to some strong memory impressions," finishes Sam, noticeably uncomfortable under Miller's analytical gaze.

"But you can't quantify them or assign them to an experience category," says Miller.

"Not yet, but maybe if I …"

"Look Sam," interrupts Miller. "I don't mean to sound harsh, but you know that we aren't supposed to waste time on frivolities. We're supposed to train them so that they can remember all the significant and insignificant details during their day-to-day experiences. That kind of focus helps them latch on to the impressions and experiences and better hold on to how they feel in any given moment. The good ones can almost relive the experience."

Harriet purses her lips, remembering how Mona described honey. But she decides not to share this with Sam or Miller just now.

"I know, I know," says Sam, waving his hand to dismiss the lecture.

"I don't see anything wrong with asking about dreams to get your pupil to open up," says Miller more gently. "But the chances of him remembering enough detail for you to accurately be able to categorize the memory and the sensations ... I just don't think it's possible."

"I think he could with time," replies Sam.

"Really?" asks Miller. "It seems risky to me. If the directors found out, you could lose your job. Don't get me wrong, I'd love to do more with the students. I always think it would be fun to work with them in groups or in the regular classroom. I wish we could take them on trips like schools used to. Keeping them on campus all the time seems almost like prison, even if it is so much safer than the world outside. Anyway, I just wouldn't want you to get in trouble."

"Alright, I won't waste any more time on it then."

They eat in silence for a while.

"It's only," says Sam at last, "it's only he has so much fun talking about his dreams, it's almost contagious. I thought it might be worth pursuing."

"It might be," admits Miller. "But is it worth you maybe losing your job? There aren't too many companies that do what we do, and they all know when someone gets blacklisted. Besides, you want to be a director someday, right? You don't want to be seen as someone who breaks the rules."

Harriet looks at Sam, surprised at the revelation.

Sam smiles shyly.

"Sam, I know you've been asking around about what it takes to move to the next step," Miller says. "You've even taken some extra training on some of the more technical aspects of the work, haven't you?"

Sam says nothing.

"There's no shame in it," Miller says, trying to ease some of Sam's embarrassment. "I've done the same. Look, if you've got the ambition to apply for the next director position, that's great. Just don't let this preoccupation with dreams—as interesting as it is—get in your way. Once you're a director, you'll have more leeway to explore new ideas."

"Good point," replies Sam. "Anyway, Harriet, you were going to tell me about one of your superstars, weren't you?"

"I don't know if she's a superstar," Harriet ventures tentatively. "But she's showing a lot of promise. She's particularly strong when recalling smells and tastes."

"Hmm, that's not surprising. Most of the top pupils I've had showed early promise with recalling olfactory sensations," says Miller. "Does she show promise in any other areas?"

"Well, she's excellent at a number of the memory games. The dot game in particular."

"Really? How many can she remember?" asks Sam.

A student who excels at memory games is nothing too special. They've all had them before. Harriet is pretty sure that Sam is just humouring her by pretending to be interested.

"Thirty-four," answers Harriet.

Sam's eyes widen and Miller lets out a gasp.

"That is impressive," says Miller. "You should flag her for additional lessons. I think she might …" Miller is cut off by a chime letting those people in the cafeteria know that it is now 1300 hours. "Sorry, Harriet. I'd love to chat more, but I have some afternoon sessions to prepare for. Sam, good to see you." Miller takes her half-finished lunch and leaves.

Harriet smiles, feeling proud that one of the top instructors, Miller, is impressed with her student. It was a bonus that Miller suggested additional lessons. Harriet hadn't thought of that, and it would be nice to spend more time with Mona to see if she had any other hidden aptitudes or talents.

CHAPTER FOUR

Plomp Dreams

"What's behind the door?" asks Owen.

"Owen, I need you to concentrate on the lesson. You've asked what's behind the door before a number of times, and my answer is always the same: 'you'll find out when you're ready to go in,'" replies the instructor.

"Yeah, you always say that," says Owen, downhearted to be pushed back into the boring lesson work.

"How many times have I said it?" asks the instructor, a smile twitching on his previously impassive face.

"Twelve. Thirteen, if you count just now," replies Owen.

"When was the first time?"

"At the beginning of last cycle. It was the first day we met. Our first lesson together." Owen replies.

"As I recall, it was the first thing you asked. You asked it before you'd even shut your door, before you sat down, before you even looked at me."

"Well," replies Owen, "I've always wanted to know."

"Did you ever ask any of the other instructors you had before me?"

"Of course," smiles Owen. "All of them! Lots of times. One even told me what was back there, but I wanted to confirm what he said with you to make sure.

Sam examines his student carefully. Owen's face starts to betray that he isn't telling the truth. Most people would miss it, but Sam has been Owen's instructor for two full cycles now, and he has made a study of the boy. He's started to learn to tell the difference between a recollection and something more spurious. It's subtle, but Owen briefly pushes the tip of his tongue between his teeth before he adds an artificial detail to a story.

"Oh really? So what's back there?"

"I'm not a total plomp," replies Owen. "If I tell you you'll just deny it, so that I'll second guess what the last instructor told me."

"You're pretty clever then."

"So are you going to tell me?" asks Owen again.

"You know I can't. Let's get back to the lesson. If we keep getting sidetracked, you'll finish late again."

Owen looks down, dejected. "Alright," he says.

"At the end of our session yesterday, I showed you a series of pictures. How many did I show you?" asks the instructor.

"Fifty," replies Owen without enthusiasm or interest.

"I showed you forty-nine. What was depicted in the first six pictures?"

"House, flowers, bed, test tube, bandage, insect," Owen rhymes off the list quickly in a monotone voice. Already he is starting to fidget in his chair.

"Try to sit still, Owen," warns Sam. "Now can you tell me a detail about every second picture?"

"The insect was funny-looking and pale. I've never seen one like it before. It was hard to tell in the picture if it was the actual size or if it was blown up because the background was all black and there was nothing else in the picture.

"The test tube was sitting in a rack that could hold five more just like it, but it was the only one. It was filled with dark red liquid, which was the only colour in the picture. The rest of the items were white or grey like this." Owen reaches out and touches the sleeve of Sam's tunic. He has to lean forward in his chair to reach and he gently rubs the material between his thumb and forefinger.

Sam is about to scold Owen for not completing the exercise, but he suddenly becomes aware that Owen is mesmerized by the feel of the fabric. He watches as Owen slowly opens and closes his eyes, seemingly oblivious to any other stimuli apart from the feel of the coarse, light grey fabric. Slowly, Owen sits back and touches his thumb and forefinger to his cheek, moving them in a slow circular motion.

Owen looks up at Sam and says, "That fabric must not feel good on your skin. It's too rough. It's like the sacks that the rice comes in, only not so much so." Then he touches his fingers to his own cotton shirt and back to his face. "My shirt is much nicer," he says after a pause. "You should ask them for a shirt like mine."

Sam is startled by Owen's reaction. As Owen continues to describe the pictures, Sam can't help but feel that Owen was somehow holding the memory of the feeling of each fabric in his fingertips, then testing them against his face. Without thinking, Sam worries the cuff of this tunic between his fingers and reaches up to his own face, but all he feels is the heavy fibers of the shirt and the smoothness of his clean-shaven face.

"Oh yeah!" exclaims Owen, snapping Sam's attention back to the exam room. "There were bees in the flowers! All buzzing about collecting nectar and pollen. They were only little ones and hard to see, but they were there."

"How were the bees different from the picture of the other insect?" asks Sam, happy to have something that Owen seems excited to concentrate on.

"How were they the same? They couldn't have been more different! The bees are black and bright yellow, with fat little bodies and buzzing wings. The other insect was white, with almost clear legs. It had no wings and its feet looked like little hooks." Owen's face screws up with a look of disgust. "The bees are almost like little pets or stuffed toys. I wouldn't want to touch the other one."

Sam smiles. "Do you know why you have such a strong sense of revulsion to the other picture?" he asks.

Owen shrugs.

"It's because it was a picture of a louse. An enlarged picture, of course, but still a louse," Sam explains.

"What's a louse?" asks Owen.

"It's a parasite. A bug that lives in hair or fur and sucks blood from its host. Even if you've never seen one in person, or had lice yourself, it's pretty common to find them disgusting—it's an instinct."

"What does 'instinct' mean?" asks Owen.

Sam is aware that Owen is, once again, pulling the conversation away from the exercises they are supposed to be pursuing, but he can't help but answer the question. After all, instinct is related to memory, isn't it?

"Instinct is something that the brain does without thinking. It can be a simple behaviour, like your revulsion to the louse, or something more complex, like …" Sam stops and thinks for a moment. "Like the bees in the picture!" He is excited to bring the conversation full circle and pull Owen back to the lesson. "Bees instinctively know how to communicate with one another by moving their bodies in a little dance. It's how they tell each other where flowers are. Now can you tell me how many flowers there were in the picture with the bees? What colours were they?"

"Two red, three yellow, and one purple," replies Owen quickly. He is wrong but carries on to his next question before Sam can correct him. "What do you mean bees dance? That's so funny! I bet they play music with their wings and have little parties in their hives! I'm going to try to dream about them tonight."

Sam is about to use his instructor voice again, but at the mention of dreams, he relaxes and looks at Owen, who is staring off into space, eyes wide, smiling in wonder. "What do you mean, you're going to try to dream about them?" he asks.

"Just what I said," replies Owen. "Tonight, when I'm falling asleep, I'll try to remember everything we talked about today, especially the bees. I'll remember the picture and their cute fuzzy bodies. I'll listen to the hum of the air circulation machine and imagine it's the hum of one thousand bees in a hive, then maybe I'll dream about dancing with them."

Owen is still staring into space smiling. He is swaying gently in his seat, already dancing with the bees in his dreams. "Last night I had a dream that I was falling and it was so scary that it made me wake up. I jolted up in my bed and startled Nick in the bed next to me. Dreaming about bees will be much nicer."

"Owen, we're not supposed to talk about dreams," says Sam, glancing up at the recorder on the wall, painfully aware that he has wasted almost all of this session. "I know in the past sometimes we have, but that was against the rules. We could both get into trouble."

"You can get into trouble?" asks Owen with his annoying habit of latching onto the one piece of information that Sam wished he would miss.

"Listen, there are rules that you have to follow, right?"

Owen nods.

"The same is true for me. We all have rules that we must follow. One of the main rules is that in the exam room we are supposed to spend our time on memory exercises and training. That way you can improve your skills and I can evaluate your progress. All the time we spent on dreams, or having this conversation, is just wasted time that we should have spent more productively."

"You sound like an instructor now," says Owen, looking down at his feet.

"I am an instructor," replies Sam sternly. "And you are a pupil. Those are our roles." He is now very nervous that anyone reviewing the session would rightly admonish him for not only wasting a session, but also for the casual relationship he'd developed with Owen. This is exactly what Miller warned him about. He should have listened to her.

"I know. It's just that sometimes you don't sound like the rest of the instructors I've had. Sometimes you sound like you want to be friends, like when you told me about bees dancing or about instinct being like the memory of a whole species. It's like you had a story you wanted to tell me. I like telling stories too, so I thought …"

"It wasn't a story," interrupts Sam. His voice is now hard and definite, betraying no warmth or friendship. "It was information. I will expect you to remember it for our next session. I will review the recording of this session and ask you about the specific order of information that I gave you and about …" he trails off.

Owen has tears in his eyes.

"There's no need for that," says Sam, regretting his earlier tone. "We will continue next time when you are more composed." He stands and opens the door to let Owen leave. Then, without thinking, he leans down and says, "I'd like to hear about the dancing bees in your dream, so try to come early to our next lesson."

Owen turns and smiles.

"I expect you to approach these lessons more professionally in the future," says Sam for the benefit of the recorder and whomever might review this session, giving Owen a conspiratorial wink.

Owen walks away from the lesson and down the corridor, smiling.

o o o

"What did he say to the child?"

"I'm not sure, he was leaning into the corridor and the recording device doesn't extend beyond the range of the room."

"A foolish oversight on your part!"

"Really? I thought your training was meant to prevent the instructors from ever going through that door. He shouldn't even have stood up to let the boy out."

"Still, if your systems …"

"You are upset with the instructor for his lax approach and his indulgence of the child, you are upset with the student's progress to date, and now you are focusing your frustrations on me and on the protocols that are well established. Do not blame me for the faults you perceive in others."

"Perceive! The faults are clear. The boy is … is … what do the students call him? A plomp! He is a plomp! And his instructor is no better, continuing to indulge the child at every turn."

"Are you finished?"

"What?"

"Have you finished or shall I let you rant more?"

"Fine. Go on with whatever you're going to say."

"Good. The boy is behind. We have already agreed on that. But his instructor has talent and may be able to pull some good out of the boy yet."

"How so?"

"Did you notice anything positive about the boy today?"

"He performed adequately with the pictures until he got distracted again."

"What about when he touched the instructor's tunic?"

"A fine example of the instructor failing to adhere to the rules on boundaries."

"Perhaps you are right and that was all it was, but I think the instructor sees something our recording devices are missing."

CHAPTER FIVE

Awe Filled

"The war was terrible." There is a long pause before she continues. "That's cliché. Is that cliché?"

"The war was terrible," he repeats her assertion flatly.

"Yes it was. Quite terrible. Tell me, do you remember it well? You were probably just a few years old, weren't you? No, no, don't tell me, you'll just make me feel older than I am.

"It was terrible and you're too young to know or at least too young to remember. I imagine that you've heard lots of people like me say 'the war was terrible.' We all say the war was terrible, don't we? As though we have no other words to describe it. As though we agreed years ago to tell anyone too young to remember, too young to have lived through what we lived through, that the war was terrible." She stops and pauses for a long while. Her eyes are so dark that they look black, but despite her age they are sharp and never break the strong lock they have on him.

"Do our words start to lose meaning for you after a while? Do you think, 'It can't have been that bad, you're rich, you were rich then too, you survived'?" she asks. "Every time you hear those words, I bet the whole concept of the war becomes a little less terrible to you. You grow older. The war fades further and further into the past. Just another set of experiences that you've never had, described only with a few simple words like terrible, frightening, horrible, hungry … how can they have any real meaning to you? You look them up in a dictionary, but I've lived through them. I know what they mean. The things that you may have read about, or heard about, or seen in old broadcasts, I've seen them and lived them and felt them. To you, they are memories of boring days in school, of slogging through textbooks, maybe even of some rationing—your mother using powdered milk for baking and leftover drippings for shortening. To me, the memories are real. They are memories that are still so vivid and close that I relive them in my sleep and sometimes when I'm awake too.

"Do you know what another word for 'terrible' is? Awful. I don't mean awful like you use it, how someone your age would describe a bad meal. During the war we ate food that was so disgusting you couldn't comprehend, and we were glad of it. When I say awful, I mean that the sense of terror was so great that it inspired awe. We have words like that, words that describe a feeling so intense that it is beyond definition. Words like 'awe' and 'sublime.' You cannot really understand what they mean if you haven't felt them yourself. But once you feel it you can draw that memory back and live it again and again, like holding a picture or smelling the perfume of someone you used to love.

"And you know all about memory, don't you? That's what you specialize in here at this clinic. If you call it a clinic."

"We do," he replies. The ambiguity of his response is not lost on either of them.

"Well, that's why I'm here, isn't it?" she says flatly. "I've gathered enough awe-filled memories in my time to overflow whatever magic little bottles you store them in. And I've had far too few sublime memories." She pauses and breaks eye contact for the first time.

He looks at her. She sits straight in her chair. Although she is seemingly small and frail, she speaks with the crisp authority of someone used to taking the reins even in the hardest of situations. Until a moment ago, he would have been surprised that she would ever show emotion. Now he can see that she is slightly shaken. He has the impression of an iceberg (though he has never seen one): hard, cold, and mighty—until the first few shadows of cracks appear. Then it is only a matter of time until she breaks apart in huge, terrible pieces, resembling nothing of her former majesty.

He is suddenly sorry for her and wants to reach out a hand to stop the slight tremble in hers, but years of cultivating a professional demeanour on his part, and years of being stoically composed on hers, keep him from moving to her. Instead he calmly stands and turns his back to her, giving them both the pause they need to regain control. He walks away from her, over to the wall on the far side of the room. A slight wave of his hand, past an almost invisible sensor, reveals a compartment hidden in the wall. The compartment contains shelves lined with unlabelled pills, each neatly and precisely arranged in uniform vials. He carefully chooses one and empties two pills onto a small, elegant silver tray. Turning back to his client, he sees that she has fully returned to her usual self. Her eyes once again lock on his, betraying none of the former break in composure he had just witnessed.

He moves forward and smoothly offers her the pills.

"No, thank you," she says.

His admiration for her grows.

"I've seen what reliance on pharmaceuticals can do to people. I have family who are so full of chemicals that they can do nothing but blubber to themselves. Useless. I can't abide uselessness, in others or especially in myself."

"Something different, perhaps? Less strong? Or perhaps a small drink?" He doesn't usually offer clients alcohol. The real stuff is a luxury item that is both expensive and difficult to procure. The synthetic stuff is so terrible that he would be embarrassed to have the Company associated with it, let alone to offer it to a woman of such high class.

"I'll take a small glass of something that isn't too strong, if you have it," she replies.

Another deft movement of his hand reveals a small, but well-stocked liquor cabinet in the wall. He carefully checks the mirror at the back of the cabinet as he chooses a glass. He is pleased to see her reaction betray a hint of surprise. Trained to notice subtle changes in people when they are thinking about a pleasant memory, he watches her reflection as his free hand passes over each bottle.

"A small glass of port seems appropriate," he says, offering it to her.

"Very clever," she replies. "Very clever indeed. I would like to know your trick." She takes a small sip.

"I remember reading somewhere that you enjoyed fine port," he lies.

"No, you don't. I know every word written about me—the good and the bad. They've written about my youth, about how I kept my family alive—most of them, anyway. How despite the odds I rebuilt our business, reclaimed the 'former glory of our family name,' and grew our empire beyond even the grandest vision my grandfather ever had. I've also read that they say my family was complicit in the outbreak of the war, that our fall was the fault of my father wishing to profit from a wartime communications and industrial monopoly, that we got what was coming to us. I've read that they criticized me for building on the bones of my family's enemies, for profiting from the chaos that followed the war, for helping to install puppet politicians too eager to please their benefactor. I've heard them say that, in my youth I was the power behind the throne—and the woman literally in bed with the Chancellor. They've called me everything from magnate to monster."

She pauses for another sip. "There is truth to some of it, both the good and the bad, but no one has written a word about my drink of choice. In fact, no one outside my family, my close circle of friends and confidants, or those in similar positions of power, has ever seen me drink or eat."

"Why is that?" he asks, taking a sip from his own glass.

"To drink or eat in public is to admit to either a want or a need. I do not wish for people to see that, like them—like everyone, I suppose—I require food and drink. As I said, I've seen what chemicals can do to people. I would never allow anyone to assume, even from the smallest sip of port, that I lust for drink or pills. I must seem invincible to the public, whether as a magnate or a monster. Respect and fear work to the same end for me."

"You've achieved your goal," he says. "I was shocked to see you on my appointment schedule. Certainly, we cater to your class of individual, but you have never graced us with your presence. It is an honour, albeit an unexpected one."

"Unexpected for a reason." For the second time, her eyes pull away and stare into the distance. "So many parts of my life are over. I am old now. Old and vital, they may say, but old nonetheless. My business empire is well established and will outlast me. I have kept it from the grasping hands of my idiot children and found more capable successors.

"Yes, the business part of my life is over and despite earning both the title of magnate and monster, I will look back at what I've accomplished and sleep well at night. But there are other parts of my life that, while over, still haunt me."

"The war was terrible," he interjects, beginning to understand what brought her here today.

"Yes," she says, as if startled. "Terrible at its start, terrible at its end, and terrible in those first hard days afterward. I relive them, you know? Those terrible times. I still feel the sense of awe and wonder at how humans can cause so much misery. I feel it." Her fist pounds her chest hard enough to make him jump in his seat. "I feel it with every inch of my being. It wakes me up at night. It pulls me from myself during the day. I can no longer hold it back or hide it. It's grown too strong and now has a will of its own.

"A relatively short period of my life, yet it seems to take up the majority of my thoughts these days. I can't escape it any longer. I can't push it away with work and I won't slowly kill myself by numbing my thoughts with drink or pills.

"Nor do I want to." Again, she locks eyes with him. "Your business is memories. I want new memories. I want to have happy memories to replace these awe- and terror-filled moments that haunt me."

"Certainly, we can provide you with a variety of very pleasant memories," he responds in a cool voice that relays confidence and expertise. "But I must caution you. We do not generally remove memories from anyone over the age of fourteen, due to the risk of causing damage to the brain. Moreover, memories that elicit the type of emotional response that you are describing are often deeply rooted in your mind, making them dangerous to remove."

"Dangerous, but not impossible?" she asks.

"I'm afraid that I could not in good conscience sign off on such a memory extraction. It is not a matter of money," he says, politely dismissing it before she raises the issue. He pauses and raises a hand to the side of his face, subtly touching the small, almost invisible, earpiece to better hear his partner's instructions. "It is a matter of safety. Extractions work best on children and youth. At their ages, the mind is so resilient and the physical structure of the brain is still developing. This gives young people a certain ... cerebral plasticity, which safeguards them from many of the potentially damaging effects of memory extractions."

"So I risk some brain damage," she counters. "Certainly not a desired outcome, but one that I am willing to live with if it means purging myself of the painful memories I carry."

He now realizes that he underestimated both her resolve and her desperation.

"Madam, you are a remarkably intelligent woman. I can only surmise that you have done your research before coming to our Company." He pauses again and listens to his partner. "You know that the primary risk with a latent extraction is the loss of additional memories. Secondary, less common, but more severe risks include temporary or permanent damage to the faculties that control motor and speech skills."

"As I said, risks that I am willing to take," she replies with the same determination.

"What the public studies do not say is that the importance of the memory—its depth for lack of a better word—is directly linked to both the likelihood and severity of the damage caused by extraction. If tomorrow we were to remove your memory of me, it would likely cause few, if any, lasting negative effects. However, the memories you describe from the war are not just powerful on an emotional level, they are integral to who you now are. Your personality is intertwined with and likely dependent on those memories."

She scoffs, but before she can interrupt, he continues.

"I do not speak metaphorically," he explains, now perfectly in tune with the voice and instructions of his partner. "Rather, were I to scan you, I would almost certainly find that these memories are physically dispersed throughout your brain, inhabiting and overlapping the same cerebral systems that hold key aspects of your personality, your intelligence, your drive, quite likely even your consciousness. At best, extracting these memories would turn you into a blubbering idiot, like those useless relatives you describe. At worst, it would kill you or so badly damage your mental faculties that you would end your days supported by machines, unable to function in any way as you do now."

"I see," she says, looking down at her hands. "Well, thank you for your time, at any rate."

"There is one other option," he interjects. "We cannot remove your bad memories and add pleasant new ones. We can, however, implant strong memories to combat the terrible ones that plague you. They will have to be—what was the word you used? Ah yes, sublime. They will have to be deep experiences of pure happiness, excitement, love, and joy to counteract the memories you already have. Moreover, they will have to be meaningful to you in a deeply personal way."

"Is that possible?" she asks with renewed hope in her voice.

"Yes, although it is a more involved procedure that requires us to map intense memories onto your existing personal experiences. Put simply, we will find memories that align with the pleasant memories that you already have and we will implant them in you, strengthening and building on your good memories, as well as adding new ones that would have a deep emotional impact on you.

"To work best, we will concentrate on memories that map onto experiences you had prior to or during the war. I understand that this may prove difficult as you likely have very few pleasant memories from that time. But those few that you do have, we will build on, adding layer upon layer until they are as strong and vivid in your mind as the memories that brought you here today.

"The process will take more time, but will achieve permanent, lasting results that a simple memory implant will not, at least in your case."

They sit in silence for a while as she mulls over his proposal. Finally, she stands and extends her hand to him.

"The reputation of the Company is well earned," she says. "I am ready to begin immediately."

○ ○ ○

"You are somewhat taken with her."

"I am not too proud to admit it. Yes, she is impressive. Her reputation alone enticed me to take the meeting personally, rather than assign it to one of the directors or senior associates. But meeting her in person was something else. I cannot fully describe it, but even at her age and as weakened as she seemed, I was left with the feeling that she could crush me like a bug."

"Well, financially, she could. She could destroy the Company if she wanted and not see a dent in her own bottom line. We had best make every effort to ensure that we are successful."

"Are you worried about the procedure? You've performed similar operations a number of times, always with excellent levels of success."

"It is not the Selective Memory Implantation, but the calibre of memory that worries me. Even from the recording of your interview, I could see that the memories she is describing are deeply embedded, exercising a great deal of power over her emotional state. Frankly, I am surprised that it has taken her this long to show the first signs of breaking."

"So, I am not the only one taken with her. But yes, you are quite right, the implants will have to be of the finest quality. We will likely have to cultivate experiences in order to map onto her past memories. This will require a great deal of effort."

"I'm not sure that will be enough. We will be combating memories that still elicit specific sensations. She is not simply remembering—she is re-living. There is an important distinction. Giving her a happy memory of a day at the beach will not combat the terror she still feels. Even the layering process will just result in a strong memory of a pleasant day or two, not the full sensation needed to eclipse the memories of dread and terror."

"Agreed. I think we both know what will be required for this client."

"I must remind you that cultivating the strength of happy memories that connects the individual to a particular sensation will likely cause the same irreversible brain damage that you warned the client about."

"You have explained that to me in the past, yes."

"It will also require a very strong subject from which to cultivate the memory."

"I have one in mind. She has shown a particular aptitude for connecting memories to actual sensations."

"Mona."

CHAPTER SIX

Sweet Success

After lunch, Mona and the other students in her pod move to one of the classrooms for their afternoon lessons. The teacher hasn't arrived yet, so there is a lot of noise as students take their seats, trade stories about the morning sessions, or continue the games and conversations that they started during lunch.

As usual, Stephanie is bragging about her accomplishments in her session with her instructor that morning. She has a small group of loyal followers and hangers-on gathered around her as she explains how she, once again, impressed her instructor and surpassed expectations on a variety of tests

Mona can't help but roll her eyes as Stephanie puts on an air of casual superiority, saying things like, "We did that lesson months ago." Whenever another student seems to challenge her by asking about what tests she'd taken or what lessons the instructor gave her, Stephanie shuts them up by explaining in a superior tone that her instructor designs new tasks that test her limits.

"My instructor is always trying new things too," responds one of the more skeptical students, maybe trying to rebuild their own self-assurance in the face of Stephanie's nearly overwhelming self-confidence.

"Oh really?" counters Stephanie. "Well I've already breezed through most of the things that you all are still working on. Now I'm following a very advanced course of study—much more challenging than simple memory exercises."

This shuts everyone up, leaving Stephanie with the quiet reverence that she feels she deserves.

Mona rolls her eyes again. The individual sessions with instructors are always private, so there is no way to verify Stephanie's story. Still, she can't help but feel that Stephanie might be telling the truth. Could she really be head and shoulders ahead of everyone else? Mona isn't sure what's more annoying: the fact that Stephanie might be lying to sound important, or that she might be telling the truth. She's surprised to find that it hurts her pride to think that Stephanie might be so far ahead of her, that she herself might not be the top of the class.

"Do you think that Stephanie is really so far ahead of us?" Mona asks Owen. Owen blinks a few times as if re-centring himself—he has a habit of daydreaming.

"I dunno," he says with a careless shrug. He then goes back to humming tunelessly in his seat.

It annoys Mona even more that Owen doesn't seem to care. How could he not want to know if Stephanie really was so far ahead of the rest of their pod? For a brief moment, Mona has the cruel thought that maybe Owen really is just a plomp.

She is about to turn around and ignore him when he suddenly says, "It's really nice to eat lunch with you again today."

Mona is taken aback. His comment seems random and removed from her concerns over Stephanie's boasting. She stammers, not really knowing how to respond. All the while, she is trying to form her words, Owen just sits and smiles patiently.

"I liked it too. Maybe we can eat together again tomorrow," she finally manages. When she started eating lunch with him a week ago, she was afraid that others might make fun of her. To her surprise, Owen was really good company, always telling stories and jokes without ever being mean. Eventually, she realized that she didn't care so much what the others might think about Owen or about her for eating lunch with him.

"I'd really like that," replies Owen. "By the way, did you know that bees like to dance? I found out last week and meant to tell you about it, but I only now remembered."

Mona laughs at the absurdity of Owen's comment, but before they can continue their conversation, three instructors enter the classroom.

The students all go silent and sit very still. As far as Mona knows, no one has ever seen the instructors outside of the individual sessions. But here they are, two women and one man, standing in front of the class wearing the plain grey uniforms that they always wear. Mona is even more surprised to see that one of the three is her instructor. Her eyes widen and she is suddenly very afraid that she has done something wrong and will be kicked out of the school. Her mind races with all the possibilities. Will they ask her to leave? Will they tell her to get out? She thought she'd been progressing quickly. Has she fallen behind? Will she have to go back to the orphanage or live on the streets like so many other children?

The three instructors stand very still with their backs against the lesson board and wait as a severe-looking individual dressed in a dark suit enters the classroom. Mona recognizes the man from when he came to her orphanage years ago. He has not changed. He is tall and thin and has the same hungry look about him. His gaze makes Mona uneasy. Owen actually shuts his eyes and drops his head down to the desk to avoid looking at the man in the suit or at the instructors. Mona wonders if Owen recognizes his instructor too. Are they both plomps? Will they be kicked out?

She feels her breathing coming in shorter and shorter breaths. Her eyes dart around the room to the other students, searching for some recognition from one of them, or some sign that they know what's going on. All she sees are worried looks and nervous faces. Even the overconfident Stephanie looks as though she might cry.

The man in the suit pulls the larger teacher's chair over to a corner of the room, sits, and takes out a computer touchpad that the instructors call a clipboard. The screen suddenly seems to occupy all of his attention. Once he is comfortably seated, one of the instructors steps forward to address the class.

"Good afternoon, students," she says in a formal authoritative voice. "I apologize for the interruption to your regular lessons, but this will be quick. We are pleased to say that a number of you have been excelling in your lessons and studies." There is a slight murmur around the room.

Mona looks over at Stephanie, who is now trying to put on a confident smile despite her obvious nerves. On Mona's other side, Nick smiles up at the instructor who is speaking. Mona cannot be certain, but she thinks she sees the corners of the instructor's mouth twitch upward in response. *That must be Nick's instructor*, she thinks. Next to her, Owen continues to keep his eyes shut and his head down.

"As you know, we are at the end of a cycle. We will be changing some of your instructors in the next cycle," announces the instructor. Mona isn't surprised at the news; it's normal to get a new instructor every two or three cycles. But it's strange that an instructor would come to their class to announce this mundane change.

"Beginning in the next cycle, three of you from this pod and one student from another pod will also take on additional lessons with your instructors. These four students are some of the brightest that we've ever seen."

This news elicits much more of a response. The students all start looking around and murmuring. Mona isn't surprised to hear both Nick and Stephanie's names mentioned in hushed tones, but she is a little surprised to hear her own. In fact, it seems to be coming from a lot of the other students.

"Quiet down please," the instructor continues. "The extra work with instructors will help with the continued development of the talents of these students. It will ensure that they progress quickly through the program—perhaps reaching new levels that we have not yet seen."

Mona is suddenly nervous in a whole new way. She realizes that no one is being punished; on the contrary, some of the top students will be rewarded with extra sessions with the instructors. Compared to the regular schoolwork and chores that all the students have to do, the individual sessions are fun. *Particularly when you have a good instructor like mine*, thinks Mona. She wants desperately to be one of the students selected.

Hoping for some sign, she tries a shy smile at her instructor, but Mona can't tell if she notices or not.

"Naturally, pursuing this extra study means that these students will spend less time on other daily activities, such as these classroom lessons," the head instructor continues with a motion to the classroom that seems to dismiss both it and its contents. "This is a great honour. We have chosen only the best and most promising students in the entire school. The fact that three come from your pod reflects very well on all of you. Beginning next cycle, Nickolas, Stephanie, and Mona, you will have extra sessions with instructors. Congratulations."

Stephanie lets out an audible squeal at the mention of her name. Nick stays calm but is clearly trying hard to hold back a boastful smile. Mona simply sits in her seat and lets the news sink in. She is one of the best students in the school, hand-chosen for additional study. She is still not sure what all this means, but she is overjoyed to be selected.

The man in the suit stands up and nods to the instructors as he leaves the room. With him gone, the atmosphere relaxes. The students begin to chatter excitedly among themselves as the instructors pull the three selected students aside for a moment.

"You three should be very proud," says the female instructor who has done all the talking to this point. "We are so happy that our students were selected." She pats Nick on the shoulder. Mona's instructor finally betrays her true feelings and smiles broadly, giving Mona a thumbs-up that feels as good as a hug to Mona.

"The extra work will be hard," says the male instructor, speaking for the first time. "But we know that you can handle it." He smiles at Stephanie, who is nearly floating off the floor with pride.

"You guys are just so great," says Mona's instructor. "So, so great."

"Now," Nick's instructor says loudly, quieting the classroom and causing students to return to their seats. "I have even more good news. Thanks to the three exceptional students in your pod, you all get the afternoon off for free activity!"

The students all cheer at the unexpected free time and rush to get their things before some adult can call them back for chores or schoolwork.

On their way back to the dorms Owen leans in toward Mona and whispers "Congratulations!" For a moment she is worried that he will have been hurt not to be selected with her, but one look at his smile lets her know that he is genuinely happy for her.

"Are you still hungry?" she asks.

"Not really, why?" replies Owen.

"It's just that I got a note last week saying that I can have a slice of toast with honey on it," smiles Mona. "If I share it with you, will you tell me more about the dancing bees?"

Owen's eyes widened. "Sure," he blurts out.

○ ○ ○

"Why give them extra free time? Surely we should begin the new program right away?"

"Two reasons. First, I do not want to have those students selected ostracized from their classmates. I want heroes, not pariahs. Second, I want to see what our four top candidates do with their free time. Their chosen leisure activities may give us a better sense of how to map the memories they develop for our client."

"Very good, but about that, why choose four candidates? I thought that we were in agreement that the girl was the ideal subject."

"We were and she still is. But I do not want to discount our other top students. There is always the risk that Mona will fail us in some way. Using four students is merely a precaution."

"I see. Very well. I still don't see the benefit of the leisure time, but I trust your judgement."

"That's refreshing to hear. Now on to the client."

"What about her?"

"We need more from her. We need to map some of her experiences so that we can connect the memories that we plan to cultivate with real events as she recalls them. We need to find commonalities so that the process stands the best chance of being effective."

"Leave that to me. I will schedule another meeting with her."

CHAPTER SEVEN

Tainted Sweets

Mona waits, sitting at the edge of her bed, watching the clock in the girls' dormitory tick away the minutes until the morning alarm. She is excited. More excited than she can remember being since the day over five years ago when the man in the suit came to the orphanage and picked her, along with three others, to come to his special school. Owen was there that day too, but he'd been so quiet in the orphanage, and even during their first year at the school, that all Mona really knew of him was his name and the reason he'd been selected.

At the time, Mona had no idea what the school had to offer. All she knew was that it had to be better than the orphanage with its rows and rows of small, hard-mattressed bunk beds in a room with dozens of boys and girls of all ages. Now she had a comfy bed in a room with four other girls, regular meals, and a bathroom with hot water that lasted long enough for everyone to take a shower.

She knew that there was worse than the orphanage. Many children had spent a long time living on the streets before they found a facility with a bed for them. Some were kicked out of the orphanage for fighting or stealing, or just because they got too old. Mona would often see them hanging around the back of the building, hoping for a handout. Sometimes they'd have angry black bruises or red scars from fighting for food on the street.

Mona was very young when she came to the orphanage. Like many of the children there, her parents, or anyone who could look after her, had either died or couldn't afford to keep her any longer. Despite her talents, she only had vague memories of a time before the orphanage, and they were painful and difficult.

Even though the war had ended years ago, many poorer people were still living with its effects. From the front windows of the orphanage, Mona could see crippled beggars asking for change from the poor folks who had to leave their homes early for work, coming back late each evening to eat rationed meals. Many of the men and women who had lived through the war or who were born just after it ended had developed dry, hacking coughs from the fallout of the bombs and artillery fire. If they were lucky, they'd live with those coughs the rest of their lives; if not, the cough would go deeper into their chests and would start to rattle and sound wet. Once that happened, they would have only a few years, at best, before they were in the ground. Even those who could afford medicine or surgery rarely seemed to recover once the cough began to rattle.

Mona could remember the old custodian who worked at the orphanage coughing in that hallway after the children had gone to bed. The kids all sang a rhyme about that cough and the people who had it:

Stood tall like a soldier when I was young,
Said we'd all come home, but I'm the only one.
Now there's dirt on my hands from working all day,
Time to wash all my cares away.

So I walk through the streets with grey in my lungs.
Tell mama I'm home, her last living son.

Pa gave me a lucky penny so I'd stay strong,
Kept the copper in my boot all day long.

Wore the penny down smooth from marching all day,
Only money I ever got worth a damn anyway.

Now I walk through the streets with grey in my lungs.
Tell mama to come visit her last living son.

Hung up my boots when I came home,
Couldn't find me a wife so I gotta live alone.
Lost the lucky penny that used to keep me safe,
Now I've got one foot in the grave.

Blood on my hands and rattle in my lungs,
Tell mama she's lost her last living son.

Mona didn't know who made up the rhyme, but she was pretty sure back then that it was about the old custodian. He'd cough and wheeze into his handkerchief, turning it from white to grey, to sticky black. The children were instructed to treat him with respect, but not to shake his hand or take any of the candies he offered them, for fear of catching the cough too. Despite the warnings, most of the children were happy to take the occasional sweet, reasoning that only those born too close to the war or too close to where the bombs had hit ever got the grey cough.

It was Owen who found the custodian's body one day. It was exactly three days before the man in the suit arrived for the first time at the school. Owen had been inconsolable, not eating anything and not sleeping at night. The staff were all worried that he'd get sick or disturb the other children. They wanted him out of the orphanage, but he was far too young to kick out on the streets and he never misbehaved or fought with the other children, so their hands were tied. That is until the man arrived to take Mona and the two others.

He wore a smart navy-blue suit and a medical mask that covered half his face and muffled his voice when he talked. He was tall and thin. A few of the children were afraid of him, but most were eager to please him so that he would take them some place, any place better than the orphanage or the streets.

On his first visit, he said that he was looking for keen students who showed aptitude with remembering dates, numbers, facts, and other academic bits of information. The children were all gathered in the dining area. The man showed them all a series of cards with letters, numbers, and symbols on them, then he asked each of them to write down what was on the cards, in the order that he showed them. From the first group of students, only seven were selected. Mona was one of them. The staff kept Owen out of the dining hall that day; the man never even saw him.

On the man's next visit a week later, he asked to see the seven children individually. They all sat in the hallway and waited their turn to meet him. Everyone knew the man was somehow important and everyone could see by his clothes that going with him meant something better than staying at the orphanage and waiting to get dumped on the streets. One by one, each child was asked into the room with him. One by one they left, until it was only Mona and a much older girl. The older girl was busily brushing her hair and arranging it into braids to look younger and prettier. Mona didn't think the man cared about her appearance, only about how smart she was, so she concentrated on remembering the cards he had shown a week before.

When it was her turn in the room, she snatched up the pencil and blank piece of paper in front of the empty seat and began transcribing the symbols on the cards before the man could get a word in. She drew the symbols on nineteen cards before she stopped and started to cry. She couldn't remember the next symbol and she was sure that meant she'd failed and would have to stay in the orphanage.

The man simply smiled. "Impressive." He made a few notes on his clipboard and asked if she could remember more complicated pictures.

Mona said she didn't know. She'd stopped crying now and was starting to feel like maybe the man was happy with her.

He tested her for the next forty minutes, much longer than any of the other students. It was the first time she played memory games or was asked to recall exact specifics from earlier that day and week. By the end of their session, the man stood and asked Mona in a formal tone if she'd like new clothes, her own comfy bed, warm showers, good food, a better education, and the chance to sit outside on real grass. Mona was ecstatic. That night, she cried in her bunk out of sheer happiness and relief.

The night before the man was to come and take Mona and two other students he'd selected back with him, it was Owen that was crying in his bunk. He let out slow, gulping sobs that kept most of the children awake until finally one of the staff came and took him away. He slept in the infirmary the rest of the night.

When the man arrived the next day, the staff paraded Owen out and said that he was a new arrival. They asked the man in the suit to test him too, saying that he was smart and could remember vivid details from when his father died.

"When did he die?" asked the man.

"When I was two," replied Owen.

"What can you remember about that day?" asked the man in the suit, sitting down and pulling out his clipboard.

Owen went on to recount the horror of finding the dead body slumped over in a closet. He recounted the look, the feel, and the smells all around. It was done in such great detail that Mona could picture Owen's father alive and well, then dead on the floor. She could picture Owen's dead father so vividly that she was starting to feel as though she knew him, as though she'd seen him every day—she could practically hear his rattling cough and smell the sweet candies he compulsively ate to cover the stench of rot growing on his breath.

Owen finished his story by saying that his grandmother wouldn't even allow Owen to take any of the candies his father would offer. Mona knew then that it was a lie. Owen was recounting details about the custodian and finding his body only a few days before. She watched as the head staff member patted Owen on the shoulder and mouthed the words 'good job.' They'd planned this. They'd coached Owen on what to say in order to get rid of him.

It seemed their plan had worked, as the man in the suit was visibly impressed and decided that Owen should join the other three. Soon all four had packed up their meager belongings and were loaded into a small bus, which was already packed with a number of other children.

"I can't remember anything from when I was two," sneered one of the other children from Mona's orphanage.

"Neither can I," replied Owen in an offhanded way. "They made me make something up." He sat down with a plomp, oblivious to the looks he was getting from some of the other children.

"Cheater," whispered one kid.

"Liar," cursed another.

"They wouldn't take my brother, but they'll take him!"

Mona could feel the animosity toward Owen growing, but he seemed blissfully unaware as he looked out the window and drew a picture of a dog with wings with his finger on the condensation.

She was embarrassed for him that day. In truth, she'd been embarrassed for him on a number of occasions since they both came to the school. For a long time, she didn't want anyone to find out that they'd both come from the same orphanage, as if their shared history would somehow make people think she was a plomp too.

Looking back, she now feels more than a little guilty for wanting to distance herself from Owen.

They were only six or seven years old when they left the orphanage. Mona didn't know her exact birthday, but she knew it was in the spring because when she turned two, she remembers people singing to her on an old blanket in a park. The tulips were out. It is one of her only pleasant memories from the time before the school. She'd been at the school for a little over five years, so she must be close to twelve now. She is pretty sure Owen was around the same age, though he always seems a little younger.

The hands on the clock continue to count down the minutes until the alarm will sound and the students will wake to get ready and head off for their morning chores. Mona would usually be on cleaning duty, mopping the cafeteria floor or wiping down the tables before and after breakfast. Then she would help restock the kitchen before showering, changing, and heading to the one-on-one lessons with the rest of her pod. But not today.

Today she will change, eat breakfast, and head straight to her one-on-one lessons. This will mean a lot more time with her instructor, and less time with the rest of the students in her pod or from other pods on a similar schedule. She wonders if she'll still be able to have lunch with Owen.

In their extended free time yesterday afternoon, Owen had told her about bees dancing to communicate and about how people have instincts that are sort of a collective memory for what might hurt us or make us sick.

"That's why you can look at something and think it's disgustingly gross without even knowing what it is," he explained enthusiastically. Mona tried to explain that she instinctively had a fear of bees and wouldn't want to get close enough to any of them to see if they actually danced.

"No, no," explained Owen. "You had to learn your fear of bees. You probably got stung when you were younger and now you see them and remember the hurt. Bees aren't bad though, so you wouldn't instinctively be afraid of them."

Mona was about to protest, but she remembered sitting in the garden near the wall on one of her first days at the school. She was delighted just to feel the sun on her skin and smell the honey scent in the air from all the flowers. It was completely different from the grey walls of the orphanage or the stink of the city streets she'd known. Here there were colours and scents and insects with beautiful silken wings—things that would be caked with dust and trodden underfoot in the city.

She would slowly walk around the small garden smelling each flower.

That is until she accidently stepped on a flower with a bee in it and got a nasty sting on her leg. Since then, she'd always been very careful to watch her step and give any little buzzing insect plenty of room.

Looking back on Owen's explanation and his insight into her own fear of bees, Mona decides that he isn't a plomp at all. Sure, he makes up funny stories and daydreams, but he isn't stupid or useless like some of the other students say he is. He is actually imaginative and can be quite bright and attentive when something interests him. It was too bad the instructors didn't recognize it, then he could be one of the four top students and maybe Stephanie would get put back with the rest of the pod. Mona smiles at the idea. But despite not liking Stephanie that much, she is excited about what the next few hours will bring. Excited but nervous at the same time.

Sitting on the edge of her bed waiting for the first day of the new cycle to begin, Mona can still feel the thrill of knowing that she is one of the best students in the school. She is as excited now as she was earlier hearing her name announced in the classroom. She just can't wait to get started.

CHAPTER EIGHT

Falling and Flying

"Have you ever had a dream where you are falling?" asks Owen. He has arrived early for his session with Sam. He had to rush through his chores to get here early and he's sure that someone noticed him leave or that he'd have to redo some chores because he didn't do a good enough job the first time. Still, he's not worried about the potential negative backlash. He's too excited to tell Sam about his dream.

"As a matter of fact, I have," replies Sam. "I think that it's a fairly common dream."

"Does that mean that everyone has that dream?"

"Well, maybe not everyone, but I certainly think that most people do at some point in their lives," explains Sam.

"I have the falling dream a lot," says Owen. "Usually, I have it just after I go to sleep. It feels like I'm falling backward through my bed, into the dark, then, just before I think I'm going to hit the ground or splash into water, I wake up."

"That's exactly what it's like for me too," replies Sam. Owen smiles to hear that he and his instructor have something in common

Sam is as happy as Owen is. His student is engaged. He wants to get started with the lessons, but Owen's sense of fun and wonder can be infectious, and Sam knows that starting the session by talking about a dream, Owen will share something truly unique. The lesson can wait another few minutes, he decides. Let's hear what Owen dreamed up.

"The falling dream is scary," continues Owen. "Every time, even if I know I'm dreaming, I wake up with a jolt and almost jump out of my bed."

"That's pretty common," replies Sam. "For me, it usually feels like I've tripped over something and I wake up kicking my legs, as if I'm trying to regain my footing."

"That's funny," laughs Owen. "It must look like you're running or dancing in your bed."

"I guess it does," smiles Sam. "Luckily, no one is there to laugh at my bad dance moves. Why did you bring up the falling dream? When you first came in today, I was certain that you were going to tell me about a dream with dancing bees in it."

"Well, I had the falling dream last night," explains Owen. "Like always, I dreamt that I was falling backward, and I couldn't catch hold of anything to stop myself. I wonder if I was moving my hands or arms in my sleep like you move your legs.

"Anyway, I was falling backward, only this time I didn't wake up, I just kept falling. It felt like I fell through my bed, through this warm dark cloud and into a bright blue sky. I was so high up that the ground was just blotches of green and brown. I could see for miles in every direction and the whole world looked sunny and warm."

"That doesn't sound too frightening," says Sam. In truth, to Sam it sounded beautiful. He could feel his face mirroring Owen's calm smile.

"It wasn't anymore," continues Owen. "I still knew I was falling, but the ground was so far away that I didn't have a sense of speed or danger. It wasn't like a normal falling dream, where it feels like you're going to hit at any minute. It was ... it was almost fun."

"Would you say you were flying?" asks Sam. He is fully engrossed in the description of Owen's dream and is waiting to see what other fantastic events will unfold.

"No," giggles Owen. "I wasn't flying. I was falling. But for some reason, I wasn't really that scared. I was a little worried about how I was going to land, but that's when the bees came."

"Bees?"

"Yeah bees, really big ones!" Owen holds his hands out to indicate that the bees were at least nine inches long. "Big, big bees with fat furry bodies. Just like the bees in our garden, only the size of a kitten or a puppy. They were soft and cute too."

"You touched them?" asks Sam. "Weren't you afraid that they'd sting you?"

"Not really. And I didn't touch them; they touched me. They flew around me, dozens of them, and they grabbed me by the hands and shoulders, by my shirt and shoelaces, by my belt, and some even pushed into the small of my back. Suddenly, I felt like I was slowing down. It was like they were floating me safely to the ground.

"I guess I should have been afraid—I mean, they would have had really big stingers—but instead I just felt warm, happy, and safe."

Sam watches Owen carefully throughout the entire description. He watches as Owen's eyes glaze over. He observes the boy lose himself in the memory of his own dream. As Owen describes the controlled descent, he unconsciously stops and makes buzzing noises as his hands dance through the air, gently holding the fuzzy bodies of imaginary bees.

Sam is fascinated to see Owen so engrossed in his description. He watches as Owen gingerly cups air in his hands and brings it to his face, feeling the soft fuzz of one of the bees against his cheek.

"Their little bodies were so warm and soft that I think I knew I didn't need to be afraid. They buzzed so beautifully that it was like a song that I already knew. I could feel it inside as much as I could hear it."

Owen reaches out his hands. Sam laughs but can't help but pretend to pat the imaginary bee.

"Can you feel how soft they are?" asks Owen.

"I almost can, the way you describe them," replies Sam, realizing that it is true. *Are his fingers actually feeling warmer?*

"I wish you could," says Owen. "I wish you could feel how soft they were, I wish you could hear the happy buzz they made. I wish you could feel what I felt—like there was no reason to ever be afraid.

"Why are dreams like that? I mean, I was falling and I wasn't afraid. I was surrounded by huge bees and I knew I was safe." Owen looks puzzled. "I just knew it was true that I was safe. I just knew that I didn't need to be worried or afraid. I wish it was like that all the time. There are lots of times when there isn't really anything to be frightened of, but still I feel nervous somehow."

"Can you remember a time like that?" ask Sam.

"Oh, sure I can," replies Owen. "Lots of them. Just the other day some of the instructors came into our classroom and I felt really nervous."

"Well that's normal," explains Sam. "We instructors rarely visit students outside of these one-on-one sessions that it must have seemed very unusual to you. It's only natural that something so outside the ordinary would make you feel anxious or nervous."

"It wasn't the instructors that made me nervous," replies Owen. "It was the man in the suit."

Sam tries not to betray his surprise.

"He didn't really say much of anything, or do anything," continues Owen. "But I was scared all the same. I just closed my eyes and kept my head near my desk. It was the same classroom as any other day, but when he came in, it didn't feel like normal anymore. It was strange and different."

"Did he do anything that frightened you?" asks Sam. He knows he shouldn't pry into this area, but he is fascinated by Owen's visceral response to one of the Company's top associates.

"No. But yes," says Owen. He thinks for a while then tries to explain. "You know how you asked if I was afraid of the bees in my dream and I said I wasn't?"

Sam nods.

"I can't explain why I wasn't afraid, I just knew that I didn't need to be, so I wasn't. It was the opposite with the man in the suit. Nothing he did made me feel scared, but it was like my body just knew that it should be afraid, so I was. It was like what you described the other day. I think I had an instinctive feeling to be afraid."

Owen stares down at his hands for a minute or two, gently running his thumbs through the fur of the imaginary bee that he is still pretending to hold.

Sam is taken aback. The students would have no cause to fear any of the instructors or anyone else in the Company. Usually, the directors and associates don't interact directly with the students, preferring to meet with the instructors or review the recordings of the sessions. Sam has himself only met with the top associates on a handful of occasions, usually to give an update on the progress of one of his students. He'd actually secretly been dreading such a meeting to discuss Owen's lack of progress.

Sam had reason to fear his bosses, but Owen shouldn't be consciously or unconsciously frightened of them.

Taking another approach, Sam decides to ask Owen about his dream, hoping that this will steer them away from any further discussion about the instructors or the associates.

"Did the bees dance for you?" he asks, glancing quickly at his watch to make sure that the session hasn't yet officially started and that their conversation still isn't being recorded.

Owen's face lights up. "Yes!" he exclaims. "They brought me to their hive. It was full of golden light from the sun coming through the honeycomb. The whole place smelled sweet with honey and the bees showed me one of their dances!

He jumps out of his chair. He laughs and wiggles and makes buzzing noises, all the while still cupping his hands, gently holding one of the bees from his dream. Sam can't help but laugh as Owen does laps of the room, periodically looking up past the grey and white walls to the golden honeycomb prisms of his dream. Owen takes in deep breaths through his nose, smelling the honey and nectar in the air. He pats the bee in his hands and finishes by plomping down on the floor and smiling contentedly.

Sam is sure that Owen is reliving the best moments of his dream. It is the strongest recollection that Sam has ever seen, from Owen or any other student. Owen looks so happy and peaceful, as if nothing bad has ever, or could ever, happen to him. He seems content in every sense of the word.

"I wish real life were like that dream," says Owen, finally breaking the peaceful silence. "I wish I could feel like I never had to worry or be frightened, like all I had to do was dance in a beautiful room filled with the smell of honey and happy sounds.

"It's so far from the grey city I remember from when I was younger, before I came here," continues Owen as he stands and walks back to his seat. "It's so far from the classrooms and this grey room. It's so far from the dorms and the others in my pod who don't want to talk to me or who think I'm a useless plomp. It's so far. But in my dream, it seemed like I was there, like I could always live there. Like this world, the world where people get the coughing sickness, where they die and you get taken to the orphanage, like this world was the dream and that other one was real."

Owen stops and gently reaches over to Sam, placing the dream bee in his lap.

Sam looks down. He doesn't know what to say or how to tell Owen that he sometimes wished that the world was different too. Instead he pauses for a moment and then says, "Thank you, Owen. Thank you for telling me about your dream. It sounds wonderful."

Sam's watch lets out a solitary beep, letting him know that the session is about to officially start. Soon the recording devices will be turned on.

"We only have a minute before our session starts," he smiles at Owen. "You know that you aren't supposed to make up stories or tell me about dreams in the session."

Owen nods.

"I think that we can get around that by meeting for a few minutes

before each session so you can tell me about anything you'd like. Then
when the session starts, we can do some exercises and talk about things
that might help improve your scores. Who knows, if you improve them
enough, maybe we'll get extra time to work together and we can fit in
more time for stories and dreams."

Owen is visibly pleased by the suggestion. In truth, so is Sam. As they
start the regular work, Sam can see a renewed focus and energy in Owen's
answers. His recollections are stronger and he is able to provide Sam
with a higher level of specificity and detail than he normally does. He
also performs better on almost all of the memory games and stays more
focused throughout the session.

When Owen leaves and Sam steps through his door to the changing
area, he is pleased with himself. He has found a way to encourage his
weakest student to work harder. However, he is also pleased to have come
up with a way to meet with Owen and secretly continue working on his
dreams.

He can't put his finger on it, but Sam is convinced that dreams, or
at least Owen's dreams, would make valuable memories. If there were
some way to capture the feeling of peace and contentment that Owen
described—that sense of safety and ease—Sam is sure that there's
something to it, but he knows he'll need more time with Owen without
the bosses interfering in his sessions.

What then? He thinks. If he can prove his hunch, then he can bring
his discovery to the bosses. Maybe they'll make him a director? Maybe
he'll get a raise too? Sam decides that it's worth whatever risks might be
involved.

o o o

"An improvement this session."

"Yes, what did you do?"

"Nothing."

"Surely you spoke with his instructor. What's his name? Sam, isn't it?"

"It is, and no, I have not had a chance to call Sam into a meeting, although I was in the process of scheduling time with him. I wonder if it is still necessary."

"Hold off to see if the boy continues to improve."

"You seem more patient with him than normal. Why is that?"

"I am less concerned about the boy's progress now that we have identified our four top candidates for our client. I only want to make sure that he doesn't have a negative impact on the girl."

"I think that the opposite is more likely. I think that Mona will have a positive impact on Owen. Perhaps we are seeing the first signs of her influence in his latest session."

"I doubt it. More likely you were right, and the instructor's talent is beginning to shine through."

"Really? A rare compliment."

"But deserved. Why do you now think the girl is more of an influence than the instructor?"

"Did I tell you that she and Owen spent most of their free time together since we made the announcement a few days ago?"

"You certainly did not!"

"Because I thought you would react poorly and have them separated. I can see by the change in your pallor that I was probably right. Yet now we see that their new friendship may, somehow, be helping the boy improve."

"Hrmph. I don't like these sorts of … experiments. She is too valuable."

"Do not worry about her. The program I have designed for her will only help strengthen her skills and add to her value. I'm certain that within a few cycles she will be our strongest producer and your client will be raving about our Company to everyone she knows."

"You can be so convincing that sometimes I must remind myself that you are in charge of programs and I am the outward face of our Company."

CHAPTER NINE

Naming Friends

"**M**y friend Owen told me about the funniest dream he had. It was about dancing bees," says Mona.

"Is Owen your friend?" asks Harriet.

Mona thinks for a little while before responding. "He is my friend," she says, smiling. "And he's not just a plomp, he's actually really clever."

"That's wonderful," replies Harriet, smiling to herself at the student-word *plomp*. "You've never really talked about the other students in your pod. I wasn't sure that you had that many close friends."

Mona is a little startled. She never thought of herself as not having friends. Owen was the loner in their pod. He sat by himself at lunch, and he was always the last chosen for any group work; Mona sat with a group of students and she was always among the very first chosen for group assignments.

Was she chosen by her peers because they were her friends, or was it because she was an excellent student and they would be sure to get a good evaluation on their work? Owen was ostracized for being a plomp, but was she only included for being the opposite of a plomp? The more she thought about it, the more she realized that she didn't really engage in the lunchtime conversations or jokes—she mostly just sat and ate her meal. If the other students got to know Owen as she had over the past cycle, they would probably love his stories and jokes. What did she bring to the table?

"Are you alright, Mona?" Harriet asks. She reaches out and places her hand on Mona's knee.

Mona is aware that this type of affectionate gesture would not normally have been permitted, but she guesses that her instructor has been given special privileges too since the announcement.

"I'm alright," replies Mona. She tries to casually look away and blink back her tears. "You're right, I may not have many real friends, but I am Owen's friend and he is mine."

"It's okay not to have many friends, you know," explains Harriet. "I only have a couple of close friends myself, and really only one here at the school ... well two if you'd consider calling me a friend."

Mona relaxes a little and smiles. She'd never thought that an instructor could be her friend.

"Friends know each other's names," counters Mona mischievously. She knows that asking the instructors about any personal details, just like asking what is behind the second door, is off limits.

"My name is Harriet."

Mona is thunderstruck. Harriet laughs as Mona opens and closes her mouth in silence.

"Well go on, say something," she prompts Mona.

"I thought that ... well the rules ... they told us," stammers Mona.

"Now that you are in the special group of students, the regular rules do not apply in the same way," explains Harriet. "There are certainly still rules. For instance, I have to ask that you keep my name a secret and not to tell anyone in your pod that you know what it is. They still aren't allowed to know the names or their instructors."

"So, it's a secret between friends," replies Mona.

"Exactly!"

"That does make us friends then," smiles Mona.

"Do you have secrets with Owen?" Harriet asks.

"Yes," Mona thinks for a moment about what she knows about Owen's past and the story he made up at the orphanage to get transferred to this school. "I can't share his secret. I'm sorry."

"That's alright, Mona. I wouldn't want you to share a secret—otherwise how could I trust you with any of my secrets?"

Mona is thrilled. Not only is Harriet her friend now, but she's treating her with respect and kindness. She realizes that this is what she'd been hoping would happen for a long time, even if she had never admitted it to herself.

"I would like to hear about how you and Owen became friends, if you don't mind telling me that?" asks Harriet.

"It just sort of happened. We ate lunch together one day," replies Mona.

"Mona, it's not like you to gloss over details. I'm sure you can do a little better than that."

Mona thinks for a while then says, "He asked me to wait for him so that we could go to lunch together. I didn't want to at first—not really anyway—but there was something in the way he asked me. I could tell that he was really lonely. He usually eats by himself or with the kids from younger pods. No one in my pod wants to eat with him."

"What made you decide to, then?"

"Like I said, it was how he asked," Mona pauses. "Not what he said exactly, but how he said it."

"Was he sad? Can you describe it?"

"Not just sad, something a little more. He was quiet and the way he asked made me feel like he was very, very far away reaching out, even though we were standing next to each other at the bottom of the stairs that lead up to the dorms." She pauses.

"It sounds like he might have been a little bit desperate to make a friend," suggests Harriet.

"What do you mean 'desperate'?"

"Desperate is a feeling you get when something seems hopeless," explains Harriet. "It is a feeling you get when you would do anything or try anything to escape the situation you are in. People sometimes say, 'It was a desperate effort' or 'In a desperate attempt to.' Another similar word that people often use is despair. Despair means losing all hope. So, I guess you could say that people often act desperately, before falling into total despair. Does that make sense to you?"

"I think so," replies Mona. "Can someone be desperate to eat at a table with someone else?"

"Probably," replies Harriet. "People can certainly be desperate not to be alone. Or they can feel despair because of extreme loneliness. Do you think that's what Owen was feeling?"

"I think he might have been. He's funny and really nice to everyone, but some things seem to affect him more than others. It doesn't really bother me to eat lunch without someone to talk to, but I guess I usually eat at a table with other people so maybe I don't notice that I'm really sort of eating alone. I guess when Owen asked me to eat lunch with him it made me feel bad that he was almost always alone. It reminded me of when I've felt like that too."

"That sounds like empathy to me, and I think it's very good that you felt it and that you have become Owen's friend," Harriet replies, making a few quick notes on her clipboard. "Can you elaborate a little more on how Owen reminded you of a time when you were desperate or when you felt despair?"

"It's not fun to remember that. It was a long time ago," responds Mona, looking down at her shoes.

"Mona, believe me, I understand. I prefer asking you about happy memories and the fun times that you've had. For instance, I still want to hear that funny story that Owen told you about dancing bees."

"It was a dream he had," corrects Mona.

"It sounds like it was a good one, and I'd love for you to tell me about it at the end of your session. But right now, I'd like for you to tell me more about when you felt sad or alone or desperate. I don't mean to dredge up painful memories for you, but you need to understand that all memories are important to our work."

"Why is that?" asks Mona.

"It's hard to explain," replies Harriet. "The work we do with you is meant to help people. We study how your memories work so that we can help other people with their memories. Most of our clients—the people we work with—want to remember pleasant things, like eating honey or making a new friend. So, we mostly help them with those memories." Harriet pauses.

Harriet and Mona exchange a look. Harriet wants to tell Mona that a few years ago someone figured out how to copy memories and share them from one person to another, but she knows that she is not supposed to tell Mona about the specifics of what the Company does. It's not that the process is harmful, it's just that it can be frightening for children.

"Does that mean that our memory games help you figure out how to help other people hold on to their good memories?" asks Mona.

Harriet is relieved that Mona has come to this conclusion, it is not entirely accurate, but it will serve to help Mona understand. "Exactly, very good," she lies.

"So why do you want to know about my bad memories?" Mona asks.

Here Harriet is on safer ground. This new process was just explained to her as part of her briefing on how to continue with Mona's training.

"Well sometimes people get sort of stuck in bad memories. They only remember sad or scary things and they can't remember what it's like to be happy," she explains.

"That's terrible!" exclaims Mona.

"It can be really bad for some people," continues Harriet. "A lot of people can get medical treatment to help. Sometimes they take medicine, sometimes they talk to a doctor and the doctor helps them work through their bad memories, but sometimes nothing works. We're trying to help those people. That's why you were chosen."

"How will you help?" asks Mona.

"Well, it's a very new process, but we need to figure out how someone with an excellent memory, like yours, can connect a bad memory to a good one." Mona looks confused as Harriet says this, so she tries again to explain. "When something makes you sad or mad, it doesn't make you feel that way forever, does it?"

"No," responds Mona.

"Sometimes you feel better just because enough time goes by, but sometimes something or someone makes you feel better—like I'll bet you did for Owen when you ate lunch with him. He was lonely, now you're his friend. He's lucky that you were there to help him."

"But I didn't do much," replies Mona.

"Maybe it didn't feel like much, but I bet it meant a lot to him," explains Harriet. "It will be the same for the people we are trying to help. They are stuck feeling sad or lonely. We need to understand how our brains can move from being sad to being happy. Imagine how Owen must have felt when you said you'd eat lunch with him. I bet he started feeling happier right away."

Harriet watches as Mona smiles at the memory. "I'd like to help," she says.

"So, will you tell me about a time you felt despair? I know it might not sound like fun, but remember you don't feel that way now and understanding how you went from feeling bad to sharing funny stories with a friend will help us make a sort of a map to happiness for someone else who might be stuck feeling sad and alone. Can you do that?"

"I'll try," replies Mona.

Mona pauses for a moment to collect herself, then she begins.

"I've always been able to remember things—even before I came to the school—but some things I find really hard to hold on to. We do a lot of work to concentrate on details and sensations. I can't remember all the details from when I was really little, back before I went to the orphanage, but I can remember some of the sensations. Is that okay?"

Harriet nods.

Mona closes her eyes and continues. Pulling up these memories is much harder than reaching back and remembering how many red dots were on a white page or the colours of individual flowers in a picture of a bouquet. These memories seem buried somewhere inside her. They are part of her, not just external details that she is recalling as part of some test. She has to relive them to remember them and it hurts to bring them up.

"I was cold. I was hungry. I was tired. The cold was a sort of deep-down cold, where you don't shiver anymore. It felt like it was a razor running right through me."

Mona starts to shiver slightly, and Harriet can see her face getting paler, but she presses on.

"When I'm hungry now, my stomach sometimes gurgles. But back then it just hurt. All the time. I felt like I would eat anything. I remember eating scraps of bread with lumps of green mold on it. I knew it was disgusting, but I was too hungry to care."

By now Mona is bent over in her seat, shielding her stomach with her hands like someone protecting an open wound.

Harriet wants to inch closer, to tell her she can stop, to hold her and tell her it's over, but she can't. Her instructions were specific. This is a necessary step in the new memory mapping process. It is difficult, but it will make all future work easier and will ensure stronger connections to memories.

"And I was so tired," continues Mona, slumping even further in her chair. "It was so hard to find a safe place to sleep, so I had to stay awake, but sometimes I'd fall asleep on my feet and wake up with my face against the cold pavement. After a while it was hard to tell the difference between being awake and asleep. I felt confused and scared, and then eventually like nothing mattered. I remember just wanting to lie down and sleep. I didn't care how cold I was anymore or how hungry. I just wanted to sleep and have it all go away.

"Then I saw this lady. She was walking right by me, humming. There was something familiar about the humming, I think. It's hard to remember exactly what she looked like or where we were. I just knew she couldn't see me and that I had to make her see me before I fell asleep. I ran.

"I guess I stumbled or fell. I don't know. My feet were so cold I couldn't feel them anymore. I think I fell down in front of her. I think she stopped and picked me up. Whatever it was, I suddenly felt soft and warm. I think she was humming to me—I don't know.

"The next thing I remember was waking up in the orphanage in their little infirmary. I asked about the woman, but no one answered me."

They sit in silence for a minute. Finally, Harriet stands and walks over to Mona. Kneeling down in front of the child, she leans in and gives her a hug. They are both crying softly.

"Thank you, Mona. I know that was hard. Next session we'll talk about something much more pleasant—something fun, I promise."

With Mona in her arms, her little body still feeling cold and frail, Harriet starts to hum.

o o o

"That was unusual."

"It was perfect! Did you see how her memory elicited that emotion? Not only in her, but in her instructor too?"

"She elicited a response. I have no doubt that Mona felt a strong memory, but the sheer lack of details! She is always so good at delivering specific and strong details!"

"In this case, and perhaps only in this case, a lack of specific details may work in our favour. My client spoke of the terror and dread of war. I am sure that she must have felt despair at some point. I am sure that, like the girl, she had to act desperately in order to save her life or save the life of someone she loved."

"Based on what you've told me about her past, I'm sure she has."

"Exactly, and now she feels deep regret and remorse for some of the actions she was forced to take."

"I wouldn't be able to tell you what she feels."

"Then trust me. And trust me that we have our starting point from which to map the memories. My client experienced despair. So has Mona. The fact that the details are vague is good, it means you can make a plan to map directly onto a deep sensation, without running the risk of muddling memories of two unrelated events."

"You may be right. Have you been studying my techniques? I'm flattered."

"Do you think it will work?"

"Yes. The more I consider it. If we start with a strong sensation, from there we can build a new neural pathway that leads to more pleasant memories."

"Good, continue."

"Imagine that you are standing on a road and you come to an intersection with a choice of where to go. You can see that the road to the right is treacherous but still fairly clear. The road to the left has been almost completely washed away. You have no real choice but to take the path to the right, correct? It is the same way with your client. At the time she formed her memories, she could only choose to move forward and deal with whatever treacherous path lay in front of her. When she looks back, she sees her younger self, desperate and frightened, but resolved to survive.

"We can scan her to pinpoint the moment where she first experienced a sense of despair. We will call that moment the intersection, to continue to use our metaphor. While your client may only have had one path to follow, we will add another. We will clear the washed-out road and make it lead somewhere more pleasant than the path she remembers taking. Rather than being forced to take desperate actions leading to later regrets, we will map and implant memories that link despair to relief and then to joy, love, whatever we want. The memory implants will be false, as they always are, but the new neural pathway we create will be built on real sensations and experiences, ensuring a permanent solution to the client's problem."

"I see. An elegant solution and all based on my observation about the importance of a strong emotional reaction."

"Very well, I'm not just flattered, I'm impressed."

"I will be sure to inform my client of the progress we are making toward a lasting result."

"May I also suggest that you find out about some of her pleasant memories? We can work to give Mona similar experiences to build a sort of critical mass so that the pathway we are creating leads to implanted memories that align closely with the client's own memories. This will help ensure the implanted experiences feel more genuine and real."

"An excellent suggestion."

CHAPTER TEN

Off Track

Harriet is lucky enough to live in one of the pristine new buildings that the Company had constructed for its employees back when they first began dealing in memory extraction. Even in those early days, before the Selective Memory Extraction and Implantation technology had fully developed, memory manipulation was a highly profitable field. The Company, as every employee called it, made huge sums of money extracting particularly painful or unpleasant memories from soldiers and survivors recently back from the war.

Memory extraction was a booming industry in the first few years following the war, with new firms starting up every day. However, it wasn't too long until the bubble burst and major problems with memory extraction began to become apparent.

About a decade after the war, veterans who underwent the extraction procedure began to experience serious and troubling side-effects. Often the procedure would affect more than just the targeted memories, leaving the patient with large gaps, sometimes years of their life, that they could not recall. Sometimes patients would wake from the procedure unable to remember their husbands, wives, or children. Some patients would suffer physical side effects, including severe tremors in their limbs, trouble understanding speech or writing, and occasionally even paralysis.

When the first patient died twelve years after the end of the war, the newly-formed government passed a law banning memory extractions on persons over the age of fourteen, unless the event to be removed occurred less than six months before the scheduled procedure. The procedure could still be performed on children, as scientists agreed that their brains were malleable enough to recover and that the removal of a particularly traumatic memory would allow the child to grow up to live a more productive and happy life. No one seemed to care that the scientists coming forward with the information were employed by the top firms offering memory extractions.

After the new laws were passed, many smaller firms went under. The larger ones began to specialize in what was now called acute memory editing. They advertised that they could remove the pain of a bad breakup or reduce nightmares associated with a car crash, but given the cost of the procedure and the public perception that it was dangerous, many of these companies also folded.

From the dozens of firms offering memory manipulation in the first decade after the war, only a handful survived into the second decade. The Company that Harriet works for is one of them. Like the others, the Company differentiated itself by moving from memory extractions to implantations. It focuses today on implanting pleasant, happy memories. The Company is now considered a global leader in this area.

Harriet had originally been hesitant to work for a company that extracted memories from children to be implanted in the super-wealthy. But the more she learned about the process, the more she was reassured that it was minimally invasive and had little to no lasting effects on the children.

Harriet read in her orientation materials that, unlike the old-fashioned memory extractions, which selectively damaged neural pathways to essentially delete unpleasant memories, the process the Company employed today involves conducting several complex scans of a student's mind while they focused exclusively on a specific happy memory. These scans were then analyzed by a massive computer bank, which constructed a digital memory that could be 'downloaded' through a medical procedure into the mind of a client. The child didn't lose their happy memory, nor did they suffer any ill effects; the clients were able to pull forward false memories from the child that would feel as real as any from their own lives, to enjoy a strong recollection of love, comfort, joy, excitement, or anything else their hearts desired.

As for the children, Harriet was assured that they were selected for their aptitude from orphanages and hospitals, or they were sent by parents who could no longer afford to feed them or send them to school. In return for sitting in a room with lab techs and scientists and being asked to concentrate on their happiest, best memories, they receive food, clothing, a safe place to sleep, and an education.

During her orientation with the Company, Harriet and the other new instructors heard from a former student who had gone on to have a career in politics. He explained how his memory training and education helped him breeze through university and get a job as a political aid for the Chancellor himself. His memories of his time on campus in the Company's school were, not surprisingly, very detailed, but also overwhelmingly happy.

"If I were a client looking for memory implants," he explained. "I'd ask to have the memories of a student from your school. I'd ask to be able to feel what it's like to build a relationship with an instructor and see how pleased they are when you succeed. I'd ask to feel what it's like to live with a small group of kids my own age with plenty of time for free play and study. I'd ask to sit in a garden far away from the dangers of the city, feeling the sunshine on my skin and the fresh, clean air in my lungs.

"But I don't have to pay for any of those memories. They live within me. They are as much a gift as my education and training. I've used the memory exercises I learned here to make myself a key player on the Chancellor's inner team. To those who worry about the well-being of the children here, I say the fact that they are here ensures their current and future well-being."

Everyone at the orientation applauded.

Then there were the financial reasons to get a job with the Company. Harriet's take-home pay is modest, but the benefits of working for the Company are almost too many to name. Probably the greatest benefit are the living arrangements.

Prior to working for the Company, Harriet lived in a one-bedroom apartment in the city with her sister due to the high cost of finding a safe living space. Her sister owned the apartment, so Harriet slept on the couch and kept her few possessions in two suitcases.

Since the war, almost everyone had moved close to the city. The outlying areas beyond were largely deserted, having been reclaimed by the Chancellor and his government to be converted into arable land— an enterprise that was wildly successful according to all official reports, but a dismal failure if you judged it by the price of food or the ongoing rationing of so many basic products.

Harriet could remember the embarrassment of not being able to afford her own place. She was a university graduate—a fairly rare thing—with a degree in neuropsychology, forced to beg for a spot on her sister's couch. But now she had her own apartment just outside the core of the city. It was connected to the Company's main campus by a private subway system, and only a short ride on public transport into the city centre. Best of all, the apartment was free. The Company didn't want to run the risk of anyone selling trade secrets, having their work or personal files stolen, or simply being tempted away by better offers, so they made sure that employees received perks—the apartment was just one. Harriet also got access to the Company's physicians, ensuring that she remained healthy even during crop blights or in the rare times that lasting fallout blew through the city.

When she was first hired, Harriet sensed that her sister wasn't happy. Amelia would argue that experimenting on children wasn't ethical. Harriet would shoot back that the Company was providing for the children, not hurting them. The procedure was a little more invasive than an fMRI. The family dinners became more and more uncomfortable and before too long the dinner invitations came less frequently. Soon they stopped altogether. As Harriet lived in a secure building, she could not invite her sister to dinner at her place without getting Company clearance—a step that she felt would have infuriated and embarrassed her sister.

Harriet felt a little lonely back then, but soon she met Sam. And part of her resented Amelia for not celebrating her success.

Still, she thinks as the subway pulls to a stop under her building. It would be nice to have dinner with her again sometime soon. Amelia lived in an oddly beautiful part of the city, near an old church. They used to walk together through the square to the market, Amelia filling Harriet in on the rich, sometimes shocking history of the neighbourhood before the war. Amelia wore her address the way many former soldiers wore their medals. Harriet could never quite figure out why.

Harriet reaches her hand into her pocket and feels the smooth screen of her company phone. Maybe it would be worth the effort to get the Company to approve a family dinner. She knows that Sam's mother visits at least once a month. She could convince Amelia if she worded the invitation carefully and met her at the security check-in.

Harriet is just about to call the building security desk to put in a request when she spots Sam on the platform. Unlike everyone else, he isn't heading home, he is waiting to get back on the train to campus, a black file case tucked under his arm. He looks preoccupied and even a little anxious as the train comes to a stop and the doors open.

Harriet watches from her seat as the passengers file out and head for the stairs up to their apartments. It only takes a minute or so and then the station is empty, save for Sam standing on the platform and Harriet in the now-empty train car. She stands and steps onto the platform, a few cars down from where Sam is waiting. Her boots clomp on the hard concrete, echoing in the empty tunnel, but Sam doesn't take notice. He simply waits by the open doors of the last car, seemingly unsure if he should turn around and head to his apartment or step onto the train.

Harriet smiles at the flustered and pained look on Sam's face. He is so deep in thought that he doesn't notice her closing in on him. She nearly laughs as he mumbles something inaudible to himself. He looks cute when he's deep in thought, and something is clearly on his mind now.

Harriet is just about to call out and startle Sam away from whatever is bothering him, when he suddenly steps forward, catches the closing door of the train, and climbs onboard.

"Sam, wait," she cries. But her words are lost in the noise of the train and the whirl of wind it kicks up. She turns to watch as the train gains speed pulling him away from her.

What had him so worried, she wonders looking down the long dark tunnel. And why was he headed back to work this late in the evening? He wouldn't have any one-on-one sessions scheduled this late, and he could finish any paperwork he might have leftover from home.

Harriet pulls out her phone and calls Sam. His voicemail picks up straightaway, informing her that he is not available but will return her call. Her brow wrinkles hearing the cheery, friendly voice on the phone that seems at odds with the worried face she saw only minutes ago.

"Just calling to see if you were free to get together tonight," she says. "Anyway, give me a call when you get this, I'd love to see you." She hangs up and walks up the stairs to the building lobby.

It isn't until after she's home and halfway through dinner that Harriet realizes that her message could be interpreted as asking Sam out on a date! Suddenly she's no longer worried about what might have been bothering him and much more worried about what he might think of her.

Beet red, she paces her small living room for a full five minutes. What will Sam think? They're just friends, after all. Close friends sure, but friends and nothing more. Harriet picks up her phone and begins to call him back to apologize for the awkward message. She'll explain how she saw him on the subway platform and watched him head back to work.

She'll say how she was worried that he was working too hard and might need a break or a friend to talk to. She'll stress the word friend and tell him that she just wanted to make sure that he was alright. That's all. Nothing more. Nothing ... she stops pacing and puts down her phone.

What harm would it do to see how he responds to the message? How would he react? Even if she didn't mean to ask him out, Harriet is a little surprised to find that she is happy with the idea of going on a date with Sam. She smiles at the thought of him agreeing to go to dinner. Maybe he might want to date her. Who knows? And if not, she could always just say that she left the message as a concerned friend. He wouldn't be the wiser and no one would need to be embarrassed or hurt. She frowns at this last thought, knowing for certain now that she, at least, would be hurt. Then as quickly as she calmed down, Harriet is pacing the living room again, worried once more about how Sam would react to her message, only this time for a very different reason.

CHAPTER ELEVEN

The Crown

"There is something more to a dream," Sam mumbles to himself before stepping on the subway train back to work.

After the quick ride, he is back in the facility, walking through the nearly empty building to the diagnostic labs. He waves at the security patrolling the halls on his way past. It is unusual, but not unheard of, for instructors to be working after regular hours.

"Just have to prep a few scenarios in the diagnostic lab for tomorrow," lies Sam as he passes a security desk. The disinterested officer waves him through with barely a glance at his credentials.

The lights of the diagnostics lab flicker to life as Sam puts down his file case. He checks his watch. It's just past 1900 hours. If all goes well, he has a few hours to kill before they begin. He can use that time to prep the machines and get the room ready for Owen. Sam is fully aware that his student will be frightened in these clinical surroundings, but he's taken a few steps to make Owen feel a little more comfortable. He removes the stuffed bee toy from his bulging file folder and sets to work preparing the room.

Owen arrives at the door, bleary-eyed and yawning, close to 2300 hours. He is holding the hand of his housemother, who looks very nervous to be parading the child about this late at night.

"Did you see any guards?" inquires Sam.

"No," replies the woman. "It's just me in the dorms this late."

"Good," replies Sam. "Owen, why don't you come into the lab?"

Owen peers into the cold, white room from the doorway, clearly too afraid to move through the door. He looks from Sam's welcoming smile to his housemother's concerned frown. Unsure what to do next, he simply bows his head and stares down at his slippers.

The housemother checks nervously over her shoulder and sucks her teeth. Sam can tell that it will only take a moment more for her fear to get the best of her; if he doesn't act quickly, she will pull Owen back with her through the halls to the dorm. She knows that she is risking her job and she knows that she can get Owen back to bed without anyone but Sam being the wiser. She also knows Sam is as guilty—no, even more guilty—than she is, so he would never tell the bosses about this.

Sam has to act quickly to remind her why the risk is worthwhile.

"You know Owen, I'm glad you came tonight. I have a gift for you," he smiles and points to the stuffed bee by the diagnostic table. Owen is visibly excited but holds tight to the housemother's hand. "And don't worry, I didn't forget your housemother," Sam says, revealing the vial of medicine in his hand.

Owen watches as the housemother cautiously reaches out and takes something small and made of glass from Sam's palm. Her eyes begin to fill with tears and to Sam's obvious surprise she rushes forward and kisses him on each cheek. Owen starts to smile. Whatever gift his instructor gave her must have been perfect. She kneels down next to Owen, still smiling and wiping tears from her eyes.

"Mr. Sam is a good man, Owen. You listen to him and help him with his work. He is trying to help people," she pauses. "You can be his assistant tonight. Together you can make a lot of people who are sick better. Would you do that?"

Owen nods. He is in awe at the reaction of the usually stern housemother. He has seen her smile and laugh before, especially when singing to some of the younger students. He has seen her be tender and kind, like when she pulls a splinter or dresses a cut. But he has never seen her cry or speak so lovingly of someone. Behind her laughter and tenderness, there is usually a sense of severity and duty—she is the first to welcome the new students with a smile, but also the first to scold them for even the most trivial of trespasses. Not so with her reaction tonight. Owen now sees a different side of her, one of warmth, appreciation, and even admiration. It is infectious and he can't help but see his friendly instructor in a new light.

More than that, she said the instructor's name. Sam. He is called Sam! Neither adult balked at letting Owen in on the secret. Clearly whatever is happening tonight, whatever involved being woken up and ushered off to this strange room, entails some level of trust. Owen can't help but feel special that they trust him. Maybe they trust him more than the students who were specially selected for additional work? Maybe he is special too?

He has never been jealous of Mona or Nick or Stephanie. It was always made clear to him that he was not one of the gifted students. Grownups even had to help him cheat to get into the school, and every day since he's been lagging behind.

"Is this some sort of special extra training?" Owen asks Sam hopefully.

Sam dismisses the housemother with a nod, and takes Owen's hand, leading him into the diagnostic room.

"Not exactly," replies Sam. "I don't actually think you need extra training. I think that you have something special that you can teach me."

"What could I teach an instructor? I'm not even that good at the memory games."

"Well, I'm not sure what I'm looking for exactly," says Sam. "I just can't help but think that you have some hidden abilities that no other instructor even considers."

"What kind of abilities?" asks Owen.

"Let's see if we can find out. Would you mind hopping up on the table?"

Owen looks nervously at the table and the large machine that hangs over it.

"Tell you what," says Sam. "Let's run the machine on your new bee first. Can you plomp him up there?"

Owen obliges and Sam lowers the machine over the bee. Under Sam's careful instruction, Owen places what Sam calls 'the crown' around the bee. The crown is attached to the much larger machine that hangs from the ceiling. The crown and the larger machine are connected by a mechanical arm that moves with silent, fluid actions at even the gentlest touch.

Owen looks around the room. It is sterile and white, not unlike a doctor's examination room. The floor is a dark grey. In the middle of the room is a standard medical table, and above it the large machine connected to the crown. The machine is off-white. It has smooth circular contours that are about six feet wide where it connects to the ceiling, but taper in stages as it extends down to the exam table. It looks almost like a conch or a shell of some sort, but a little too regular in proportion. The mechanical arm extends from its tip, a good four feet from the exam table. It reminds Owen of the arm the dentist would manipulate during the students' annual check-ups, only it doesn't have a light on it, instead it has the crown. The crown is a dull, silvery-grey ring. The inner side of the ring is covered by a row of sensors that are a darker charcoal colour. Nothing about it or the larger machine seem overly frightening to Owen as he and Sam check that the crown is properly placed around the bee.

After a few adjustments, Sam lets Owen hit the button to lock the arm in place, limiting the motion of the crown to only a few centimetres in any given direction.

"The crown is too big for just the bee's head, but the machine should be able to scan its memories anyway," explains Sam. "Now what should we ask the bee to think about?"

Owen considers the question for a while and finally replies, "Let's ask about how bees learn to dance?"

"That's a great idea," replies Sam before addressing the bee. "Mr. Bee, please clear your mind as best you can. Don't think of your day, or your chores, let your thoughts fall away. Breathe deeply, in and out. Close your eyes if you like. One more breath, in and out. Now please try to recall when you learned to dance. Think of the movement of your body. Think of the smells of the hive. Think of the other bees there, did they help teach you? Were they learning too? Think of the colours and the sensations. Think of how you were feeling before you began, during, and after."

Owen notices that while Sam is talking to the bee, his hands are moving around the control panel, adjusting levels and hitting the buttons displayed on the control screen. First, he dims the lights, then the machine starts to hum gently. Then, just as Owen begins to feel at ease in the low light and the noise of the machine, it is over.

Sam smiles at Owen and flips on the lights. Together they move the crown back up to the machine. Sam gently picks up the stuffed bee and hands it to Owen.

"That's not too bad, is it?" says Sam.

"No, I guess not," replies Owen.

"Are you ready to give it a try?" asks Sam.

"Does it hurt?" asks Owen nervously.

"Not at all," Sam explains. "It's no more unpleasant than some of the memory exercises that we do. All I'm going to ask is that you recall something for me while I conduct a mid-level scan."

Owen considers this for a moment. "Sam," he asks, using his instructor's name for the first time. "Will we really help someone feel better?"

"Honestly, Owen, I'm not sure," replies Sam. "My idea might be foolish and useless—a lot of people who are better at their jobs than I am think it is. But I can't shake the feeling that there is more to a dream than they think."

"A dream?" asks Owen.

Sam blushes a little. "You're not the only one who likes to talk about dreams when he shouldn't, Owen," he explains. "I've nearly gotten in trouble for spending too much time in our sessions with you on them. But I've never had a student like you before. I've never known anyone with such fantastic dreams, such silly dreams, and such imaginative dreams."

"That's the first time I've been called silly and fantastic," says Owen, smiling. "And I know what it's like to have people think that the stuff you talk about is foolish. It doesn't feel good."

"No, it doesn't," replies Sam.

The two look at each other thoughtfully for a moment.

"Let's prove them wrong!" says Sam breaking the silence.

Owen smiles.

They work together to adjust the machine to fit Owen, resting the crown just above his eyebrows, snug, but not tight on his head. Sam lowers the lights and leads Owen through a number of breathing exercises. After several minutes, they begin.

"Owen," says Sam. "Please relax your mind, relax your body. Breathe deeply and slowly."

Sam watches as Owen moves into a sort of trance. Suddenly he is worried—his pupil has never been good with concentration. How will he perform today? No, no he reminds himself. Today isn't a typical memory scan. Today is something new. Owen is just right as he is. Sam just needs to trust Owen, and to trust his own gut.

"Owen, you don't need to speak. I just want you to cast your mind back and remember the last dream you had."

With those last words, Sam watches as Owen blinks sleepily a few times and a smile drifts over his face.

Sam starts the scan. Owen never moves, even as the machine comes to life and begins making a quiet humming noise, even as Sam moves around him, checking connections and adjusting the fine-tune settings on the crown. It isn't until a full ten minutes after the procedure is complete, once Sam has cleared up the room and hidden all the traces that it was used outside of regular hours that he finally rouses Owen.

"You did very well, Owen. Where did you go?"

"Back to the hive to watch the bees dance."

"So, it was a good dream that you remembered then?"

"The best," says Owen sleepily, yawning and swaying on the diagnostic table.

"Let's get you back to bed, so that you can dream again."

Sam carries the sleeping Owen back through the halls to the entrance to the student areas. The housemother is waiting impatiently for them. She wraps Owen up in her arms and shuffles off to his dorm without a word to Sam.

Just as well, Sam thinks. *What would I have told her anyway?* He holds the record of the scan in his hand. So much data to pour over, so many signals and false starts he'll have to analyze. But deep in his mind, he is positive that amid all the noise and indecipherable chaos from the brain scan, there will be a signal, a shining beacon—not a full memory in the same way that one remembers a number, a room, or even something as detailed and personally significant as a sunrise can be—but something that will lead Sam to what he is hoping to prove.

"There is something more to a dream," Sam mumbles to himself. Now he just has to find out what it is.

o o o

"What do you mean unauthorized?"

"I don't feel that I should have to explain the word to you, of all people."

"Who was it?"

"One of the instructors performing a standard location scan."

"On a student?"

"Well, they didn't scan one of the night guards."

"After hours?"

"I am beginning to think that you could benefit from some of the memory training games that we teach the students—you seem to be having trouble remembering the details of the report I just gave you."

"There's no need for your so-called wit. I am just having trouble coming to grips with the obvious and glaring breach. We need to fire the instructor immediately!"

"Aren't you curious why he chose to risk his job to perform a routine scan?"

"Not in the least. You authorize scans and set the schedule. You monitor the results and work with the instructors and the other technicians to identify, isolate, and extract the most promising memories. It seems obvious to me that anyone not involving you in these processes is hoping to extract memories on their own, perhaps to sell them to a competitor."

"That is the most likely possibility."

"Is there any other?"

"You and I have always maintained a firm grip on the Company."

"You are the only other person I trust."

"Thank you, the feeling is mutual. That said, with my control over the curriculum and the extraction process and your control over the public face of our firm and the interactions with clients … well, we haven't left much room for innovation."

"What are you saying? Your technologies are far more advanced than those of any of our competition! And I've …"

"You've taken equally innovative steps to keep tabs on our competitors and to ensure that no one is able to keep similar tabs on us."

"Precisely why this security breach troubles me."

"So, we agree that together we have total control over all aspects of the Company?"

"A firm grip as you said; you as Chief of Technology and me as Chief Executive."

"As of late, I am worried that our firm grip may have become a stranglehold."

"How's that?"

"We shot ahead of the competition after the Chancellor's party introduced the new regulations. My innovations, your connections—together we were miles ahead of the pack. But now they have begun to catch up—quickly in some cases. Some are specializing, some are innovating, but most are gaining ground on us. I am most worried about those firms that are exploring new ideas and new areas. Those firms are taking risks and trying new things. When one fails, the others learn from their mistakes and improve on any potential that can be found in their failed processes. Innovation is driving innovation, and soon we will be sharing the apex."

"So, you innovate again."

"I cannot. At least not in isolation. And neither you nor I trust anyone to come into the Company."

"Then, what, we wait to become obsolete?"

"Don't be dramatic. We promote from within. We continue to keep a careful watch on our employees, but we let little things, like this scan, slide at least until we divine the reason behind it."

"I see your logic, but it makes me very nervous."

"Good. That will help focus you on investigating if we have a mole, an innovator, or just a willful and obtuse employee on our hands. I will review the data that our instructor extracted to see if I can determine why he felt the need to be so clandestine about his actions."

"I thought you said he removed the data and covered his tracks?"

"Please. You underestimate the protocols that I put in place."

"But you're still not going to tell me the name of the potential mole?"

"Do you really think that I would underestimate you? We both know that as soon as this meeting is done, you will call up your own surveillance system to learn who did this, when I found out, and how quickly I brought it to your attention."

"Well?"

"I found out two hours ago and brought it to you as soon as I had a plan in mind for how to proceed."

"As I said, you are clearly the only other person I could ever trust."

CHAPTER TWELVE

New World

M ona steps through the door to the exam room. As with almost every other day, Harriet is waiting for her. Mona sits. On one side of her is the door she came through, on the other is the door she has never seen behind. The room is the same grey-white as always. She kicks her legs back and forth in her chair and looks up at the ceiling, waiting for Harriet to begin.

Mona is feeling slightly impatient. Although she has been selected as one of the top students in the school, she has not noticed that much has changed: her school workload has not decreased, despite her hopes; she has had a reduced chore schedule, but that has been replaced with more one-on-one sessions with Harriet; and nothing else is all that different. She and Harriet still do the regular memory exercises, some of which have become more challenging. Occasionally, Harriet asks Mona to recall more painful memories, which can be difficult, but more often than not, the sessions are very similar to how they were before Mona was identified as one of the four most promising students.

In short, Mona is bored.

Harriet has not seen signs of Mona's boredom in the quality of their work together, but she has begun to notice that Mona is less engaged. Not less attentive—Mona never seems to miss anything or fail to recall the details of their conversations, but she has taken to yawning more as a subtle, maybe even unconscious protest to the monotony of their sessions.

Not today, smiles Harriet.

"Mona, are you ready to begin?"

"I guess so," replies Mona, the words coming out in one continuous sigh, her eyes still fixed on the ceiling. Harriet knows that Mona has counted all the tiles and can recall which are discoloured and which have been more recently replaced.

"Good, let's go then," says Harriet, standing up and taking three quick steps to the instructors' door. Before Mona can ask what she's doing, Harriet is through the door, leaving Mona alone behind her. She suppresses a giggle, knowing that her student has gone from bored-stupid to dumbfounded.

Mona sits wide-eyed for a moment before following Harriet through the door. It is an odd sensation to step into the next room. Mona is struck by a feeling that is part excitement and part apprehension. Before her is a room like any other, small and not dissimilar to the examination room. On the surface, it is nothing special, but deep down it is more than it appears. This room is off-limits. Mona can't help but wonder if this is a minor transgression that might be frowned upon but will be forgiven, or if this is a major violation that will get both Harriet and her in trouble. Her doubt makes her hesitate for a moment before curiosity wins out and she steps into the room.

Just after the door shuts, Mona is suddenly aware of an odd sensation. For a split second she feels almost dizzy. Like some unseen force is pushing on her stomach and trying to make her turn to her right. It's very subtle—Harriet doesn't seem to notice as she moves forward in the empty space—but to Mona it feels that something has shifted slightly, almost imperceptibly. She wonders whether it is just the excitement of entering a new part of the campus.

Harriet smiles at her and touches a spot on the wall. A small door swings open revealing a cubby-hole. At the same time a plastic card pops out of a slot on the wall. Harriet takes a bright yellow scarf from the cubby and puts it on, adding a flash of colour and a sudden sense of fun to her plain uniform. She then removes the card and uses it to open the next door.

"Ready to begin?" she asks Mona again, holding out her hand. Mona smiles and reaches out, letting Harriet lead her through the doorway into a new room.

Harriet herself can't help but marvel at the ingenious design of the building. Usually the small changing area leads to a common locker room, where instructors can shower or change into their regular clothes. Today, however, it leads to a hallway leading to a small concrete courtyard. This is a part of the building she is familiar with, but it is one floor up from the changerooms and harder to access. She has heard of other instructors who've left the exam room only to find themselves in the sterile hallways leading to the head offices of the chief instructors. Usually these stories are tearfully recounted by staff as they clean out their lockers, security guards waiting to escort them out of the building for good.

No one is really sure how the bosses change where the doors lead. There are very few windows in this part of the administrative buildings, so it's hard to tell if the rooms rotate slowly, allowing access to different areas at different times of the day. Harriet has never noticed any sudden movements either in the main building or in the exam rooms—no sudden feeling of being pulled up, down, left, or right, like you get in an elevator or on a train. Still, she has had some moments of dizziness or vertigo. She usually chalks up these rare experiences to hunger or fatigue. But maybe there is something more to the strange architecture? Regardless of how the rooms change, the overall effect is one that makes Harriet feel a little apprehensive as she steps through, not to the locker room but to the corridor somewhere above it. She had known this was coming, but she still feels a little out-of-place in areas of the building that she does not have a reason to frequent on a regular basis.

Mona is oblivious to any of Harriet's apprehension. This whole thing is new to her and she is determined to remember every detail. Harriet leads her down a number of hallways, all painted the same dull colours as the exam room. They pass through a few small rooms that require Harriet to swipe her key card again in order to open doors leading to more dull hallways. Despite the plain colours and lack of significant details, Mona is enthralled. Every twist and turn is something new, every doorway leads to an area she has never seen before.

Finally, Harriet opens a door and leads Mona down a hallway that is not just plain white and grey. One side of the corridor is filled with long, high windows letting in bright light from a beautiful green garden. Mona counts her steps along the hallway, measuring the garden, which is about twenty-five feet below the window. It seems to begin at the base of a wall which runs perpendicular to the passageway they are in and runs out past where Mona can see the hall curve off to the left, away from the greenery. After thirty-seven steps, she's measured off the width of the small garden in the main school. This garden extends much further to a small copse of trees.

"I've never seen so many plants and flowers," exclaims Mona, stopping to look out the large windows. "They go on and on!"

"I'm told that the garden is the start of five hectares of land that the school uses for farming," explains Harriet. "It's very valuable and most of it is off-limits because of the delicate nature of the hydroponic and greenhouse facilities, but the founders of the Company wanted to keep a garden as a quiet space for some of the clients to enjoy."

As Mona looks closer, she can see a few people sitting here and there on benches dotted along the pathways that weave through the different flowers and bushes of the garden. It looks like a quiet, contemplative place, and she is interested to see that the two or three people scattered around the garden appear to be resting in the sun reading or just enjoying the vivid colour and variety of the flowers. One older woman stands out to Mona as she reclines on a bench. Mona watches as the warmth of the sun seems to melt the worry from the woman's face. For a brief moment, she smiles into the light. Mona is struck by a sense of peace and contentment. But as quickly as it had melted away, the look of worry returns, and the woman's face tightens again, her countenance revealing nothing but stoic control.

The woman looks up and sees Mona and pauses for a moment as if she is about to call out. Mona notices cracks in the control on the woman's face—her eyebrows draw together in concern, sadness, or both. Then she stands abruptly and, despite her advancing age, walks briskly and unaided away from the bench and through a doorway.

"These people have painful memories?" asks Mona.

"Most of them, yes," replies Harriet.

"And they stay stuck in them, even when they sit in the sunshine surrounded by flowers?"

"Yes, many of them do. The things that happened to them, what they experienced, well," Harriet searches for the word.

"It haunts them," says Mona.

"That's it exactly," replies Harriet. "How did you come up with that word?"

"I was remembering one of our sessions, where you asked about my favourite food and I told you about eating honey. You asked if I could still taste the honey. I said no, but that I could taste the ghost of a flavour. If something so good but so small can linger like a ghost, then something bad could too, I guess. If it was bad enough—if it was terrible—it could be a ghost that haunts you, right?"

"That was very well put, Mona," replies Harriet, taking Mona's hand. "You have a gift for understanding how people might be feeling."

"I don't think I understand how the old woman who left the garden was feeling."

"Maybe not exactly," says Harriet, as the two walk down the hallway. "But you have a sense of what it might be."

They walk together in silence for a while. The windows end where the hallway curves off to the left. Then there are stairs leading up and more stairs leading down. They pass an open interior space where people are hard at work on machines that look large and exceedingly complicated. They pass glass walls with rooms on the other side containing long tables surrounded by dozens of empty chairs.

Finally, they come to a door leading to a shed-like room. Inside Mona can smell mud and grass from the work boots left under a bench. There are raincoats still wet from earlier in the morning when the gardeners must have been out watering and tending to the plants. With only one small window letting light in from the garden outside, the space feels even closer with a pleasant, humid heat. The work clothes and the wooden walls absorb the sounds from the garden, and without the regular noise of air circulation machines, the space is pleasingly quiet.

Mona shuts her eyes to better enjoy the new smells and the watery tingle of the moist air on her skin. She hears Harriet's soft-soled shoes step on the floorboards and the sounds of her hands smoothing down the rough material of her skirt as she bends down to be level with Mona. The soft light fabric of Harriet's scarf gently brushes Mona's hair, landing without sound and barely noticeable weight, on her shoulder. Were she not concentrating so much on the feel of this space, Mona would likely not have felt it at all.

Harriet looks carefully at Mona, noting the pace of her breathing and the way she holds her hands out from her sides, fingers dancing slowly to take in the feel of the thick, warm air. It seems a shame to rouse her; all Harriet wants to do is let Mona sit in this quiet space for as long as she'd like, without distraction or worry. Finally, she sighs and puts her cool hands on Mona's warm shoulders.

"Mona, I want you to remember what despair feels like," instructs Harriet.

Mona's eyes snap open and lock with her instructor's. Harriet lets her pupil refocus before breaking the silence again.

"I'm sorry to ask this of you. I really am," says Harriet, her voice wavering slightly from the truth of her statement. "I know that it is unpleasant, to say the least. I know that this new space is warm and cozy. But we need to know how strong that difficult memory is within you. Can you feel cold in such a warm place? Can you feel desperate when you are safe and sound? Will bringing back the memory dull the sensation over time?"

"It won't," Mona says flatly. Her voice is firm and definite. "It will feel the same as always."

"But I only asked you to recall that feeling once before," replies Harriet, a little more than confused. "How can you know that it will feel the same?"

"Because it is my ghost and you made me remember it. You made me bring it back. The sun couldn't warm that lady in the garden because she was haunted … I guess I'm haunted too."

Mona does not break eye contact with Harriet as tears start to well up and roll down her cheeks. Her voice doesn't waver or break.

"After you made me bring that memory back, it started to follow me," she explains. "Sometimes I dream about the cold and the hunger. I run to the lady, only she doesn't see me this time and I wake up cold and afraid."

Mona's arms are now ice cold under Harriet's hands. To Harriet's surprise, the whole room feels cooler too. The space grows much less comforting as Mona continues.

"The hunger is like glass inside of me," she says, buckling over so quickly that Harriet has to catch her from falling. "When I move, it cuts my insides."

Mona is so light in Harriet's arms; far lighter than Harriet remembers. She is pale and the skin on her face looks as though it's been drawn tight around her skull. Mona's fingers are curled in tight and are ice to the touch. Still she continues.

"When I dream, I see the lady, but she doesn't see me. I run toward her, but I fall …"

Harriet is afraid. She does not know how this can be happening. What happened to the happy smile on the healthy face of the youthful girl?

How has her skin gotten so cold, her body so light, her fingers stiff and brittle like the leafless twigs on a winter's tree?

"I don't reach her," mumbles Mona. "I don't reach her …"

Desperate, Harriet half-carries, half-drags Mona out into the sunlight. "It's warm, Mona," she says, her voice pleading to be heard. "Feel the sun, smell the grass. You're safe here. They put this garden here for you. When you're cold or afraid, you can come to this place. I will find you. I will take you here."

Not knowing what else to do, Harriet holds Mona and hums.

They stay together like that, Harriet kneeling, arms wrapped around Mona's cold torso, until finally Mona reaches out and feels the warm ground beneath her. Her fingers begin to relax and dance among the longer blades of grass and the small purple and white clovers.

She looks at Harriet and blinks. "What is this place?"

"It's a new memory for you," replies Harriet, relieved to see the colour back in Mona's face and to feel the heat from her skin.

They stand and Harriet leads Mona up a small path to a grassy hill.

The garden is not much bigger than the one in the school, but it is designed to feel more secluded. The wooden door to the shed and a brick wall behind them are the only visible sections of the building. The rest is greenery.

The small hill is in the middle of an open space of grass surrounded on four sides by small groves of trees that hide the other parts of the building. The path is trodden grass, not gravel like the other gardens Mona has seen. It leads up the hill then down through the trees. Mona and Harriet follow it to a space in the grove with a small pool of clear water, fed from a stream cascading down a low rock face. It is the first waterfall Mona has ever seen, and despite the fact that it is only a few feet high, with a trickle of water barely strong enough even to be called a stream, to her, it is beautiful.

"I like this place," says Mona. She sits on the grass by the pool of water and turns her face to the sun. Her hand makes slow figure-eights in the cool water. "I like this place," she says again more slowly as her body warms and relaxes.

"This is your place," replies Harriet. "It's just for you. This is so that you can have a memory of someplace that is safe and warm. I hope that you can bring it back like any other memory, whenever you need to feel happy and at peace. But we can also come back here together, whenever you like."

Mona smiles. "Could we visit it tomorrow?" she asks.

"Of course."

o o o

"Perfect."

"I agree. It's rare that you get so personally involved in the development of any memory programs, but I must say your input on this one yielded the exact results that we were hoping to see."

"Thank you. I had a feeling that creating a garden for her would work. I modelled it on one I used to play in when I was a few years younger than her."

"So, this is your memory too? Did you want to share it with Mona or with the client?"

"Well, obviously I hoped the girl would enjoy it … otherwise how could it be the basis for what we plan to build for our client?"

"But if Mona enjoys it too, then what's the harm? Do you have a soft spot for the girl?"

"Don't be absurd. If I show her any favouritism it is only a reflection of the potential that you and I both see in her. Now, did your instruments pick up anything of note?"

"It is difficult to say. The instruments in the shed certainly picked up on huge levels of anxiety and fear, but it is not clear whether those readings came from Mona or her instructor. The instruments simply cannot be that precise when we have to hide them like that."

"Yes, the instructor is rather close to the girl."

"Not a bad thing. I think it actually helps Mona transition from despair to comfort. The instructor is a sort of catalyst that pulls her from an unpleasant state to a peaceful state."

"I only wish we had more accurate readings to confirm that Mona is linking her old memories of despair to new memories of comfort and happiness."

"We will have to perform some mid-level scans in the coming weeks, but I can tell you this: the thermal sensors we had in place registered a temperature change not only in Mona's body but in the ambient temperature in the shed as well. The air got colder when she accessed the memory."

"Is that even possible?"

"Until today, I would have told you it was not."

CHAPTER THIRTEEN

Needing Sunshine

"**H**ave you enjoyed the gardens?" he asks, offering what has become the standard sip of port she takes during their meetings.

"I've been here off and on for three months," she says, ignoring his question. "How soon until the procedure is ready?"

"Madam Andriss…"

"Simply Andriss will do. People hear 'madam' and they expect an old female matriarch. I may be over seventy, and I may have produced offspring, but I will not be reduced to the role of doddering old grandmother." Andriss smiles sarcastically at her host. "I'm sure that you will not find it hard to believe that I have never made anyone sugar cookies."

They share a chuckle before she continues.

"I apologize for my earlier impatience; you and your staff have been excellent hosts." She sips her port and looks out the window to the gardens below.

They have taken to conducting these meetings in his office. This is not the norm, he reflects. Rarely would anyone but Morgan be invited into his private office, but his esteem for Madam Andriss has grown from respect to admiration over the time that they have spent together. During the past few months, they have had several meetings. Often, they talk of her past, allowing him to glean necessary details to help inform Morgan's work. But more recently, they have discussed family and business. Andriss has insights into politics, the economy, the collapse of long-established trade deals, future tariffs, and most interesting of all, changes to the make-up of the Chancellor's inner party. Her insights are always well-reasoned and well-supported by seemingly insignificant details found in Party papers and on the news nets. It is as if she is able to read invisible signs hidden in full view, there for all the world to see, but for only her to comprehend.

As if reading his mind, Andriss breaks away from the window and asks, "Have you sold your company's shares in rice?"

"I have."

"Good. I tell you that it may seem foolish now, but the deal with the Eastern Bloc is failing and you will find the Party pumping government funds into the production of other grains soon enough. Look to new foodstuffs but avoid investing in synthetics."

She finishes with a sigh, looking tired once again.

"I wish I could wrap myself up in business like I used to," she confesses. "But I find my memories haunting me more and more. Even in your lovely gardens."

"You have taken Morgan's advice and started taking constitutionals?"

"I visit the gardens when I'm here," replies Andriss. "Much good they do me. I won't argue that they are beautiful, even restful. For a moment the other day, I felt the sun on my face and could almost feel the weight of my memories slip away. But the mere thought that they were off my shoulders was enough to open the door and let them pour back in. No, I cannot be distracted from them. My past is mine and it stays with me." She pauses for a moment, remembering the girl in the window, and sets down her unfinished port.

"It stays very close to me these days," she says. Her eyes are not focused on the garden beyond the window, nor the room around her. It is as though she is seeing things that once were happening again, like an old scar opening new, raw, and fresh.

Stowe thinks of standing and making his way over to her. He has had this thought many times in their sessions together. He knows that no action of his will alleviate her pain, but he feels that the act of trying may help in some way. These are new thoughts for him; he has never been accused of being emotional or sensitive to the feelings of others. *It must be a sign of his respect*, he tells himself as he reaches out and puts a hand on her shoulder. *Still*, he reflects, *how odd it is that he wants to comfort Andriss. Just as Morgan noted recently, it was odd that he wanted the girl to share a happy memory similar to his own.*

Andriss is pulled back to herself. She looks at the hand on her shoulder, then across to the body attached to it. Instantly she regains her composure, her eyes clear and her voice crisp and definite.

"Stowe," she says, addressing the man in front of her, "I need a permanent solution. If my pain is mine to bear, I need the new memories you promised me. I need them closer than my pain to shield me from it."

Stowe sits back in his chair. *This is what I want*, he thinks. *This is why I am drawn to her. It is not empathy for her, it is a desire to have her control, her sense of purpose, her drive. They are the strengths I've always seen in myself magnified and made manifest in this woman.*

"I will speak to Morgan," says Stowe. "We are very close, and you are our top priority."

"Good," replies Andriss quietly, once again looking out past the garden and the buildings far off at something that also seems to be in the room with her. "Good," she repeats almost inaudibly. "I need to feel something else while I still have time."

o o o

"Morgan, I assume you were watching my session with Andriss?"

"I always review your sessions with our most esteemed clients, Stowe. They help me work with our directors to ensure that we are harvesting the best memories to meet the needs of our customers."

"But you watched this one in real time, no doubt."

"Yes."

"How are we progressing?"

Morgan sighs. Stowe's constant insistence that progress advance like clockwork can be trying.

"We are ahead of schedule, as well you know," replies Morgan, after a sufficient pause.

"Good, good. I don't know why, but I hate to see Madam Andriss like that," replies Stowe.

"You mean in pain?" asks Morgan, genuinely curious about Stowe's reaction.

"No, not that. Pain is a whetstone to people like Andriss. This is something else. She is weakened, lessened by what she is feeling."

Ah, thinks Morgan. *You are worried that if a woman of such fortitude and drive can be reduced in such a way that it could also happen to you. How rare of you to show your cards, Stowe. Usually the only feelings we get from you are frustration or anger. It seems the Andriss file is touching you closer to home. But I suspect you also feel for her too, despite the lie you tell yourself.*

"I will authorize additional resources to get the girl ready," says Morgan. "We are on the right path; we just need time to see it through properly. Half-measures will do no good. Madam Andriss requires our best work to date, I'm sure you'll agree."

"Nothing less than our best. I am in full agreement."

CHAPTER FOURTEEN

Reliving the Moment

H arriet examines herself in the mirror while remembering the events of the day. She tries to use the exercises that she has taught Mona, but with so much that happened, the little details seem lost and she is left with a general happy feeling. Happiness mixed with a few nerves. She never would have guessed that her conversation with Sam would have led her here tonight.

She remembers Sam saying, "I can't believe this place," just after they sat down together on the bench outside the little wooden shed that led into the garden.

Harriet smiled at that. She was happy to be able to share the garden with Sam. It was Mona's garden, really. Harriet felt that it was odd that they provided such a beautiful spot for the benefit of only one student. Looking around it was clear that the grounds were maintained, but that there were very few signs that the garden was used by anyone else. Even the paint on the bench cracked and flaked when she and Sam sat down, a sign that no one else had sat here for a long while.

Why not use it? Why not share it? When Harriet proposed the idea, Mona was delighted.

"You mean we could bring Owen?" replied Mona, barely containing her excitement. "He'd love the waterfall and all the flowers. There are bees here too. Owen loves bees."

"I'm sure that I could arrange for Owen to come with us," said Harriet. "We'd have to invite his instructor along as well," she added, wondering if that were true, but secretly hoping that it was.

Harriet was surprised at how easy it was to get administrative permission to bring Sam and Owen along with them. It seemed as though any request that involved Mona was granted with barely a second thought.

She even pushed her luck and asked her director why so many allowances were being made for Mona.

"Mona is one of the top students we have," replied the director. "Our instructions are to trust your judgement when it comes to the curriculum. You are aware that you are building memories for clients. You know Mona best and know what will make her happy. Our instructions are to foster happy memories that can be mapped to help our clients."

That was that. Harriet didn't want to argue or press the point. If she got special permission to do things that made Mona happy, then she would use it. If it also meant making another student happy, well that was an added benefit. Just like the added benefit of spending some time with Sam.

She couldn't deny that Mona was happy. Harriet watched as Mona led Owen through the doorway to the garden. His jaw practically dropped off and without warning he spontaneously hugged Mona before running up the hill.

Harriet saw Mona blush a little before chasing after Owen shouting, "Wait, Owen, wait! Let me show you the waterfall!"

While they watched the two children laugh and play in the sunlight, Harriet and Sam sat on the bench and talked.

"I got your message," said Sam after a pause in their regular chatter about work and the day's events.

"Oh," replied Harriet, trying not to betray her anxiety.

"Were you asking me on a date?"

Harriet remembers the feeling of warm blood rushing to her cheeks.

"Because I'd like that," said Sam. "I mean, if that's what you were asking."

"Then that's what I was asking," replied Harriet, maintaining her cool despite the flutter in her stomach.

They sat together as Mona and Owen explored the different parts of the garden, peering at butterflies on flowers or dancing in and out of the shade of the trees. For all the world they looked like two children lost in play. Harriet was grateful that they had a chance to visit this special place together.

"I had called to see if you were okay," explained Harriet. "Then I sort of got off-track."

"Glad you did. And I'm fine by the way," replied Sam. Within a few minutes of their awkward fumbling, Harriet was relieved to find that she and Sam were back to their normal comfortable banter. Nothing changed. Well, nothing that she would not have wanted to change.

"I had to go back to work to run a few tests, is all," continued Sam. "I was actually hoping to run some of my findings by you. Not here though. Maybe tonight?"

"It's a date."

"I suppose it is," smiled Sam.

o o o

Harriet smiles at the memory of the day.

Suddenly, there is a knock on the door and Harriet is pulled back to the present. She realizes that she is not quite ready.

"Just a minute!" she shouts, as she gathers up the books and clothes that she has yet to tidy neatly away. They'll just have to go in the cupboard by the door for now.

Another polite knock.

"Coming, coming," she says, wiping the crumbs off the kitchen counter that faces the front entrance.

"Come on, Harriet," says Sam, his voice muffled by the door. "I've seen your place before. It's exactly like my apartment—except for the unfolded laundry on your sofa," he adds with a chuckle.

Harriet scrunches up her face in a half-embarrassed, half-amused smile as she leans back on the closed door.

"I don't think I'm going to let you in," she teases.

"Well if you don't," replies Sam, "then we won't be able to finish our conversation."

In the mix of nerves and excitement getting ready for tonight, Harriet had almost forgotten her earlier conversation with Sam in the garden. But with his reminder, her curiosity is again piqued. It's unlike Sam to keep a secret. She wonders if it has anything to do with when she saw him heading back to work after hours one night?

"Alright, you can come in," she says, opening the door.

Sam smiles and steps in. He takes a moment to look around as if seeing her apartment for the first time.

She tells Sam to sit down as she finishes prepping in the kitchen. For a while they make idle conversation about their work and what they did that week, but soon Harriet's curiosity gets the better of her.

"So, what did you want to run past me?" she asks.

Sam pauses for a moment then pulls his coat off the chair where he had laid it. For a moment, Harriet is confused and thinks he is leaving, but instead he rummages through a pocket and pulls out a memory file.

"Can I use your clipboard?" he asks.

Minutes later they are sat close together on the couch as Sam pulls up files from a scan he performed. Harriet watches as he shows her how he sorted through the data and muted the background brainwave activity that makes the scans look random and messy. Little by little it starts to become clear as layer upon layer of activity is isolated and removed from the baseline.

"At first, I was looking for the signatures that allow us to identify strong memories," explains Sam. "I thought that the dream would show up there and I could isolate Owen's feelings of comfort and happiness."

"I don't see it in the data from the scan," says Harriet, moving her figure around the screen. "Everything looks pretty normal, no spikes or hot spots. Nothing is lighting up like it should."

"That's what I thought too. I was ready to give up when I found this." Sam wheels his finger around a spot on the screen. Harriet watches closely as the spot enhances and a pattern starts to emerge from the seeming chaos of neurons firing.

"Do you see it?" Sam asks, his finger following the bright spots as they flare on the screen.

"There are so many. Is this a memory? How can it be affecting so many areas at once? It should be a localized pattern that the clinicians can scan and copy."

"It's not a memory! It's not anywhere near the memory centres or any other area that we usually include in our analysis for further scanning and mapping," Sam explains.

Whatever this is, it is not like anything she's seen in the normal mid-level scans that she has assisted with in advance of the more complex mapping procedures. She has never seen so many hot spots. Sam could be mapping multiple memories at once, but that doesn't make sense because Owen would have had to have been remembering many events in a high level of detail to get these results, something that she would have thought to be impossible.

"I know what you're thinking," says Sam, seemingly reading her mind. "It's not multiple memories. The flares are too sudden and brief, not the gentle warming of pathways that we usually see when a student focuses on a specific event.

"Then what are these?" asks Harriet.

"I think they are experiences. I think that I was scanning Owen while he was actually experiencing intense, pleasant emotions!"

"But how? We can scan memories that link to emotions. Those are the pathways that we build in our clients to give them the sensations they are looking for. You can't actually copy an experience over, can you?"

"I'm not sure. I think I got this on the scan because Owen was dreaming. He was awake, but he was able to escape into a dream and actually experience it again," Sam pauses to let what he just said sink in. "Owen isn't just daydreaming; he goes into this trance and he's lights out. He's awake and you can pull him back, but he's off somewhere else." Sam taps the clipboard. "He's here and he's having very strong experiences. He's feeling something genuine in the present, not merely remembering it."

Harriet is about to protest, but then she remembers how Mona made the room feel colder, how she grabbed her stomach like the memory of hunger was stabbing her. She is certain that Mona was reliving those events, but was she actually experiencing the feelings as if they were happening to her again? Suddenly, Harriet is feeling very worried and guilty. She made Mona relive those moments, many times. Before each visit to the garden Mona sat in the shed and brought about the memories of despair and terror, but until now Harriet had only thought of them as strong memories, not fresh wounds.

"What's wrong?" asks Sam.

Harriet realizes that she has been silent for a few minutes.

"Nothing, I was just wondering if Mona's memories bring about the same response," she replies.

"Don't worry, I don't think that Owen is going to outshine your superstar," says Sam, misinterpreting Harriet's concern. "I don't even know if any of this is useful or if I'm still just wasting my time. It's just that I can't help but feel that there is something more to Owen's dreams."

Looking down at the replay on the screen, Harriet can't help but agree. If there was a way to map Sam's scans, it could lead to a powerful memory. No, the recipient wouldn't just have a memory—they would have the ability to relive an experience right down to any feelings of excitement, happiness, joy, or ecstasy. Or fear, thinks Harriet. Or terror.

Or despair. Or any number of emotions. Even sensations like hunger, cold, or pain.

"I'm not sure what I should do with this," says Sam. "I wanted to show it to you. I needed a second opinion. I don't have enough to bring it to any of the directors. Not yet at least."

Sam pauses and looks at Harriet. "Are you okay?" he asks.

Harriet is miles away, back in the exam room, back in the garden shed, reliving each time she asked Mona to suffer, remembering how she held her afterward and took her to the garden, watching as peace and calm washed over her. Why would they need any memories other than the happy memories of days by the waterfall or playing with Owen in a garden? What good are memories of pain?

○ ○ ○

"What do the scans reveal?" asks Stowe.

"It is not definitive yet," replies Morgan.

"Don't give me that! The instructor is sure they have merit. He showed them to a colleague."

"One of your bugs?"

"I've been following our mole carefully. I'm willing to concede that he does not seem to have any intentions of selling our corporate secrets to another firm, or of smuggling out scans or our students."

"Do you know what he is doing?"

"I think he is trying something new. He thinks he's on to something, but he doesn't know where to go next. I want to know if he's chasing his tail or if he's got something we can work with. I want to know what you think of his scans."

"The scans are … promising," replies Morgan. "But they are very different from what I would expect to see in a normal scan."

"How so?"

"It is difficult to tell. Suffice to say that Owen is not, what's the word?

Ah yes, he is not, as the students say, a plomp," smiles Morgan.

"I've never seen any potential in him."

"Nor I, in truth. But I'm glad I argued with you that we shouldn't write him off. Sam sees something in him, and he is finding out how to bring Owen's hidden talents to the surface."

"So, what next?"

"We need to see if what Sam is working on is really worth something."

"And how do we do that?"

"Force him to move to the next level."

"Very good. I will apply some pressure to see if that gets him moving. What about the girl? Her progress seems good; I want to keep ramping it up if you think she can take it."

"She is strong. More than capable of following the curriculum that we have planned out," explains Morgan. "I worry that her instructor, Harriet, has grown too attached to her, though. Some of what we were planning may be … upsetting."

"How much does the instructor need to know about the next steps?"

"Very little for a while, but she is smart and capable, she may begin to suspect …"

"I like the instructor; she makes the girl happy. Let's continue to use her as long as we can. It's best for the girl."

"For the client you mean?"

"Yes, of course."

CHAPTER FIFTEEN

Fevered Dreams

M ona feels tired and weak, but for the first time in the last few
days, she is hungry.

"Can I have some soup?" she croaks. Her throat is sore and dry.
Hearing her, Harriet wakes up from the chair by the infirmary bed.

"You're awake!" says Harriet. "How do you feel?"

"Tired," replies Mona. "And hungry."

"That's good," says Harriet, visibly relaxing. "The nurse will be in to
check on you. In the meantime, let me get you some water and crackers."

"Were you here with me the whole time?" asks Mona, as Harriet stands
and walks to the doorway.

Harriet just smiles and steps out into the hall.

Mona tries to think back and remember exactly what happened. She
can remember waking up coughing violently. Stephanie told the other
girls in the dorm to stay back. She said that Mona had the grey cough
and that if they went near her, they could get it too.

In between coughing fits, Mona told Stephanie to shut up. But she was
worried too. She tried to see if she could feel a rattle in her lungs, but all
she felt was the pounding in her head and a dry fire in her throat.

The other girls in her dorm were huddled together against the wall
when the housemother came. She scolded them for not coming to get her

and told them to get back in bed as she shuffled Mona out of the room.

The housemother brought Mona to the infirmary and tucked her into one of the four hospital beds. Then she left to get the overnight nurse. After that Mona's memories start to muddle together—just short periods of lucidity mixed into a jumble of confusion and sickness.

It makes Mona very uncomfortable to feel that there is something she can't remember. Since her time at the orphanage, she has always been able to remember anything significant that happened to her. With her memory training at the school, she has expanded her abilities and can now remember almost everything that she experienced in a given day, from the exact words in a conversation to the feeling on her hand of the cool pool water in her garden.

Trying and failing to remember the events of the past few days makes her feel powerless, like she's lost control or had something taken from her. She can feel herself break out into a nervous sweat. She clutches the sheets up and looks fretfully around the room. The strangeness of the infirmary only adds to her anxiety. This is not her bed. This is not the girls' dorm. There are no familiar sounds. The widows here look out to a completely different part of the school.

Mona pulls the covers over her head and tries to shut out the outside world. Concentrate. Concentrate and remember. And suddenly she feels panicked and hot under the tangle of blankets.

It was a fever. She could hear the nurse talking to her housemother. A high fever. They would need to keep Mona overnight. All night she tossed and turned, sweating through her sheets, her body aching and shivering.

The next day was no better. She couldn't keep food down and even drinking water hurt her throat. Her lips got so dry and cracked that they bled, but she was too tired and ill to care. She fell into fitful sleeps where she had terrible dreams about being trapped in the dark while all around her unseen voices whispered and plotted. She would wake up tangled in her sheets from thrashing around in her sleep, half her body uncovered and freezing, and the other half bound up and boiling. She was often too weak to free herself and had to try to call out to the nurse in her rasping voice.

On the second night, she had a dream that she was falling backward into some kind of thick hot liquid. She was being pushed down and down as her limbs grew numb with the weight of the substance around her. It was hard to breathe. She couldn't decide if she was drowning in mud or being buried alive in hot sand. She couldn't move her limbs far enough to reach up and pull herself out.

Then she felt something firm and cold press against her. It soothed her and she felt the tension ease around her body. It felt as though the heat was being pulled from her forehead. Slowly she began to relax. Her breathing became easier and she could move her body again, but she didn't need to. The pleasant cool sensation was spreading as she was being lifted out of the pressing heat. Soon she was lying down comfortably but exhausted. She slept then. A deep, calm, dreamless sleep.

The next thing Mona could remember was waking up hungry and tired, with Harriet asleep in the chair beside her, one arm reaching out to hold Mona's hand.

Harriet appears at the doorway again carrying a glass of juice and some honey on toast.

"Do you feel any better?" she asks Mona.

"I do," replies Mona. She could smell the honey. She closes her eyes and imagines that she is back in the garden sitting by the cool waterfall with Owen and Harriet, the scent of a hundred flowers in the air.

"Do you want to try to eat something?" asks Harriet, sitting on the edge of the bed next to Mona.

Mona sits with her eyes closed for a moment. She remembers the cool sensation that cut through the heat and discomfort and pulled her back from all the confusion and terror of her dreams. It felt like the cool mist of the waterfall. It felt like the warmth of the woman who carried her to the orphanage. It felt like the hand resting against her forehead now.

Without a word, Mona leans forward and wraps her arms around Harriet. Harriet hugs her back.

"I almost forgot to tell you," says Harriet when Mona finally lets her go. "Owen has been asking about you; he was very worried. His instructor gave me this card he made for you."

Mona opens the handmade card. Inside it is full of funny, colourful pictures and made-up rhymes. She recognizes some of Owen's silly jokes, but there are also some well-wishes from other students in her pod. Mona is touched.

"He's so funny," she says, with tears in her eyes. "Listen to this."

> There once was a bee,
> Who liked to hear a grasshopper sing.
> She sat on his knee,
> And buzzed a melody with her wings.
>
> I can't remember their song,
> So, I'll just write you this letter,
> And say I hope it's not long,
> Until you feel better!

"How creative, and he got so many students in your pod to write you notes as well," laughs Harriet. "He seems like a great friend."

"He's my best friend," replies Mona.

CHAPTER SIXTEEN

Tumbling Down

"Andriss, I hope you do not object, but I have brought my partner along with me today. Morgan is the mind behind the magic that we do," Stowe pauses for a moment and shakes his head gently from side to side. "My apologies. I forget that you are not some simple client that I must impress by making Morgan seem like a magician or an artificer. No doubt you have heard of my colleague, both by my own report and through your own sources. Andriss, Morgan. Morgan, Madam Andriss."

Stowe turns and gestures to Morgan, who in turn gives a curt nod.

"A pleasure to meet you, Morgan," says Andriss, reaching out her hand. "Your reputation proceeds you. But I didn't think you personally met with clients?"

"Not on normal occasions," explains Stowe. "Morgan's work does not usually require direct interaction with our clients; however, in certain cases when expert advice is needed …"

"Do not let my colleague oversell me," interrupts Morgan. "Any number of my staff could perform this procedure. Stowe here simply wants to give the impression that you are receiving special attention." Morgan gives Stowe a wry smile.

"I judge by the fact that you agreed to perform the, well, whatever it is we are doing today, that you agree with your colleague that my business is worth a little charade on your part," fires back Andriss, eliciting a smile from Stowe.

"I'll admit that I was curious to meet you after Stowe's reports," replies Morgan. "The pretense of performing a scan seemed like a good enough excuse."

"And what is the purpose of today's exercise?" asks Andriss.

"We need to have a base scan of some of your memories to map out how best to implant the new memories we are developing," explains Morgan, opening a small white box and removing a portable scanning device. "We call this a crown. I will ask Stowe here to help you adjust it while I prepare my equipment."

"So, you will ask me to rehash my past while you scan my mind? I came here to have you give me new, sublime memories, not to relive the awful ones that plague me."

"I do apologize for this, Andriss," says Stowe, as he adjusts the crown on her head. "Believe me, it is a necessary evil. Were there a way to avoid it, we would not ask this of you."

"I do not wish to presume to know how you feel, Madam Andriss," Morgan adds. "But many of our clients describe themselves as caught in a storm, with the pain and terror of their memories whirling around them, tossing them like a ship on the sea. I personally do not enjoy the hyperbole of their comparison. I feel that many of them merely wish to add one more indulgence to an already decadent life."

Morgan pauses, looking up from the equipment at Andriss. Andriss' eyes are clear and hard as pieces of dark granite.

"But there are also cases like yours," Morgan continues. "Stowe assured me that your suffering is genuine, and I can see even from our brief meeting that you have not over-exaggerated your present condition. Perhaps you are a boat being tossed in the violent waves of your memories. By performing this scan, we will be able to locate the eye of the storm, and from there plot a course to calmer waters. Does this make sense to you?"

"More than you may think," replies Andriss.

"Good," says Morgan. "Then we can begin. My technicians would usually ask you a series of questions about your past, in order to hone in on the specific memory or memories that will serve as the anchor points for your new implants. I do not believe that will be necessary in your case."

"Why is that?" asks Andriss.

This time it is Stowe who answers. "It is clear to me from our previous conversations about your past that you are fully aware of the specific event that is central to your pain," he explains, gently placing his hand over hers. "When you say the war was terrible, I believe that you are not referring to the feelings of hunger or fear that you no doubt experienced. I believe that you are concentrating on one specific memory. Something that occurred which inspired a feeling of awe in you—a sort of divine understanding of the terrible power that comes from despair."

The three sit in silence for a moment. Andriss closes her eyes and seems to shrink in her chair.

"I would never have pegged you as being so good at reading people, Stowe," she says at last. "More fool me. Were I younger, I would have to hire you to work for me or else make every effort to destroy you—I could not afford to have a potential rival who could see through me so easily."

Morgan's hands move silently to make the final adjustments on the portable scanner.

"I had a sister before the war. Now I do not," explains Andriss, her eyes closed and her voice barely above a whisper. "She was younger than me by a few years, and so much prettier—all smiles and laughter, where I was so serious and studious, even then. When she walked into a room she was like sunshine. Everyone adored her, but no one more than me.

"I was her protector and her best friend. For, you see, she needed a protector. She was so trusting and silly. She could not fathom that anyone would look at the world and not see all the beauty and songs that she did. She would weave her own silly songs too, creating them from thin air," she pauses with one hand raised slightly, fingers dancing to a tune locked in her memory.

"My father had so many enemies, even before the war began. Even before his greed nearly ruined us, there were those both inside and outside his corporation who would take any opportunity to destroy him. Family can be a terrible thing. And my family is one of the worst. My father's cousins fought him openly for control of his assets. His own brother and sisters were more sinister. They tried to use me against him, but when I fought back, they turned on my sister.

"What could a child who loved gardens and music know of family politics? They tried to use her for their own ends. They would have been able to if I were not always by her side. I shielded her from them and kept her from being their weapon against my father.

"God, I loved her. Even when the war started, she would sing and dance and carry joy into each room of our home. When we had to flee, she made it a game for the other children. She could weave some strange magic and turn a bomb shelter into an enchanted cave or an attic into a belfry in a castle. I knew the reality, of course, but it was nice to be able to join her fantasy, if only for a brief respite.

"Once when the bombers were right overhead and we were all huddled together praying to make it through the night, she turned the explosions into a beat for a silly rhyme."

Andriss pauses and reaches back into the past. When she speaks again, her voice is soft and warm, the voice of her younger self:

> *Fie dee diddle dum*
> *diddle dum doo.*
>
> *If I were a lobster*
> *and you were a bear,*
> *me with a red shell*

and you with brown hair,
we'd have nothing to talk about
and no one would care,
so fie dee diddle dum
diddle dum doo,
I know even then
I'd still love you.

If I was the sea
and you were a skiff,
you could float on my waves
and I'd give you a lift,
if you left for the shore
you know I'd be miffed,
but fie dee diddle dum
diddle dum doo,
even when you leave
I still love you.

You said if I were an animal
you'd want a tomcat,
but I always felt
I'd be a wombat,
I'd live down south
so that would be that,
and fie dee diddle
drum diddle dum doo,
even in Australia
I'd still love you.

But you're not a bear
or a ship on the sea,

and I'm not a lobster,
I'm just wombat-less me,
well it might be just us
but at least that makes we!

So diddle dum fie
or just diddle dum doo
together we're better,
and I'll always love you.

There are tears on her cheeks when she stops.

"A silly little thing," she says. "Not unlike my silly little sister. But it saved us that night. She fought back the terror and let us be happy and safe in her make-believe world for a while."

"How did she die?" asks Stowe.

Andriss looks straight at him and suddenly Stowe is certain that she was the cause of her sister's death, whether through direct action or deliberate inaction.

"The bombing that night collapsed a large portion of the shelter where my family and some others were hiding. I can still hear the cacophony of the bombs landing right overhead. Comparing the noise to thunder is so inadequate. You couldn't just hear the explosions, you could feel the noise of them pulse through your body, shaking your bones so hard you felt they might break. Pushing the very breath from your lungs with the force of their explosions.

"Of course, that was also happening to the buildings above us. Their steel skeletons were snapping from the explosions or else melting in the heat of the firebombing. We heard the buildings falling on us overhead. The whole while, she was whispering in my ear, repeating the last lines of her stupid poem 'together we're better, and I'll always love you.'

"When the concrete ceiling split, we ran. I grabbed her hand and pulled her behind me. I was only fourteen and she was younger—ten, maybe eleven. We were just children really. Just children, and I could not keep hold in the swell and push of all those bodies. She fell behind."

Andriss stops and reaches into her pocket, removing a lily-white handkerchief with the name Eleanor embroidered on it. She dabs her face and tries to calm her uneven breathing.

Morgan sits motionless, eyes fixed to the readout on the screen.

Stowe squeezes Andriss' hand in his own. There are tears in his eyes too, so he keeps his head turned from Morgan.

For a long while no one moves or talks, until finally Andriss speaks. Her voice is steady and calm, but with the same inevitable finality of sand passing down through an hourglass.

"The roof was going to fall in on us. I could see we had only a few seconds. My sister had fallen in the turmoil. She was calling out from the dark corridor, hurt and afraid. All around me were the crying faces of my family, dimly illuminated by the orange light from the fires burning outside. We had one more door to get through to reach relative safety. I led my family out of the destruction and rubble. We barely made it out before the rest of the shelter collapsed in on itself, burying the living with the dead.

"My sister died, and we lived. I made the decision to leave her there. Her and countless others. Her voice, just one of many crying out for help. But unlike the others, she was calling out my name.

"It was a hard decision, you see," she says, trying and failing to sound matter of fact. "Hard but practical and necessary. Father wasn't around to make the decision. His own foolishness had already led to his early death not long after the war started. I do not grieve losing him. A foolish man. Stupid and useless, like my remaining relatives, but worse, driven by ambition but lacking all the necessary faculties to realize anything but his own destruction—and the nearly total destruction of our family.

"Mother was no better. Like the rest of my family, save myself and my sister, she was paralyzed by fear and grief. I knew that there would be time to grieve later. That is, if we did not hesitate and made the hard decisions then and there. If we faltered, if we wavered and delayed, then there would be no time for any of us, not for me nor my family who preferred to wring their hands and hope that someone else would take the reins. So, I acted. I made the decision.

"I have no illusions of heroism. My actions were awful and selfish. The terror and despair that I feel today is of my own making. I don't want to forget my sister. I just want to let her go without so much hurt to either of us."

Without a word, Stowe lets go of Andriss' hand and removes the crown, handing it to Morgan, who packs up the portable scanning equipment. When they are done, Morgan turns to Andriss and says, "Thank you, Madam Andriss. You will be happy to know that our mapping is complete."

"Good," replies Andriss, her voice shaking again. "I do not wish to do that again."

"The next time we meet will be to begin the procedure," explains Morgan, moving toward the door. "When I scan you again, it will be to confirm that these memories are merely shadows behind the sublime experiences that we have developed for you."

"When will that be?" asks Andriss, her voice betraying a hint of desperation.

"We are ready to harvest the memories before the end of this month. Soon they will be yours. Your happy memories in place of those that weigh on you today."

CHAPTER SEVENTEEN

Lightning Bugs or Fireflies

T he door opens to the garden. It is the first time that Mona has been back since she's left the infirmary. It has only been a few days, yet somehow to her it feels much longer. Mona is still feeling a little weak from her illness, but earlier when Harriet asked her if she'd like to return to the garden today, she jumped at the chance.

She smiles stepping through the door into the late afternoon sunshine. Eyes closed, she can smell a hundred different flowers: the strong overarching scent of honeysuckle, the gentle perfume of the rose bushes near the shed, the pine-citrus of the small marjoram shrubs on the perimeter of the garden, and the subtle sweetness of the juniper bushes in the shaded grove near the waterfall. The watering system must have been running only minutes before they arrived, because the air is still misty. Mona can almost taste the mix of scents in the water droplets still floating in the air.

There is a wonderful moment of silence as Mona breathes in her surroundings. Then she opens her eyes and smiles at Owen.

"Come on," she says, grabbing his hand. "Let's go to the waterfall!"

The two run up the hill in the middle of the garden and down the other side toward the path that leads to the pool and the waterfall, leaving Harriet strolling slowly behind. Oddly, Owen's instructor did not join them today.

Owen whoops his delight and starts jumping and skipping faster than Mona can keep up.

"Are you alright?" he asks as Mona stops short of breath by the edge of the pond.

"Yes. Only a little tired. That's all." Mona can feel fine beads of sweat on her forehead. "I think I'd better sit down for a minute. I keep thinking that I'm all better, but I get tired so easily," she explains.

"It's okay," replies Owen. "We can sit here for a bit. I like watching the waterfall make ripples in the pond. See how they push out and get bigger and bigger until they reach us? It's fun to imagine that we are sitting on the edge of a giant ocean and that the waves are travelling to us from somewhere far off." He pauses for a moment. "Do you think that somewhere in the world there is an island that is making all the waves? Do the people that live there go down to the beach and watch as the water ripples gently away from their home?"

"I don't think that's how waves work.," Mona knows that Owen is being silly. They learned about weather patterns and how waves are formed by tides and the wind months ago. Still, it's fun to listen to Owen weave a story out of the ripples on a pond.

"Well maybe the island is where all the wind comes from then," replies Owen. "Maybe it's got geysers that erupt pushing out the water all around the island and making the waves and wind that we feel even miles and miles away!"

"Then how come no one has ever seen this island?" asks Mona, smiling in anticipation of Owen's response, which she is sure will be even more fantastic than his original premise.

"Well, lots of people have tried. Hundreds, maybe thousands. Explorers and scientists all load themselves into the best ships and sail into the wind." Owen picks up a fallen leaf and carefully folds it in his hands, forming a rough boat-like shape.

"They set off," he continues, gently floating his leaf-boat on the surface of the pond. "They could always tell where the island was by heading straight into the wind and waves, but that made the going hard. The rough seas made most ships turn back before they even got close to the island. For a long time, even the most courageous scientists and explorers who were prepared to brave the storms were eventually pushed back by the power of the headwinds."

Owen blows gently on his leaf-boat, shifting from side-to-side to maneuver it closer and closer to the waterfall, but eventually the ripples are too much for it. The boat bucks up and down on the miniature waves, taking on water until Owen stops blowing it forward and lets it drift safely away to the edge of the pond.

Mona reaches down and scoops the little boat out of the water.

"Did anyone ever make it to the island?" she asks, happily playing along with Owen's fantasy.

"Not yet," replies Owen. "One group of explorers came close once. They were in a special ship that could race into the wind and hop over the rough waves." Owen reaches down into the cool water of the pond and pulls out a stone in his closed hand.

"Their ship was fast and light and brought them closer than anyone had been before," he continues. "When they finally got close enough that they could see the island, the captain turned on the new engines and the boat began to leap the waves and pull closer and closer to the island." As Owen tells his story he turns a flat stone over and over in his hands.

"Did they make it?" asks Mona, hoping that Owen has changed his mind and that the story will continue with the scientists exploring the strange island.

"They came close," replies Owen, standing and skipping the stone on the small pond. "But their new engines were too powerful and they skipped right by the island, without being able to find a place to stop safely. The crew all wanted to try again, but the captain was afraid that they might crash their boat on the island and never be able to get back home again. So, he turned around and let the wind and waves carry them home."

"I wish they got to see what was on the island," Mona says dreamily. "I would have liked to hear about that."

"Well, when we leave school, we'll have to find the captain and convince him to take us. We can be the first to set foot on the island and explore it. We'll take pictures of all the new animals that we find and map the forests and mountains. And because of your memory, you'll be able to remember all the details of our trip and write a book so that other people can experience the island too!"

Mona smiles and looks at the pond. Owen is so convincing that she can almost imagine the small pool of water continuing on forever, reaching out in every direction, spanning the globe. Somewhere in the distance she can picture a strange island, with wind-swept shores and massive spouts of steam erupting from the ground. Past the wind and bubbling geysers lies a forest or a jungle filled with animals that have adapted to life on the strange island: elephants on long spindly legs, lizards with round leather wings that they use to glide on the thermals from the hot springs and geysers, and insects with bodies that are clear by night and colourful during the day, allowing them to hide and hunt without being seen.

There is a gentle mist coming off the waterfall that feels pleasant and cool on Mona's skin. The smell of juniper is a little stronger in the grove and it mixes with the fresh scent of the water running over the rocks. Everything feels cool and wonderful.

Mona can remember the hot thick feeling of being sick, and the heaviness of her limbs. She can remember how hard it was to breathe, like she was being smothered. Then she remembers the cool relief, feeling something soothing against her skin. She lies back on the grass and closes her eyes. Her body is relaxed and comfortable, she feels cool and safe. Everything about this place seems to cradle her, the soft grass, the sweet smells, the cool mist and the playful bubbling of the waterfall. Most of all, having Owen sit next to her telling his stories and making boats out of leaves. She feels so far away from the discomfort and confusion she felt during her fever.

Mona doesn't feel herself fall off to sleep. She is so happy and comfortable that slumber sneaks up on her. Whether awake or in the loveliest dream, Mona finds herself resting next to the pond, listening to the waterfall in her garden, with Owen nearby skipping stones or spinning new stories out of the air. She lies like that happily until a hushed voice wakes her.

"Mona," whispers Owen. "Mona, wake up and see."

Mona rubs her eyes and blinks. It's dusk and the garden is darker, but a small light is blinking in Owen's cupped hands.

"What is it?" asks Mona, sitting up and inching closer to Owen.

"I think it's some kind of fly," replies Owen. "Only look! it blinks on and off, like a light!"

Sure enough, the little insect in Owen's hands lights up a beautiful bright green and flies lazily away, winking on and off as it goes.

"That was incredible," says Mona, half awestruck by the new creature she just saw.

"Look there's more of them," says Owen, pointing to the path that leads back out to the main garden. "Come on!" He grabs Mona's hand and they are away running.

When they reach the base of the hill in the garden's open grassy space, Mona's breath catches in her throat. All around them there are hundreds of little lights, blinking on and off, illuminating the petals of flowers or small patches of grass. She sees Harriet sitting on the grass near the top of the hill. Mona waves at Harriet and giggles. Harriet waves back, then brushes her hands over the grass, sending dozens more blinking bugs into the evening sky.

Holding Owen's hand, Mona runs up around the garden then up the hill. All around her more and more lights twinkle and whirl, until the entire garden is filled with a magical light.

"People call them lightning bugs or fireflies," explains Harriet. "They light up to attract one another. Aren't they beautiful?"

"I've never seen anything like this," gasps Mona as she tries to take in the full beauty of her surroundings.

"They must have come out to visit you two," suggests Harriet. "You're very lucky, I haven't seen fireflies in years."

Mona watches as Owen whispers inaudibly to a new little lightning bug resting in his hands. They seem to be drawn to him—his calm wonder and his readiness to accept everything fantastic pulls them in. After a moment, he smiles and gently blows on his hand. The little lightning bug takes off and joins the others. It might be Mona's imagination, but to her, it seems to burn brighter than the rest.

o o o

"You're alone?" asks Stowe.

"The instructor is just outside the door," replies Morgan. "I thought that you might like to confer a little before we invite him in."

"Very well. I am still not sure if this plan is ready, but you say that the scans are convincing?"

"Very much so. I believe that we should proceed with an extraction."

"Are there any dangers?"

"This is uncharted territory. I cannot say whether the process carries more or less risk, but as I have indicated before, there is a chance that any negative side effects will be permanent."

"So, we could lose a student."

"We've lost others before. Not many, granted, but the mortality rate has never been a major concern of yours."

"Those are my words."

"Have you changed your mind?"

"No. But I do not like to risk losing on an investment."

"Innovation takes risk."

"And resilience. Very well, bring in the instructor."

Sam steps into the room. His mouth is dry and his hands feel cold and sweaty at the same time. He is getting fired. Definitely. There is no doubt. Someone figured out what he has been doing. Somehow, they've learned that he has been working with Owen, scanning him and mapping his dreams. Now he's been summoned here to speak with the bosses.

Sam has a number of bosses. Technically, Miller is sort of a boss. She is a senior instructor and, while she doesn't give Sam his assignments, he knows that he should listen to her and follow her instructions. Sam, Harriet, and a few other instructors also report to a director above Miller who gives them their assignments and shuffles them around so that they work with different students every few cycles. There are also the lab techs who work with the machinery and oversee the instructors when they perform scans. All of these people have titles and faces familiar to Sam. He has met them all, joked with them, gone over lessons and student profiles and scans with them. He has even assisted the techs on several extractions, once they recognized he had some experience with the equipment from his previous job. But the two people in this room are new to him. They are *the* bosses. The founders of the Company: one tall with a powerful frame, the other a little shorter than Sam, with a slight build and cold dark eyes. Apart from senior directors and lab techs, and one or two associates, Sam can't think of anyone who has ever met with the bosses and still had a job the next day. Most of the time, the offending employee is escorted off company grounds in disgrace.

Sam is sure that today he is the offending employee. Today he will be fired. If he's lucky, they won't blackball him, and he'll be able to find work somewhere else. He holds on to that hope as he waits for one of them to speak.

"Do you know why we called you here?" one of the bosses asks. The cold eyes burrow into Sam. They are dark and unblinking. Sam starts to feel like a fly staring at the black, lidless eyes of a spider. As if sensing this, the boss' long fingers spread out across the desk in a smooth deliberate motion, like a spider extending its legs to a closer strand of silk.

There is no point in lying; he is caught. Sam jumps right in.

"I have been conducting scans on one of my students outside of regular hours. The scans …" he stammers a moment before collecting himself to continue. "The scans were not scheduled or authorized. No techs were present; I did them on my own."

"What about the student's housemother?" asks the other boss, glaring at Sam. The second boss' eyes are nothing like the cold, dispassionate eyes of the hunting spider. They are clear and blue, but above all furious. Looking at this boss, Sam no longer feels like a fly with its wings tangled in a web, but like some poor fool who has wandered into the jungle and now finds himself face to face with a tiger.

"I bribed her," he confesses, his mouth dry with fear. "Extorted her, really. It is not her fault; I'm the only one to blame."

"Brave," says the spider boss.

"I don't care about bravery," replies the tiger, his fist on the table as he leans his strong frame toward Sam. "I care about loyalty. Were you planning to sell your findings to another firm?"

"No!" says Sam, more loudly than he had intended. "No, not at all."

"Then why perform your scans after hours?" asks the spider again.

"I wasn't scanning Owen's memory," Sam explains. "Not exactly anyway. I was scanning his memories of his dreams. One dream in particular."

The two bosses exchange a look.

"Morgan, this is your circus, he's your monkey," growls the second boss, sitting back in his chair. The tiger almost looks disappointed not to have a kill today.

"Very well," says Morgan the spider. "Sam, I've reviewed your findings. Don't look so shocked. Yes, you took steps to cover your transgressions, but you are no match for the systems Stowe here has in place."

"I only wanted to …" stammers Sam.

Morgan raises a hand. "We can get into the specifics of your reasoning later. What I want from you, what we want now, is for you to continue."

"What?" says Sam, flabbergasted.

"Your work shows ingenuity and promise. I designed many of the systems that we use here at the Company. I was the one to perfect some of the techniques used in the Selective Memory Extraction and Implantation procedures. Yet I never would have thought to try to scan a dream. Your innovation ... interests me," Morgan stops to let the words sink in.

"I can continue my scans with the help of a tech?" asks Sam, still not fully comprehending, but elated that he is not fired. Still, he cannot shake the feeling while part of him may be free, the spider is still wrapping silk around him.

"No," replies Morgan. "I don't believe that a technician would be useful helping you in this uncharted territory. For now, at least, I think that you should continue on your own, working as you have been, after hours."

"I'm not sure how much more I can learn from scans," confesses Sam. "I'm not an expert."

"This is a new field," continues Morgan. "We are none of us experts, but you have strong skills in this area. Do you think that you know enough to try an extraction?"

"I ... I might have enough data," replies Sam, his voice wavering.

"We don't deal in half-answers," responds Stowe, breaking his silence and making Sam sweat.

"The question is, do you believe in your data?" asks Morgan. "Have you found something new or have you been wasting all this time on a dream?"

"I'll perform the extraction," replies Sam. "I'm ... I'm sure that there's something more to a dream."

CHAPTER EIGHTEEN

Extraction

M iller taps a few buttons on her electronic clipboard. Her files from the day transfer over to the main computer banks. Tomorrow her director will assess them. The review will be glowing. It always is.

Miller prides herself on the quality of her work. Today she ran Nickolas through his paces. It was grueling for both of them. Despite his quiet confidence, Nick did not make it to the top of the class on his ability alone. Sure, he's a good student. He would be successful under the supervision of any instructor. But Miller is not just any instructor. She has her eyes on a director position. She's proven herself as one of the most capable senior instructors and she knows that having one of the top students will help secure her promotion. That's why she has been spending time after hours reviewing her sessions with Nick. Each evening, she maps his progress and revises her lesson plans to focus on how she can work on any weaker areas.

To his credit, Nick is proving to be an amazing student. He does not have the natural ability that Miller has seen in some other students, like the girl that Harriet is working with, but he makes up for it with his work ethic. It did not take Miller long to recognize a kindred spirit. Nick likes to be the best and he's willing to put in the effort to stay on top.

Miller smiles and packs up her things. Tomorrow will be another intense day, but she feels ready for it, and she knows that Nick will come prepared to work.

The hallways are deserted as Miller makes her way toward the subway back to the apartment complex. The only other people in the facility seem to be the evening cleaners and the night security. They are used to seeing Miller leaving this late. She smiles as she passes them.

"Have a good evening, Miss," smiles one of the security guards.

"You too," replies Miller.

"I'll never understand what drives you to stay so late," he says, making idle conversation.

"You've got to work hard to stay on top," she replies honestly.

"Well, the two of you must be the very best," he says, turning back to his security display.

"Two of us?" asks Miller.

"Yeah, you and the young man. He's been working late recently too. Must be following your example."

"What young man?" asks Miller.

"I think he's an instructor or a technician. Sam is his name. Pleasant fellow."

Without another word, Miller turns and heads back down the hallway.

Sam is midway through a scan when Miller finally finds him. She waits outside the door, watching through a window as he adjusts the equipment on his student. Why is Sam wasting his time and risking his job by performing after hours scans on that little plomp Owen? She watches as Sam pinpoints specific areas. It almost looks like he is preparing for an extraction.

Miller wants to step in and confront him, to stop him from getting fired, but something doesn't feel right. It isn't until the scan is nearly complete that she realizes what seems out of place: both Owen and Sam are silent. Sam is not leading Owen through any exercises or instructing him to focus on specific elements of a memory. Even more disturbing, Owen is deadly silent and almost completely still—it almost looks like he is asleep with his eyes open.

Usually students talk through their memories during the scans, repeating many of the same exercises that they do when recalling events during the one-one-one sessions with the instructors. It is eerie to see a student so utterly still and quiet. Miller starts to feel that something is wrong. Carefully, she turns the knob on the door, opening it just enough to be able to hear what is going on in the room.

The hum of the machines dies down as the scan finishes. Sam takes the time to finish his work before going over to Owen and gently rousing him from his daydream.

"Where were you this time?" Sam asks.

"I don't know," replies Owen. "It was dark but with thousands of lights swirling around like stars."

"Was it scary?" asks Sam.

"Oh no," smiles Owen. "No, it wasn't scary, it was beautiful. Like floating in a pond under the stars and seeing them reflected in the still black water all around you. Or maybe like floating in the sky with nothing but stars all around you.'

"So, you were flying?"

"I guess maybe," replies Owen. "Only, it didn't feel like I was moving at all but like the stars were alive and moving all around me."

"It sounds like it was beautiful."

"It was," smiles Owen happily, still half lost in his dream world.

"Are you ready for the next type of scan?" asks Sam.

"Hmm? I guess so," replies Owen.

"Do you think you can go back into your dream again?" asks Sam.

Owen nods and begins to breathe deeply. As Sam is preparing the equipment, Owen is already slipping off, back into the night sky.

Gently, Sam leads Owen back onto the bed. He adjusts the crown on his head, all the while describing what he is doing to Owen.

"I'm putting the crown back on now. For this type of scan, we need you to be lying down. Are you comfortable? Good, good."

Miller watches as Sam puts on medical gloves and covers his face with a mask. He is going to perform an extraction! Should she step forward to stop him?

Sam applies a topical numbing cream to two spots on the back of Owen's neck, near the base of his skull.

"Owen, you may feel a little pressure in the back of your neck," Sam explains. "Just stay relaxed and still and you'll be alright. Breathe deeply. Clear your mind. Think of the stars spinning around you. Concentrate on your dream."

Sam connects another set of sensors to Owen's forehead. Then he presses a button and two long needles come out of the back of the headrest and push into the back of Owen's neck, where Sam had applied the numbing cream.

For a moment, Owen's eyes widen and focus on Sam.

Sam gently takes Owen's hand and continues to guide him through the process.

"I know," he says. "It's an odd sensation. Just relax and it will go away. That's it, breathe in and out, in and out. Good." His voice is strong and soothing. Miller watches as Owen's eyes begin to glaze over again. His body relaxes and his breathing becomes so deep and regular that he could be asleep.

That's when she realizes that Sam is not performing a normal extraction. She pushes through the door and clears her throat.

Sam turns around. He is clearly surprised but tries to remain calm.

"Miller, I know what this looks like," he begins to explain.

"That's good, because I don't," replies Miller.

"It's an extraction, that's all. I know it's after hours, but I have permission."

"Do you? From whom?"

"I can't say just now," explains Sam. "But I'm going to proceed. Please don't get in the way, this is delicate work."

"What exactly are you extracting?" asks Miller, not moving.

"A dream," replies Sam. With that he steps forward and reaches around Miller to start the extraction. She is too shocked to move.

The lights dim and the various computers and scanners light up. It is too late; the process has started. Miller knows that if she does anything now it could harm the student. Numbly, she steps back and watches as Sam shifts his focus back to the monitors displaying complex brain scans. Carefully he adjusts the controls and little by little the noise of the scans becomes clearer and clearer until one exact pattern emerges.

Owen continues to lie motionless throughout the procedure. His breathing remains constant and his eyelids flutter and close.

The images on the screen explode in a shock of movement and colour. "I've never seen the displays look like that," whispers Miller.

It only takes a few minutes to complete the extraction. Once it is finished, Sam breathes a sigh and wipes the sweat from his forehead. He carefully unhooks Owen from all of the machines, helping him sit up on the diagnostic table. Owen seems to wake up a little. He smiles at Sam.

Miller feels a sudden rush of relief. The strange events she just witnessed are over, and everything and everyone seems normal again.

"I can explain everything," says Sam, not turning his attention away from Owen. "And I will, but for now I have to get Owen here back to bed."

Miller can only manage to nod.

"You did great, Owen," adds Sam, speaking to his student. "I knew that you would. I think we got a full dream! I can't imagine what it will be like, but whatever it is, it's going to be ground-breaking."

Sam gently helps Owen down from the bed and puts an arm over his shoulders to lead him to the hallway back to the students' section of the facility. As they reach the door, Owen stops suddenly and shakes himself free, turning and running back to the diagnostic table.

Both Sam and Miller exchange worried glances, but Owen just searches the floor around the table for a moment before recovering a plush bee toy.

Owen turns and holds up the toy.

"What's this?" he asks.

"Are you being silly?" replies Sam. "That's your bee."

"Oh," says Owen, staring at the toy. "Is it mine?"

"Yes," laughs Sam nervously. "Now come on, you should be back in bed."

Miller watches as they walk together down the hallway, Owen holding his bee as Sam leads him forward.

○ ○ ○

"We will need to bring in the instructor for a debrief," says Stowe.

"Agreed. It is very unfortunate that she interrupted the procedure. Do you think that she will be a problem?"

"I doubt it, Morgan. She is driven—ambitious really. She has her eyes on a director position. I'll imply that she is our top candidate and that part of what is expected of directors is a certain level of discretion, that should do the trick."

"An excellent solution."

"Have you had time to examine the extraction?"

"Yes, it is most … promising."

"Promising? That's all?"

"Well, it is unlike any memory that we have previously extracted. It is not a memory at all really. It is hard to analyze it: our programs do not recognize certain patterns."

"Can it be implanted?"

"That should not be a problem."

"Then why not test it in person, or have one of your techs test it?"

"That would be the simplest solution. The only danger is that we may only get one use out of the extraction. It would be a pity to waste it by not selling it to a client."

"Well we can hardly sell our clients something if we are unsure about what it is. Besides, this student seems to be good for nothing but daydreams, I'm sure he can produce many more."

"Very well, I will have this extraction tested and we will proceed to harvest more from Owen if this first attempt was successful."

"What do you think we can charge for a dream implantation?"

"Who knows? To my knowledge, no other firm has ever tried working with dreams before. It is exciting. We can introduce a new product and name our price."

No Return

Harriet sits by herself in the cafeteria. It's supper time. Usually she would already have taken the train home by now, but between her extra work with Mona and trying to see Sam, she's been staying late more often.

The work with Mona has been a pleasure. She'd expressed some concern to her director about pushing Mona too hard and asking her to remember unpleasant memories, but her director told her to keep up with the program as planned. After Mona got sick, they seemed to take Harriet's concerns more seriously. Now her sessions are all about planning magical experiences for Mona and then asking her to relive them the next day.

Sam, on the other hand, has been a little more difficult. He's been working a lot and hasn't been around as much. The past week she's barely seen him at all.

Two nights ago, Harriet bumped into Sam leaving one of the labs. She asked him casually how his day was.

"Fine, fine," was all he managed in reply.

"Are you still working on that scan on Owen's dream?" she asked.

"What?" replied Sam, as if coming to. "No, that was a while ago. I'm working on something else now."

"What is it?"

"Nothing. Look, I can't really talk about it. See you tonight?"

It was unlike Sam to brush Harriet off, and he was always willing to talk about his students or his next project. After all, he was the one who shared his thoughts about dreams with Harriet. He was the one who was bursting to show her the initial scan he'd performed. Why was he shutting her out now?

Worse still, she didn't see him that evening. Actually, they hadn't seen each other at all since then.

Harriet stirs her cup of synthetic coffee and tries to remember what the real stuff tasted like. Some days she'd kill for Mona's memory. Maybe then she could reach back and replace the metallic taste of the artificial coffee with the warm rich bitterness of a real roast.

"Coffee any good?" asks Miller.

"Not since rationing got bumped up again," replies Harriet.

"Mind if I join you anyway?" asks Miller.

Harriet gestures to the seat across from her. Miller isn't the company she'd been hoping for, but any company would do in the empty cafeteria.

"You're working late," says Miller.

"I guess," replies Harriet. "I had a session with Mona. I still need to write up my notes, but I thought I'd take a coffee break to see if anyone else was around."

"Just me here this late," smiles Miller. "Well, me and you."

"Sam's been working late recently too," replied Harriet.

Not many people would notice it, but Harriet is trained to observe subtle changes in how people sit or speak. Usually, she's looking for these unconscious cues in her students, but now she sees Miller inch back in her chair and nervously glance away.

"That's right, he has," Miller says casually, not betraying any of the subtle discomfort communicated by her body language.

"I was hoping that he might take a break too," pushes Harriet. "It's supper time, or near enough, I figured I might catch him."

"Catch him," repeats Miller looking down at her coffee. "But you haven't seen him lately?"

"No," replies Harriet. "Why? Is there something that you know that I don't?"

Suddenly Harriet is deeply suspicious. Sam's behaviour has been odd lately, but to see Miller so uncomfortable makes her feel sure that something is wrong.

"I don't know if it's worth talking about," replies Miller.

"Miller, please. If you think there is something wrong, you can tell me." Harriet is surprised to see Miller so evasive. "I know you're a senior instructor, but we're friends too aren't we?" In her experience, Miller is almost always direct and up-front with any opinion or observation. She can actually be abrasive sometimes. More than that, Miller is the model of how an instructor ought to behave. She leads by example and is often assigned to help struggling or new instructors learn the ropes. Harriet is surprised that the bosses haven't promoted Miller to director yet.

"You're close with Sam," replies Miller after a pause. "I don't want to spread rumours or anything like that."

"All the more reason for you to tell me," pries Harriet. "If what's bothering you is a rumour, I might know the truth about it. If it's true, I might be able to shed some light on it so that you can see it's nothing to worry about ... or if it is, so you'll know to report him." It hurts her to have to say this last part.

"Alright," whispers Miller, leaning in. "You can't repeat this. Understood?"

Harriet nods, leaning close to hear what Miller has to say.

"Do you know why Sam has been working late?" asks Miller.

Harriet smiles and touches Miller's hand. Of course! She thinks. Miller found out that Sam has been working with Owen on dreams and she's worried that he's wasting time or breaking the rules. It's just the sort of thing that would upset Miller. In truth, it could get Sam fired, but Harriet has seen the initial scans and she feels like Sam is on to something.

"It's okay, Miller," she says calmly. "I know Sam's been working with his student after hours. He's even performed a couple of scans. We're not supposed to do that sort of thing normally, but look, they've made exceptions for Mona, Nick, and the other top students, why not give Sam a little leeway with his student too? I've seen the first scan. It shows some potential. I think Sam might actually be on to something."

To her surprise, Miller looks neither relieved to hear that Harriet knows the truth, nor shocked to find out that she hasn't reported it yet.

"It's more than that," explains Miller. "Sam is performing extractions."

They both sit in silence for a minute or two as the weight of what Miller said sinks in.

"If he's performing extractions, then he must have authorization," Harriet ventures.

"He says he does," replies Miller. "But he's doing them solo. No techs, no directors. It's just him and his student."

"How do you know?" asks Harriet, dreading the answer.

"I saw him. I was in the room when he hit the button."

Harriet is unable to hide the concern on her face. Performing scans is one thing—they aren't invasive, and the only danger would be gathering inaccurate or corrupt data. Extractions are another matter.

Most instructors have had the chance to sit in on an extraction. Very often, they lead their students through breathing and memory exercises while a group of technicians operate the complicated machinery to perform the procedure. The process is safe, and the students leave, sometimes feeling a little groggy, but no worse for wear. That is, if everything is properly managed and the techs are there to do their jobs.

Harriet was shocked the first time she assisted with an extraction. The techs explained the procedure, but nothing prepared her for seeing the long needles push into the back of her student's neck. When she turned to the tech and asked what the needles were for, he said they entered the back of the head and actually went into the brain.

"We need to get precise information. This is the only way," he said.

When Harriet asked about the obvious dangers involved, the lead tech took her aside and calmly explained that the technicians were experts and had years of training under their belts. He'd performed the procedure dozens of times and supervised dozens more. They were there to make sure everything was safe.

Sure enough, everything was. Harriet watched as the techs went about their work, always monitoring and adjusting. Never panicked, never raising their voices, just working together with perfect efficiency.

After they had finished, Harriet asked how often they performed extractions.

"About once a week," replied the lead tech. Only when the students were ready and only after they'd had at least two months between procedures. It was protocol.

Now Miller was telling her that Sam was performing this complex procedure by himself. She knew that he had some experience from a previous job but doing the whole process alone couldn't be safe. According to Miller, he had also performed more than one extraction in the past few weeks.

Harriet didn't need to be a technician to see the obvious dangers involved. This was direct manipulation of the brain! One wrong move and the consequences were too terrible to think about.

"Was everyone okay? Did the procedure work?" Harriet asks Miller, unconsciously reaching forward and grabbing her hand.

"I think so," replies Miller. "The student, the plomp he's been working with, didn't seem any worse afterward. A little sleepy, I think, but that's normal."

Harriet breathes a sigh of relief.

"What really concerns me is what happened when I reported Sam," continues Miller. "I went straight to my director after the procedure was done. I'm sorry, I know you and Sam are close, but I had to report what I saw."

Harriet doesn't say anything, but she can hardly blame Miller. Sam shouldn't have even considered performing an extraction by himself.

"My director had gone home," Miller continues. "It was late after all. So, I wrote her a message and sent it on the secured network. I got a reply less than twenty minutes later. But not from her, from another account, labelled 'Head of Research and Innovation.'"

"I've never heard of that position," says Harriet.

"Neither had I," replies Miller. "The message just said that my concerns were taken into consideration. I thought for sure that Sam was fired. I felt bad, but what could I do?"

"What happened next?"

"I came to work the next day and there was Sam, just like always. He didn't say a thing about the night before. I met with my director about a routine matter and she didn't bring anything up," Miller looks down at her coffee. "I was starting to feel a little crazy. Like I'd imagined the whole thing. But then after my morning session with Nick, I left the exam room and instead of leaving the anteroom and stepping into the changeroom, I stepped out into a hallway."

Harriet's eyes widen as she starts to guess where this is going.

"I'd heard that they could shift around parts of the building. I guess that's why you always have to wait a few minutes in that weird little anteroom before stepping out to the changeroom—gives them time to shift things around if needed. Funny, it didn't feel like the room moved and I couldn't hear anything. Anyway, the next thing I knew, I was sitting in a room at the end of that hallway. I was sitting with one of the bosses. He said that I didn't need to worry about Sam's activities. He even went so far as to say that a certain level of discretion is needed from directors. He practically offered me the job right there."

"What did you say?" asks Harriet.

"Nothing really. I said something about being concerned about the dangers. He laughed it off and told me I was worried about nothing. He said that his colleague had assured him that Sam was properly trained and prepared. Then he dismissed me."

"Maybe he's right," suggests Harriet. "Maybe Sam got extra training. You know, about safeguards and that sort of thing." Even as she says the words she feels it can't possibly be true.

"That's what I keep telling myself," replies Miller. "But if you don't know about him taking extra training, then what are the chances he did? I don't know. The whole thing feels wrong to me."

"I'll talk to Sam," says Harriet.

Miller looks up from her cold coffee. "You can't let him know that I told you anything," she says, her voice hushed but forceful.

"Don't worry, I won't," replies Harriet. "Look, I won't ask him directly. I'll …" she stops and thinks for a moment. "I'll arrange for Mona to have Owen at her next session. They're friends and I've been able to get them time together as part of her training. I can talk to Sam then."

"Just be careful how you bring it up," cautions Miller. "I can't help feeling that something is very wrong."

o o o

"I've performed three extractions to date," reports Sam.

The two bosses sit quietly, waiting for him to finish.

"I was wondering about a volunteer to test the results," Sam continues. "You mentioned that we might need one, but I'd feel too awkward asking any of the other instructors. They'd think I lost it." He laughs. The sound dies quickly in this room. All that is left is silence.

"All my analysis of the extractions show that the memories … the dreams are of high quality. But of course, this is new territory, so without actually sampling the extractions, it's hard to tell if I've got anything good at all." Sam finishes his report and waits for one of the bosses to speak. Morgan is the first to reply.

"Three extractions. Excellent," Morgan looks down at the files that Sam provided. "I concur with your analysis of the extractions. They appear to be of exceptional quality. You've done well, especially considering that you performed the extractions on your own. When can you perform the next extraction?"

"I wanted to speak to you about that," replies Sam. "I'm concerned that I've been pushing Owen too hard. I know that extractions can take their toll on students. I'd like to give Owen a break."

"You may speak freely here. What exactly bothers you?" asks Morgan with an air of genuine concern.

"Thank you," says Sam, relieved that he appears to have an ally in the room. He had been dreading asking for the pause. "Owen has been more forgetful after each extraction. He seems to be in a haze. I'm worried that the procedure might be hurting him somehow."

Morgan smiles. Stowe sits stone-faced, his reactions impossible to read.

"Sam, can I call you Sam?" asks Morgan with a friendly tone. "What you are describing is very natural. Students usually act a little funny after an extraction. The most common symptom is being tired. Some students experience a little dizziness, sometimes some confusion, and occasionally one or two have trouble with their balance. All these symptoms are normal. They go away in a few days. They are actually side-effects of the drug that we administer as part of the intracerebral injection. It's just a numbing agent to ensure that the needles don't cause any discomfort during the procedure." Morgan's tone is soft and reassuring, very different from the spider Sam usually imagines.

"I understand that," replies Sam. "I just feel that Owen has had a lot of extractions without enough time to recover. I think they're wearing him out. And I'm concerned they might be doing more permanent harm."

Morgan's smile fades. "Sam, I know you're just looking out for Owen. Instructors usually have a close bond with their students. It's not something we always encourage, but it is something that we recognize happens. That said, I just explained to you—clearly, I might add—exactly what is happening with Owen. Pardon me, but my opinion as an expert in this area should carry more weight than the unfounded concerns of a hand-holding tutor. I have reviewed your work. I have reviewed Owen's post-extraction scans. I assure you that the procedure is safe and that you may proceed with another extraction."

"It's just …" stammers Sam, feeling caught in a web.

"It is not *just* anything," interrupts Stowe. "My colleague is a world leader in not only the extraction process, but in the technology behind the procedure. When the Chancellor started up a commission to look into the safety of performing extractions, Morgan was named chief researcher on the study. Morgan's findings helped end the dangerous practice of adult extractions and set the guidelines for all future Selective Memory Extraction and Implantation. When you question Morgan's authority in this area, you question this very Company."

Stowe pauses. To Sam, it feels very much like the pause between claps of thunder—at any moment the threatening storm will continue, and the brief respite only serves to underscore the fury to come.

"Frankly," continues Stowe in a low, slow voice, "hearing you doubt Morgan's authority at all, makes me question the faith we had in you. It makes me question why we would continue to employ someone who happily performs unauthorized scans but fails to acquiesce to a simple request from a superior."

Sam is shaking. If he loses this job, he will be destitute. He has no real savings, no family, and no skills outside of his field. Morgan and Stowe could ruin his reputation. They could conceivably have him arrested for performing unauthorized scans after hours. Until now, Sam hadn't worried about being arrested, but the mention of Morgan's ties with the Chancellor and the Party have sent a chill running through him. If these two are as connected as they claim, it would be no trouble for them to have Sam arrested or detained indefinitely. Sam has heard rumours of people being imprisoned for less, and even one whiff of something akin to criminal behaviour would make finding good work impossible.

Sam realizes that if he doesn't follow instructions, there is a very real possibility that he will end up living on the streets or working in one of the terrible factories where people still catch the grey cough.

"You've scared the boy, Stowe," says Morgan, breaking the silence. "Look, he's sweating. What a terrible instructor you would make. Any student under your guidance would tremble and stutter their way through even the simplest of exercises."

Morgan's seemingly jovial tone does not dispel the tension in the room. In fact, Sam feels that Morgan's casual chastisement of Stowe acutely adds a layer to the implicit threat floating in the air. It's as if Morgan is saying to Sam, *See how calm I am despite what you've said? Now imagine just how angry I could become. Stowe rants and roars, but if you want to see a real storm, if you want a real threat, just test me further.*

"You're both right," mumbles Sam apologetically. "I'm sure now that I'm just being overly concerned. Sentimental really. I wouldn't presume to question either of your authority. I only wanted to look out for your investment in Owen.'

"Naturally you did," replies Morgan, never blinking or looking away from Sam. "Which is why you won't have any concerns about proceeding as discussed with the next extraction."

"Of course not," says Sam.

"Excellent," smiles Morgan. "And to help reassure you that there will be no ill effects as part of the procedure, I will personally assist you."

CHAPTER TWENTY

Lost Dreams

Mona hadn't had an opportunity to hang out and chat with Owen in days, so she was excited when Harriet told her that they were going to meet Owen and Sam in the garden.

As she and Harriet wait by the door that leads to the garden shed, Mona replays the past week in her head. She hasn't been to the regular school classes in a long time. Her work with Harriet takes up all her waking time now. She knows that it is the same for Nick, Stephanie, and the younger girl from the pod below theirs. All four top students have been working hard and have been enjoying privileges like the garden. Mona overheard Stephanie brag to the other girls in her pod that she was learning to ride a horse. Mona found that unbelievable. Horses were huge animals that required large amounts of food and space, and only extremely wealthy people could afford to keep them. But part of her believed some of Stephanie's stories, especially when she saw that Nick was reading books about sailboats, calmly taking notes and practicing knots with a piece of rope that he constantly kept with him. When Mona asked him about what he was doing, Nick just shrugged casually and said, "I think they're going to take me on a trip to the sea."

With all the interesting things that had been happening around her, Mona was eager to hear what was going on with the rest of her pod. She

153

desperately wanted to see Owen and listen to his funny stories. Seeing him would make her feel normal again. So, she waited anxiously with Harriet for Owen and Sam to arrive.

"How long have we been waiting?" asked Harriet.

"Thirteen minutes," replied Mona.

"Thirteen minutes and …" replied Harriet playfully checking her watch.

"Thirteen minutes and forty-one seconds," responded Mona.

"Forty-four now," smiled Harriet.

"That's not fair!" laughed Mona. "I can't report on what time it's going to be when you check your watch!"

"I thought you were supposed to be special," teases Harriet.

"What's taking them so long?" asks Mona.

"I'm not sure," replied Harriet, her voice losing the playful tone and betraying a little concern. "It's not like Sam to be this late, and I'm sure Owen is eager to play in the garden with you."

Another three minutes pass and finally they see Sam and Owen coming down the hall. Mona rushes forward and hugs Owen. He is startled for a second, but then hugs her back, pulling her in close as if he is trying to squeeze her into himself.

"Not too hard," laughs Mona.

"You're my friend," says Owen.

"Of course I am," says Mona, laughing. Owen always says silly things, but something in his tone makes her feel strange, almost worried.

"Come on," says Mona, grabbing Owen by the hand and pulling him through the shed to the garden. "I want to see if the butterflies are out. Harriet told me that the brown ones we saw have bright blue on the other side of their wings, but you can't see it unless they open up and fly. We can chase them and see.

"We don't hurt them, right?" asks Owen as they reach the top of the little hill, leaving Harriet and Sam by the entrance. Again, his voice is strange and unsure, as if he can't remember playing in the garden or chasing the butterflies during the day and lightning bugs at night.

"Of course not," reassures Mona. "We won't actually catch them, we'll just run around and they'll fly around. It'll be like we're dancing with them. Don't you remember when the orange and black one landed on you?"

Owen just stares at her blankly.

"Remember? You told me that it was because when he was a caterpillar you saved him from a spider who tricked him into her lair by saying that she would make him a sweater to keep him warm. You found him wrapped in her web and freed him. Then he came back and landed on your shoulder so that he could whisper thank you in your ear."

"I don't remember that," says Owen. He walks away down the hill toward the path that leads to the waterfall. Looking back, he asks Mona, "Where does this go?"

Mona looks at her friend. That initial feeling that something isn't right is growing in her. She walks with Owen as he explores the garden, walking through all the spots where they played. Sometimes he smiles and laughs, remembering their games and the funny stories they made up. Other times, he just looks at Mona and mumbles, "Oh yeah, now I remember," as he stares blankly at a tree they climbed or a big rock they pretended was a troll.

Finally, they sit by the waterfall. Mona is worried that Owen won't remember anything, but suddenly he smiles at her and folds a leaf up into the rough shape of a boat.

"It's our boat," he says.

"Do you think we can reach the hidden island this time?" asks Mona, happy to see the old Owen again.

"It'll be a tricky journey," he explains, placing the leaf gently in the water. "I think we'll have to work together to escape."

o o o

"Is Owen feeling alright?" asks Harriet as she and Sam watch the two children go over the top of the hill. "He doesn't seem quite himself."

"I've had to really intensify his training," explains Sam. "I'm pushing him pretty hard now."

"Not too hard, I hope," replies Harriet.

"Me too," murmurs Sam.

"Mona's been missing him, it's good that you had time to meet today. Actually, I've missed you too. We haven't seen each other much lately either."

"I know. I'm sorry," says Sam apologetically. "I've had to do a lot of work after hours. It's the only time that I can get to perform the scans on Owen."

"I was wondering if you'd done any more," replies Harriet. She wants to ask him about what Miller told her. She wants to ask about the extractions, but she's scared that he will just deny it and push her away.

"Have you made any progress?" she asks casually. "Your initial scans were pretty promising."

"I've got everything pretty much mapped out," says Sam.

"So, you're ready to bring your findings to your director. Maybe you could book an extraction?" Harriet wants to see if he will volunteer the information.

"Maybe," says Sam, noncommittally. "Actually, I should probably go and prep for tonight's scans."

"But you just said that you have everything pretty much mapped out?"

"Oh yeah," stammers Sam. "Just about ... I still have a little more work to do."

"Sam, you're not telling me something," shoots back Harriet, refusing to let him leave. "Something is bothering you. Were you directed to perform an extraction?"

There it is, right out in the air between them. Harriet watches as Sam swallows and pales in front of her. She is sure that Miller was telling the truth now. She is sure that Sam has performed extractions on Owen, with or without permission.

"Extractions can be dangerous," she says, not looking away from Sam's shifting eyes.

"I know that," replies Sam defensively. "I'm not doing anything that I'm not authorized to do."

"Since when are you authorized to perform solo extractions?" she says, putting all her cards on the table.

"I haven't performed a memory extraction," replies Sam.

"You're lying to me," says Harriet quietly. "Why are you doing this? What's happening?"

"Harriet, I have to go prep for tonight," says Sam. "Can you bring Owen back to the student campus?"

He does not wait for a reply before turning and heading to the exit.

Harriet is left standing by herself in the garden. She doesn't move until Mona and Owen return from the waterfall. By then it is dusk and time to head back.

The garden is eerily quiet. No buzz of insects, no wind through the flowers or branches. No fireflies twinkling in the low light as they leave.

Harriet accompanies the children back down the hallway through the anteroom and examination room that leads back to the student area of the campus. She tells them to check in with their housemother before they go to the cafeteria for supper. She is relieved to see Owen acting more normally, but she cannot shake the feeling that something is wrong with him.

Mona seems to sense her unease and hangs back for a moment, letting Owen make his way down the hall toward the dorms.

"What's an extraction?" asks Mona.

Harriet is speechless. If she had any doubt about what Sam has been doing, it is gone now.

"What did Owen tell you?" asks Harriet.

"He said that Sam is doing something called an extraction," replies Mona. "He says that he dreams and a machine takes his dreams so that Sam can study them. Is that true?"

"In a way, it is true," replies Harriet.

"Does it hurt?" asks Mona. "Is it dangerous?"

"Not if it is performed properly," responds Harriet.

"Good," says Mona. "So, Owen will be able to remember his dreams again soon?"

"Of course," lies Harriet, not wanting to worry Mona. "Sometimes the procedure can leave you feeling a little funny for a day or two after. Kind of like you after you were sick. I'm going to talk to Sam to make sure that he gives Owen a break so that he can recover."

Mona smiles and waves as she walks down the hall to join the rest of her pod.

Stepping back into the anteroom and retrieving her ID card, Harriet resolves to confront Sam immediately about what he has been doing after hours. Someone needs to talk some sense into him, and if he won't listen to her, she'll get Miller and go straight to the bosses. Extractions aren't meant to have all these side effects. Owen should be fine, not forgetful and distant. If he can't remember his dreams then it could mean that he has permanent damage.

Harriet is reeling. Through all her training she has always been reassured that extractions were a minimally invasive process. Above all, she has been told that, if performed properly, they are safe with no lasting effects. If Sam messed up the procedure, the ill effects to Owen should be glaringly obvious, not the subtle hints that both she and Mona seemed to notice that something is wrong. The fact that something isn't right with Owen plants seeds of doubt into Harriet's mind. Are extractions damaging even if they are performed correctly?

After confronting Sam, Harriet plans to go to her director, then to the bosses if necessary. Hopefully, they are unaware of the potential dangers of extractions. Maybe she has been the first to notice and she can help put a stop to them before any permanent harm is done. But what if they do know that extractions hurt the students?

She swipes her card opening the door that leads to the common changeroom, but instead finds herself looking down a long white hallway. She feels her chest tighten. It seems that the bosses want to speak to her as well.

○ ○ ○

"She's on her way," says Stowe. "She'll be outside in a minute or less."

"Very good," replies Morgan. "Do you think that she is ready to coach Mona through an extraction?"

"She is very close to the child."

"That's not a yes or a no."

"I've always worried about their relationship. I've made those concerns known. Until now, I have deferred to your expertise on these matters. You explained that their relationship helped drive the student. You assured me that it would lead to better results."

"And all evidence points to the fact that I am correct."

"Indeed. But extractions are another matter. We do not always enlist the help of the instructors. Their proximity to the students can lead to … issues."

"You are afraid that her feelings for Mona will get in the way."

"Precisely. But it is more than that. She is a good instructor. Very observant. If she notices changes in the child after the extraction, she may push back. She could cause us difficulties. The child is special. Harriet sees that too."

"Well let's see what she has to say, then make our decision," suggests Morgan calmly. "Either way we have a little time. We need to complete the extractions on Owen before beginning with Mona."

○ ○ ○

The door opens and Harriet steps into the room. It is an office, not unlike the directors' offices, but much bigger, with more lavish furniture.

159

There is a couch and two armchairs around a coffee table. The plain light grey walls have nearly invisible lines running up and down them, hinting that there are hidden compartments or hallways off the room.

The floor is a darker, slate grey and, although the tiles are hard, there is a subtle warmth coming up through her feet. Adding to the warmth, the floor-to-ceiling windows along one wall let in the last light of the sunset and look out onto unfolding greenery below.

Overall, the room is comfortable and welcoming. This feeling of comfort, however, is completely undercut by the two figures standing behind the desk at the far end of the room.

Harriet does not recognize the bosses.

"Harriet, welcome. My name is Morgan. This is my colleague, Stowe."

Stowe is wearing a light grey suit. He is not much taller than Harriet, but he seems to loom over her even standing a few meters away. He has a broad frame and bright blue eyes that pull the warmth out of the room. He looks younger than Harriet expected. He cannot be much over forty, but his silver-grey hair makes it very difficult to determine his actual age. He could be older with a young-looking face or young, with a few worry lines.

Morgan stands straight and tall, thin as a pencil in a clean, black suit. It is Morgan who breaks the awkward silence.

"We called you here to discuss the next steps in Mona's program." The voice is soft and gentle, despite the severe appraising look on Morgan's face. "As you know, we are very pleased with your progress and we feel that Mona is ready for the extraction process."

Harriet swallows hard.

"We would like to request your assistance with the extractions," explains Morgan. "Your relationship with Mona and your talents guiding her through memories would greatly help with the procedure."

"What about the dangers?" blurts Harriet, surprising the bosses and herself. Before they can respond she continues. "I've seen Owen. Something is wrong with him. I think that the extractions are hurting him. I think that they are ripping something out of him."

Morgan and Stowe exchange a glance.

"You don't need to worry about other students," says Stowe. His voice is strong and definitive. "I assure you, the extraction process is safe. We have years of tests and data to back up this assertion."

"You're wrong," exclaims Harriet. "The extractions hurt Owen. I could see it, Mona could see it, and Sam can see it too. You've bullied him or scared him somehow and he won't talk about it, but he knows that you are cutting into Owen's brain."

"You are overreacting," says Morgan. "The process is safe. I designed it myself."

"Then why can't Owen remember his dreams?" insists Harriet. She had not realized how upset she was until now.

"This is not a productive line of conversation," says Morgan calmly. "I take it from your tone that you will not assist with Mona's extractions."

"Of course not! I won't let you perform them either, not on Mona or Owen! You're hurting these children!"

"You should calm down and think about what you are saying," replies Morgan coolly. "You are in no position to dictate how we will proceed with either student."

"I'm Mona's instructor!"

"You can be reassigned," says Morgan. "Or let go entirely."

Suddenly Harriet is frightened.

"You can't let me go," she blurts out. "Mona needs me."

"I was just saying to my colleague that I have had concerns about your relationship with your students," explains Stowe. "You have been far too familial with her, breaching a number of rules that were put in place in order to keep you both safe."

"I haven't broken any rules," counters Harriet.

"Please," continues Stowe. "We have video of your student calling you by name, we have video of you holding her and singing to her, we have video of you spending two days by her side in the infirmary. If I didn't know better, I would say that you were treating her like your own child."

"That's ridiculous," says Harriet, not sure herself that it is.

"Then perhaps like a family member, an estranged sister perhaps?" suggests Stowe. "What would your own sister say if you lost your job due to unprofessional conduct and failure to adhere to instructions?"

"If she knew what you were doing here, she would be proud," counters Harriet defiantly.

"I see," sighs Stowe. "That is unfortunate. We had hoped that you would be cooperative, but since you are set on a path of self-destruction, consider this your exit interview."

Harriet starts to protest, but is suddenly restrained by two security guards that appeared silently behind her. *The hidden entrances in the walls*, she thinks as they pull her back to the door.

"You will be escorted off Company property. Your personal belongings will be returned to you once your apartment has been thoroughly searched," explains Stowe. "Our staff will be instructed not to have any contact with you, and we will inform our competitors of the reasons for your dismissal."

"I hope that you can patch things up with your sister," smiles Morgan slyly. "Because no one else will take you in."

"I'll go to the authorities," screams Harriet. "This is criminal."

The door to the office shuts in her face and the guards manhandle her around pulling her down the hallway. A tall, thin man in a dark blue suit is standing at the end of the hall waiting for her. He is the same man that sat and observed the classroom when they announced that Mona was one of the top four students.

"My name is Mr. Addams," he introduces himself. "I work for Stowe and Morgan."

"I recognize you," spits Harriet.

"I'm here to help you," continues Addams. "You'll want to listen to what I have to say."

"I want to be let go," fights Harriet. "I'm going to the authorities as soon as I leave here."

"You may want to listen to me, Harriet," says Addams. "I am here as a friend."

"You're not my friend," says Harriet glaring at Addams.

"Oh, I think that I am," replies Addams. "Stowe and Morgan have close ties to the authorities and the Chancellor himself. They have very powerful friends in the government and with any branch of the authorities you might be considering going to and telling your story. You only have one friend. Me. And as a friend, let me tell you that the best thing you can do is go to your sister's place, find another job in another field, and forget everything you know about the Company, because I will be watching."

"Are you threatening me?" asks Harriet.

"For such a qualified instructor, trained to notice even subtle hints, you are being very obtuse," replies Addams. "For expediency's sake, let me say yes, I am threatening you, but not just you. I am also threatening your sister, your friend Sam, his student Owen, and your former student Mona. The only trouble is, they don't know they're being threatened, they don't know the danger they could be in, and they can't do anything about it. You are the only one who can choose to do the right thing. Am I being clear now?"

Harriet's mouth is too dry to speak. Suddenly, her knees feel weak and she has trouble standing. Shet slumps into the arms of the two guards holding her.

"I see that my point has been made," smiles Addams.

CHAPTER TWENTY-ONE

Second Thoughts

S am is shaking. How did he get here? He had only wanted to be a good instructor. That's not true. He wanted to be a director someday. He wanted to prove that Owen wasn't really a bad student. Sure, he wasn't strong compared to the others, but that was like comparing a hawk to a butterfly: one is a faster flyer, but the other paints a more intriguing picture with its wings.

All Sam wanted to do was prove that there was more to Owen than anyone expected. It had become a bit of an obsession, he had to admit, but he wasn't hurting anyone. He performed scans after hours. He reviewed the data in his free time. He wasn't looking to sell company secrets or anything. He just knew that Owen was special. Then they told him to perform an extraction.

Everything changed. Owen wasn't himself after the first extraction. Sam didn't want to admit it at the time but looking back he could see the signs that something was wrong. After they had finished, Owen seemed to forget things that had been important to him. At the time, Sam chalked it up to a side effect from the Selective Memory Extraction— something that would wear off in time. With each subsequent extraction, the lie Sam was telling himself became harder and harder to believe. He was hurting Owen. He knew it.

Sam is shaking as he preps the machines for one more extraction.

He ends the diagnostic cycle and starts the boot up for the procedure. Morgan is standing behind him, a few paces back, watching.

"You're nervous," observes Morgan casually, with a voice as cold and exact as a scalpel. "I've reviewed the tapes of your previous extractions. You were never so visibly distraught. I can only conclude that it has something to do with my presence."

It is not phrased as a question, so Sam decides not to respond.

"I was nervous when I performed my first series of extractions," continues Morgan in a more casual tone. "It was some time ago now, but unlike today, the technology was new, and the process was still being refined. But people were willing to take the risk."

Morgan moves around the room and examines Sam's work. Sam watches as Morgan walks slow circles, checking over the equipment and glancing at the monitors. With each circle, Morgan draws closer. Sam is a moth with a spider looping gossamer tighter and tighter around its wings.

"You were born after the war ended, I assume," continues Morgan. "I was too, but only just. Back then extractions were much more invasive and damaging. However, if it meant losing the memory of the pain and horror they witnessed, shell-shocked soldiers were ready to risk any damaging side effects.

"By the time I started working in memory manipulation, we were moving away from those early practices and developing new, more refined ones. That's when I met Stowe." Morgan circles around again, still talking in a casual tone. "I had new ideas and he had the means to advance them. Together we started the Company, using his political and business sense and my innovations to become a leader in the field."

Sam already knows all this. Why did Morgan feel the need to give him a history lesson?

"We were innovative, we were fresh, we were new," explains Morgan. "But now the competition has started to catch up. Where there are innovators, there are always impostors. Did you know that before the war two giant multinational companies spent millions on advertising, each trying to convince the public that they sold the best sugary drink? The products they sold were essentially identical, but they branded them as though they could not be more different. One was the original, the classic, the first, the other was the new wave, the next thing, the improvement. It's silly now—especially considering the price of sugar—but when one innovated, the other copied and soon the market was flooded. The two were not only fighting each other, but also had to contend with dozens of imposters.

"In those days of excess, companies could afford to share customers. There was so much wealth that it didn't really matter if your company was number one or number two. One could build a fortune being even further down the list. But now things have changed. We cannot afford to be overtaken. We cannot afford to have some new firm come along and do what we do, but cheaper. We certainly can never afford to have someone offer something that we cannot.

"That's where your work comes in. You have innovated. You saw something we all missed. I would be jealous, only I saw something no one else saw too. I saw you."

Sam stops for a moment and turns to look at Morgan, now standing close behind him.

"That's right," says Morgan. "I saw potential in what you were doing and let you have the leeway to pursue it. I am happy to say that it seems my gamble paid off. Once this final extraction is complete, we will have something no one ever even considered. We will have bottled a dream. But better than a dream, the full experience of a child's dream. All the wonder and beauty, all the sense of fun and excitement, and all the comfort and security. Priceless."

Morgan finishes and smiles a wolfish grin at Sam.

"But what about Owen?" asks Sam.

"Do you know what I originally called the method of extractions that we use to collect memories for implantation?" asks Morgan. "I called it harvesting. Stowe softened the word and made it more palatable by calling the process extractions; Selective Memory Extractions—what possible harm could something like that be? He said that harvesting would remind people of reaping—sheaths wheat cut down with precision. Too much a reminder of the young people lost in their full prime to the war—falling to deaths like a scythe reaping grain in the field. Extraction, he said, would remind the people of when the army could pull soldiers out of danger and return them home, whole and safe. I went along with Stowe, he understands these things. Regardless of the term we ended up using, harvesting is more accurate.

"We cultivate memories in our students. We give them experiences that our clients request or that we think will be popular. In some extreme cases, we even map the student's experiences to those of one particular client. Then we harvest the memories. Just like harvesting grain or vegetables, the soil is left bare until the bounty regrows. The process is destructive, but safe. Rarely do we have problems at all."

"Owen." The one word is all Sam can manage.

"Yes, there are cases like Owen," sighs Morgan. "Honestly, I wish there weren't. It is a shame to lose such an investment. We are harvesting more from Owen than the fruits that we grew. We are pulling up the whole plant so that it can be re-planted in a client. The process is far more damaging and the effects permanent. Nothing will grow again. But the results yield much more than memories. You know this, though."

"We aren't just harvesting memories, we are harvesting experiences," finishes Sam.

"Precisely," replies Morgan, walking around Sam to face him.

Sam blinks back tears.

"I need to know that I can rely on you," says Morgan, leaning closer to Sam. "Owen is waiting outside that door. You have two options. Either I perform the extraction without you and Owen will be terrified and you will be fired, or you assist me, Owen will have one more happy experience with his favourite person, and you will keep your job. Which will it be?"

Sam closes his eyes and lets the tears come. After a minute, he wipes his face and says, "I'll do it."

The door opens and Sam watches as Miller leads Owen into the room. She looks up at Sam, her eyes growing wide. Glancing over at Morgan, she quickly controls her reaction and puts on her regular stern, professional face.

"Thank you, Ms. Miller," says Morgan. "That will be all."

Sam watches as Miller leaves. Then he helps Owen up on to the table, making sure Owen has his toy bee in his lap. Sam begins preparing him for the extraction.

"I want you to breathe deeply," he says, starting the relaxation exercises, which are as much for himself as they are for Owen. "Good, now relax your body and think about a dream you had."

"I can't," says Owen. "I can't think of any dream."

"You have lots of dreams," says Sam. "Remember the bees or the stars?"

"No," replies Owen, looking away.

Morgan makes an impatient noise. Sam is glad to see that Morgan has once again decided to stand at the back of the room, having the good sense to stay out of Owen's line of sight so as not to upset the boy.

"Tell me about the bees," Owen asks. "What are they?"

Sam can barely keep himself together. The little boy he knew is all but gone and it is his doing.

"Do you know who I am?" whispers Sam.

Owen scrunches up his face and stares at Sam before shaking his head. "Are you my friend?"

Sam closes his eyes. His head droops toward the floor. "Tell me about someone you do remember," he whispers.

"I remember Mona," replies Owen. "I ... she is my friend."

"Do you think you could dream about Mona?" asks Sam.

"I could try," replies Owen. Oddly, his voice is distant. He is not timid or afraid. Sam thought that he would be, but that is just one more part of him that is lost.

"Then close your eyes."

o o o

An hour later Sam watches as Owen is carried out of the room. He waits until the door shuts before wheeling around to punch Morgan. His fist lands hard connecting at the jaw. Morgan stumbles backward and is forced to grab the counter to stay upright.

"I don't care what happens to me," shouts Sam. "You made me do that to Owen. You made me take away all that made him so special. He's a shell. I loved him—I still love him—and you made me do that to him. I don't care about my job. I don't care about your connections. I'll make you pay!"

To Sam's surprise, Morgan is unexpectedly calm.

"I thought that you might find this whole process too much," says Morgan, wincing in some pain. "I had hoped that you would be capable of maintaining your calm and thinking rationally, but to my disappointment you have chosen to lash out."

Sam hears the door behind him open. Before he can turn around, two sets of strong arms grab him and pull him down to the diagnostic table, pushing the bee Owen left behind to the floor. The hard landing on the metal surface knocks the wind out of his chest. While he tries to pull air back in, a hand grabs his forehead and pins the back of his head to the table.

Morgan moves forward and begins the same series of preparations that Sam had completed earlier.

"You are hurting now," says Morgan, matter-of-factly. "Fortunately, our Company has a procedure that can permanently remove painful memories."

Sam struggles as the two guards hold him down. The hand on his head is pushing down so hard, it feels like his head could burst.

"Mr. Addams, could you help restrain him?" asks Morgan politely.

Sam continues to thrash his legs and arch his back as a well-dressed man walks forward. Suddenly he feels a sharp pain in his side and the fight seems to leave his muscles.

"That's better," says Morgan. "Guards, you may leave us. But Mr. Addams, please stay behind. I may still need your help." Morgan bends over slightly retrieving the plush bee toy and, handing it to one of the guards at the door, says, "see that this is returned to the child."

Sam can just move his head enough now to watch the two guards leave.

"I know what you are thinking," says Morgan. "You're worried that I am going to remove all your memories of Owen."

Sam stares silent and wide-eyed, unable to move or speak.

"You should know that I can't do that," explains Morgan. "You'd be left with gaping holes in your memory. It wouldn't take you any time to figure out that something was wrong.

"No, I'm going to remove the memory of the past few hours. You won't suffer any permanent damage and all of this unpleasantness will be forgotten."

Sam manages a grunt-like chuckle.

"You don't think so?" responds Morgan. "You think that you'll know that something is missing from tonight?"

Sam tries to smile.

"You're probably right. That's why I'm also going to implant a memory," says Morgan, with that wolfish grin. "Not a real memory of course. A synthetic memory. They aren't nearly as good—the Company would never offer them to clients—but they'll do in a pinch."

Morgan fits the crown to Sam's head and presses a button. Sam feels the two needles push into his skin with a sharp burning sensation. It hurts much more than he thought it would. Another lie he told Owen, another time he knowingly hurt him.

"Unfortunately, the synthetic memory won't last. That is their major downfall. It won't take long before it will fade away and you'll be left with a gap in your memory. A hole where the events of tonight should be. You might even start to put two and two together, but by then, you'll be fired and unable to interfere in any of what goes on here."

Sam tries to scream for help but can only manage a low grunt. He is breathing heavily and staring up at Morgan.

"Are you ready to begin?"

o o o

"I take it that tonight did not go as planned," says Stowe, handing Morgan a glass of ice.

"Not as we would have liked," concedes Morgan, wincing a little as the cold glass touches skin.

"But you have taken care of any potential loose ends?"

"As we discussed."

"Very good. I still don't fully understand why the extraction process was so damaging to the student. Was his instructor incompetent? I would have thought that we could have expected to get more out of the plomp before he became unusable."

"We are moving into new territory. We have always dealt in memories, but now we are starting to extract whole experiences. Memories are events that can be related from one person to another. They are stories that people tell and things that people share. Our students are trained to capture the details of complex memories so that we can implant them into our clients. It is then up to our clients to attach meaning to the memories.

"Experiences are different. They are more complex and more closely linked to who we truly are. As you know, harvesting memories is a complicated process. It can be tricky. Harvesting experiences is damaging. They are so integrated into what makes up the self.

"But we were harvesting dreams. Dreams are so much a part of who Owen was. His imagination was quite active, to say the least, and he played out his fantasies while he slept and while he played. When we

171

removed his dreams, we removed the very core of his personality, the thing that connected all his memories and experiences, the very way he chose to interpret the world around him."

Morgan observes that Stowe is uncharacteristically silent.

"I have the last extraction here if you'd like to sample it," says Morgan after the pause starts to be uncomfortable. "I'll leave it on the table."

"What about the girl?" asks Stowe

"Mona?"

Stowe nods.

"So much of what is Mona is tied into everything she does and sees. She takes it all in and makes everything she experiences a part of her. The garden you designed isn't just a peaceful place, it has become a physical representation of a sense of her peace and well-being. When we perform the extraction, we will be cutting all that out—the sense of security, the sense of peace, the joy and play, even her first real friend, Owen. It will be a series of beautiful, sublime experiences, perfect for Madam Andriss. From Mona, she will receive the lost sense of the family and safety, of love and joy. It will have irreparable damage on Mona but will produce the finest memory we have ever harvested. Invaluable, priceless … we can ask anything and Andriss will pay it. And, as we discussed, the price will be more than just monetary compensation, Andriss will also lead us to a new circle."

"I have drawn up the terms and Andriss has approved them," replies Stowe.

"Then we should not wait much longer. I will schedule Mona's extraction."

"Good," replies Stowe, looking out the window to the garden. "Leave the extraction you performed today on the boy. It is past time that someone tested one of them."

"Are you planning on sampling it yourself?"

"Maybe. I would like to know more about why this boy is so special to you, to his instructor, and to the girl."

CHAPTER TWENTY-TWO

Magic Code

Mona sits and waits. This is the first time that she's arrived in the exam room before Harriet. She wishes that Harriet would hurry up. She's been worried about Owen; he wasn't at breakfast and the boys in his dorm said that he didn't sleep there last night. She's eager to ask Harriet where he is. She wants to know that he is alright.

The door opens and a woman steps into the room. It isn't Harriet.

"Hello, Mona," the woman says. "I am going to be your new instructor."

Mona chooses not to respond. Something is wrong. Harriet should be here, but this woman has come in her place. Owen should have been at breakfast, but he wasn't. Something is deeply wrong.

Mona closes her eyes and quickly runs through the events of the past few days. This is a new skill that she has been working on. It is not an exercise that Harriet assigned her, or a technique that she learned from another student. She lets all the sights and sounds, all the images and sensations wash over her, without ordering them or actively looking for any one specific detail. Instead, she relies on how she felt in the moment, letting what stood out to her at the time make its way to the surface. One word becomes clear in her mind: Extraction.

It only seems that Mona shut her eyes for a moment, but Mona has relived hours of memory. She fixes her gaze on her new instructor.

"Tell me about extractions," says Mona, her voice quiet but definite.

The instructor stops midway through arranging the materials she brought to go over with Mona.

"How do you know about extractions?" she asks.

"Where is Owen?" asks Mona, ignoring the question.

"Mona, can you answer my question?" Mona can hear that the instructor is desperate to regain control of the flow of conversation. Mona watches the new instructor shift; she doesn't want to talk about Owen.

"What's in the room behind that door?" tests Mona, pointing to the door that Miller came through.

"It's just a changeroom," replies the instructor, still sounding off balance.

"Just a changeroom?" responds Mona, skeptically.

"Yes," replies the instructor, calming down a little.

"Are you sure?" asks Mona.

"Why wouldn't I be?"

"Where's Harriet?" asks Mona, changing the subject.

"She had to take care of some personal things. She'll be gone for a few days. In the meantime, I'll be your instructor. Let's get this session back on track, shall we?"

"Okay," replies Mona calmly.

"Good," the instructor breathes a sigh of relief. "Let's start with your lesson. I understand that you are quite good at memory games. Would you like to play one?"

"I think I'd rather show you the garden," says Mona, standing and turning toward the door.

Before the instructor can stop her Mona is through the door and in the small anteroom. The instructor rushes to follow, just in time to see Mona touch the hidden button on the wall. An ID card pops out; Mona snatches it, glances at the name on it quickly, and waves it against the scanner. Opening the next door.

The instructor has to rush to keep up with Mona so as not to get locked out and left behind in the student section of the campus.

They stand together in the common changerooms that are usually attached to the anteroom. Mona takes a second to look around.

"Mona, give me back my key card!" demands the instructor.

"This isn't the way to the gardens," replies Mona, ignoring the request.

"The key card! Now!"

"They can change the rooms somehow," says Mona to herself. "What else can be behind the door?"

The instructor reaches for the card in Mona's hand, but Mona pulls back.

"This isn't funny, Mona!"

"Tell me about extractions," replies Mona, holding the card behind her. "Tell me about what they did to Owen. Tell me why Harriet isn't here. Tell me why when we went through the door it didn't lead to the hallway to the garden."

The instructor pauses, unsure what to do.

"Tell me Renee!"

"Owen is in the infirmary," replies the instructor. "Only my mother calls me Renee. Everyone else calls me Miller."

Suddenly, in Mona's eyes, Miller seems to shrink. She watches as the instructor slumps and sits on a bench next to some lockers.

"They took him there after the last extraction," continues Miller. "He's in isolation in a room by himself."

"Is he sick?" asks Mona.

"Not really," replied Miller. "It's hard to explain. It's more like he's hurt. I think the extractions hurt him somehow."

"Will he get better?"

Miller is silent. She has said far too much already, but the things that she has seen and what she has been asked to do have been weighing on her, particularly bringing Owen to the lab and seeing Morgan there with Sam. She is certain that something is going on. It feels wrong. And now Harriet is mysteriously away due to personal matters.

When they asked her to take over Mona's instruction while Harriet was on leave for a personal issue, Miller assumed that it would be an easy assignment. She's heard nothing but good things about Mona, who is supposed to be an exceptional student, naturally gifted, pleasant, and easygoing. Now Miller is confronted with a girl speaking to her in a cold, stern voice about extractions and other students. This is not what Miller expected.

Miller has worked hard for the Company every day since the day she was hired. She follows all the protocols and routines. She never deviates or disobeys instructions. She is, and has been, a model employee. Everything she's seen with Owen's case has been wrong. It's not just the lack of normal procedure that bothers her. It's a deeper sense that someone is manipulating her.

When they asked her to bring him to the diagnostics lab, she did. That's where she saw Sam crying. Whatever is happening, whatever they did to Owen, they made Sam complicit. For that matter, they made her part of it too. She brought Owen to the lab. She could see that something was wrong. She even had a sense that something was wrong days before, when she spoke to Harriet. But she did nothing to stop it.

Miller has always relied on evidence and facts in her work. Although she has very little hard evidence, she knows deep down that Morgan was somehow forcing Sam to do something that could hurt Owen. Now she can't help but wonder if she too has been manipulated in some way to help the bosses by hurting the students.

"Mona, don't let them perform an extraction on you," blurts out Miller.

Mona can see that her new instructor is breaking down. In front of her, she sees Miller, but in her mind, she can see the children she lived with on the streets who gave up and either lashed out violently at anyone who got too close to them, or more often, just lay down to sleep and didn't bother getting up to look for food or beg for money.

The memory comes back to Mona from somewhere before she made it to the orphanage, when she was too tired and hungry to remember the distinctions between individual days or weeks. The memory of despair starts to flow over her like a thick fog and she begins to feel the sadness and loneliness creeping back.

Another memory comes forward too. Mona remembers Harriet saying, "That sounds like empathy to me, and I think it's very good that you felt it." Mona remembers being hugged and carried off the streets. She reaches out.

To Miller's surprise, Mona takes her hand and leads her back to the anteroom.

"We have to help Owen," says Mona.

Miller is too stunned to say anything.

"Can you bring him a card from me?" asks Mona.

"I'm not sure," replies Miller. "Maybe."

Mona is about to step through to the exam room when Miller stops her.

"They have recording devices," explains Miller. "Once we are back in the exam room, they will know about everything we say."

Mona nods and steps through with Miller following close behind.

"I guess we can't go to the garden today," says Mona, smiling.

Miller is amazed at how quickly Mona is able to think up this charade.

"I'm sorry we weren't able to," responds Miller.

"Maybe next time," says Mona. "I'm sorry I ran through the door. I was just excited to see Owen. When will he be feeling better?"

"I'm not sure," stammers Miller, trying to keep up with Mona's ruse.

"Can I send him a card? He gave me a card when I was sick."

"I don't see why not," replies Miller.

"Do you have a piece of paper and a pen?" asks Mona.

Miller hands her a sheet of blue paper and a black pen. Mona folds the paper in two to make a card and then carefully draws a bee on the front of the card. She opens it and starts writing a note inside. She has to be clever, has to be quick, can't let the camera see the note. She needs to tell Owen to get out.

When she's done, she hands the card over to Miller.

"Harriet might like to sign it too," says Mona. "If you see her, could you ask her?"

Miller nods.

They continue their session for the remainder of the period. The whole time Mona maintains perfect composure. Miller struggles at first to stay focused, but soon she is able to follow Mona's lead and let the routine of performing memory exercises calm her.

When they are finished the session, Miller steps out into the anteroom and opens the card. Inside is a simple little poem. At first nothing about it seems out of the ordinary, but soon Miller notices that Mona has subtly underlined some letters and written others much darker. She smiles, recognizing the clever secret message.

There once was a bee,
Who liked to hear a grasshopper sing.
She sat on his knee,
And buzzed a melody with her wings.

I can't remember their song,
So, I'll just write you this letter,
And say I hope it's not long,
Until you feel better!

CHAPTER TWENTY-THREE

Empty Spaces

Somewhere there are pieces.

Owen walks around the room staring blankly at objects that he does not recognize.

"This is a …" he pauses, unsure of what label to attach to the object he is holding.

"It's not mine," he says, putting it down. "It doesn't belong to me."

Somewhere he is sure the pieces exist—the missing pieces.

He lifts another unfamiliar object up and turns it over and over in his hands. He can almost see the word for it. He can almost reach out and pull it back. He can feel it drifting in the void. The memory of what it is bouncing around in the darkness, not connected to anything.

He holds the soft … the soft … soft. TOY! It's a toy! A rush of joy fills him as he remembers the word. It's his stuffed toy! He strains to concentrate harder on the memory. He needs to pull it back and repair the connections, but they are all frayed and threadbare.

He thinks that there might have been laughter and stars. Stars that he could reach out and catch somehow. He could clutch them in his hand— small twinkling lights that he could hold on to before letting them float off back into the night. Was there someone else there?

Instinctively, he turns and looks behind himself.

Nothing.

Turning back, he examines the object in his hands. It is soft. But what is it called? He turns it over and over, trying to pull the memory back.

"No, it's not mine," he says after a while. "This doesn't belong to me. It's not part of ..." he trails off dropping the stuffed bee back on his bed and next picking up the card Mona made for him off of the shelf.

"What's this?" he asks the empty room.

Somewhere there are missing pieces. He is sure of it.

He examines the card for a little bit, before sighing and putting it back on the shelf. Then he sits down on the bed and looks at his hands. It always feels like he just dropped something, just put something important down for a minute, but what was it?

He looks under the bed.

Nothing.

Somewhere there is something missing—the pieces that he lost. He's ... he's not so sure anymore. Maybe it was always like this.

Owen pulls the blankets around himself and tries to forget that he's lost something. After what seems like a long time, he falls asleep.

He does not dream.

o o o

Somewhere there are stars.

This isn't supposed to happen. He is sure of it.

Stowe walks around his office and feels the awful void of her absence. Only a minute ago she was right next to him and the whole room smelled sweet like honey and the sky was full of stars and they were laughing.

Now he is all alone.

He can't remember what her smile looks like, but he can feel it lingering in him. Like the memory of a dream after waking up it starts to fade, and with it the sense of warmth and comfort.

Somewhere there are stars in the sky and a waterfall.

He was sailing on a ship with her. Then they were running across the flat surface of a lake. Their strides so long and graceful, they were practically flying. Looking down he could see the night sky reflected below him and suddenly he was tumbling over and over. Somersaulting through the sky with her laughing. They were holding hands. It felt so real.

He paces around his office, trying to hold on to the memory, trying to pull the dream back and stay in it a while longer, but it starts to slip away. The dream is fading.

Suddenly, he was tumbling in the dark, alone. She was no longer by his side and he felt scared. Where did she go? Why can't he remember? Is he lost?

Stowe collapses back in his chair and shoves the now empty memory file containing Owen's dream away from him, letting it skitter across his desk. He holds his head in his hands and whimpers, "Mona."

CHAPTER TWENTY-FOUR

Ringing Resilience

I t won't be enough, Mona realizes. She sits in the dark of the dormitory, listening to the slow, regular breathing of the other students who are all fast asleep. It won't be enough to save just Owen. She has to figure out a way to save everyone. But how will she get all the students out? How will she convince even the small number of students in her pod that they have to leave? Like her, most of them came from orphanages or hospitals or the streets. They had nothing, they were hungry and cold. Now they have warm clothes, good food, and people who look after them. How could she convince them to give all that up?

Mona isn't sure that the other students will believe her when she tells them about Owen. She can almost hear Stephanie saying, "They didn't hurt him, they just kicked him out because he's such a plomp!" It is an easy lie to believe. None of the other students noticed anything unusual about Owen, mostly because he was always a little unusual. Now that he is gone, they all seem to have assumed that he was kicked out. If anything, Owen's sudden absence has made Mona's pod work harder and adhere more closely to the rules—no one wants to be next. No one wants to be like Owen.

Mona lies back on her pillow and closes her eyes, not to sleep but to concentrate. The first thing she has to do, she decides, is to find a way out of the facility. Once she has an escape plan, it will make getting Owen and the others out easier. Even if she can only get herself out, maybe she can find help to get Owen and the others out. She could get the authorities to shut down the school and arrest the people who hurt Owen. But how would she convince them? They won't believe her without evidence.

If only people on the outside could see what they've done to Owen, thinks Mona. Then, suddenly, she realizes what she has to do. She has to get copies of Owen's scans. Then she can show them to people and they'll understand what has been happening at the school. But how will she get copies of the scans? Where is that information even kept?

Mona realizes that both her escape plan and her plan to get evidence to bring against the school rest on having a much better understanding of the layout of the buildings beyond the student facilities and the path to her garden. But that too is problematic. Harriet had brought Mona through the doors that lead out of the examination room a number of times. Each time they walked down a hallway that eventually led to the garden. But when Mona pushed past Miller and left the exam room, she found herself in a locker room. Clearly, someone can move the rooms around somehow. However, it gets done, it is quiet and subtle. Mona will need to figure out how the system works in order to find a way around it. Tomorrow she will ask Miller to help her.

Mona isn't sure if she can trust Miller, but with Harriet gone, she doesn't have too many options. Besides, Miller already agreed to bring Mona's card to Owen. It seems like she wants to help, like she's uncomfortable with what's happening at the school. Miller told Mona the truth about where Owen was, and Mona is pretty sure that she kept their conversation a secret. It might be out of necessity, but Mona decides that she can trust Miller. She relaxes a little and tries to get some sleep. Tomorrow she will have a lot to do.

o o o

Harriet presses the buzzer for her sister's apartment. It is very early in the morning, but the sun is up and shining in through the glass doors of the apartment building. Amelia would normally be up soon, getting ready for the first shift at work. Still, Harriet feels guilty robbing her of any sleep.

After a minute, there is a crackling static sound and the old-style intercom comes to life.

"Hello" says a somewhat groggy voice on the other end. "Who is it?"

Harriet swallows hard. "Amelia, it's me," she says.

"Harriet?" says the voice on the intercom. "What are you … never mind, you'd better come in."

There is a loud buzzing sound and the door unlocks. Harriet pulls it to her and steps into the building.

Soon she is sitting on Amelia's couch, cradling a cup of synthetic coffee and rushing through the events of the past few days that brought her here. Amelia, always patient, always kind, just sits and listens. Harriet was afraid that her sister would judge her, would tell her "I told you so," would scold her for ever taking a job with the Company. Amelia's idealism could sometimes throw up roadblocks in their relationships. But to Harriet's great relief, Amelia seems first concerned with the well-being of her sister and then with the well-being of Mona and the other students.

"We have to find a way to get Mona out of there," finishes Harriet. "She isn't safe, they'll do to her what they did to Owen, I'm sure of it."

"But you say you don't have any evidence," replies Amelia.

"No, they took all my files and searched my apartment. I don't have anything from the Company, not even a pay stub."

"Sounds like they were very thorough," says Amelia. "I still can't believe what they're doing. I mean, I knew that some of the corporations that grew up after the war were suspect—and I was sure that they were using political influences to withhold services, maintain their monopolies, or just to over-charge everyone—but I never would have guessed … I can't imagine … they're cultivating children. Growing them like chickens or cows and using them for profit."

Listening to her sister, Harriet can feel tears welling up in her eyes. There is a sharp pinch in her nose as she tries to hold them back. "What am I going to do?" she whispers.

"The first thing you are going to do is get some sleep," replies Amelia. "You are no use to anyone this tired. You look like you've been awake for days. Then, when I'm home from my shift at the clinic, you are going to tell me everything you know about the layout of the facility. Maybe there is a way we can get in and talk to one of your former colleagues, maybe there is a way we can sneak in and get a message to Mona."

Outside a church bell rings. The sound is strange and unfamiliar. There weren't many churches left standing after the war and very few still have bell towers. A few of the larger, more ornate buildings were repaired, more as national monuments or museums than as functioning churches. Harriet has always enjoyed the sound of the bells ringing from the little church in her sister's working-class neighbourhood. As far as she knew, very few people around here were devout, but they all seemed to have a place in their hearts for the small stone building, with its green copper roof and lone steeple. Harriet guessed that the people of this neighbourhood felt that the church's survival after the war reflected the same stalwart defiance they felt in their hearts.

The bells chime and Harriet thinks about how it was interesting that her sister chose to live in this neighbourhood. Moving into a space that had seen its fair share of post-war violence in resistance to the edicts and heavy-handed regulations passed down by the Chancellor. This neighbourhood had famously survived the air raids. The people had made barricades and fought hand to hand against enemy soldiers at the height of the war. Then when the Chancellor's forces rolled in to free the city, the people living here kept their barricades up, refusing to recognize the Chancellor without a free and fair election. Their defiance led to protests, riots, and eventually a military crack-down that resulted in four people being tried as traitors and shot in the square by the church.

The bells finish ringing. It is now six in the morning. Harriet looks at her sister and for the first time realizes that Amelia is not just sympathetic to the anti-Chancellor movement, she is part of it.

"Do you know people who can help us?"

"I think I know some people who can," replies Amelia. "Get some sleep. I have to get to the hospital. After my shift, I'll take you to the church and you can meet some of my friends."

o o o

"What was your sister's name?" asks Stowe.

Andriss sits in the garden with the sun on her face. The slight smile on her lips disappears when he asks the question.

"Is it relevant to my treatment?" she asks, the words sharp, almost angry.

"No," responds Stowe. "No, your program is set and ready to get underway. I was just curious."

Andriss opens her eyes and turns to her companion. They are sitting together on a bench in a glade. All around them there are flowers and bushes. The air is filled with the scent of honeysuckle. Ahead of them there is a path through the trees that leads to a quiet area with a pond and a little waterfall. The whole place is beautiful and secluded. Andriss feels that it was made just for her.

She is about to tell Stowe that she has no desire to speak about her sister or any of the earlier events of her life. She is about to tell him to keep his inquiries to himself. She is about to press him to finish the program so that she can receive her treatments. She is about to do all of this, but then she locks eyes with Stowe.

There is something out of place. Like always, he is immaculately dressed. His suit is stylish and perfectly pressed, his shirt and tie are fashionable without trying to pretend that he is young enough to be wearing the latest trends. Nothing seems physically out of place. Yet she still feels that there is something amiss. Andriss has not managed to grow her personal and political power without being able to read a room. She isn't certain what is wrong with Stowe, but she trusts her instincts enough to try and tease out more details.

"Her name was Eleanor," she says. "Ellie to me."

"How young was she?"

"As young as we all were once," replies Andriss noncommittally.

"I mean when she …" continues Stowe.

"I know what you meant," interrupts Andriss. She sighs and looks away. "She had just turned ten when the war started. We weren't too good at keeping track of time after that, but I would guess that she was eleven when she made up that rhyme for me. She was eleven when the bombs hit above us. She was never twelve."

The pain of the memory stabs Andriss and she can feel her chest tighten. The colour of the garden fades and the smell of flowers is replaced by the all too familiar memory of the stink of too many frightened people crammed into too small of a space.

Andriss pulls out her sister's handkerchief and dabs a tear from her eye. The ghost of her sister's scent still lingers on the piece of white cloth. For a moment, the memory of her sprite of a sister pulls Andriss back to the sunshine, but too soon it fades and she is left in a mixture of memories that cast a shadow even here in the perfect garden.

Andriss turns to tell Stowe that she is going back to her room. To her surprise, there are tears in his eyes as well.

"What is it?" she asks. "What could be the matter?"

"Only eleven," he replies. "So young."

"Yes," replies Andriss. "As I told you when we first met, the war was terrible."

"And you had to make the terrible decision," says Stowe.

"I did," replies Andriss. It is almost too much for her. She turns away ready to leave.

"But you had to make it, there was no choice," continues Stowe.

"I have tried to convince myself of that," replies Andriss, turning back to Stowe. "But more and more I doubt myself. More and more I wish I had made some other choice."

"What if you could?" asks Stowe.

"What do you mean?" replies Andriss.

"What if you had the choice to make again," he continues. "What if you had a real choice, what if you could save her?"

"Then I would," replies Andriss. Looking at Stowe, she is now certain that they are not speaking about hypotheticals.

"Even if it meant that you might have to sacrifice something of yourself?" asks Stowe.

"Even then," replies Andriss. "Especially then, especially if I could sacrifice something to know I saved her. Nothing would bring me greater joy."

Stowe stands and helps Andriss up. Together they walk in silence down the green hill to the path leading to the waterfall.

"Does this have to do with the program for my treatment?" asks Andriss, breaking the silence. "I thought that you said that false memories would not take hold properly. I thought that synthetic experiences eventually faded or felt fake. I don't see what good it would do to try and change my memory of what happened. I know in my heart that Eleanor is dead. I can feel it deep down in me that it is my fault. I left her behind."

"But we don't have to leave Mona behind," whispers Stowe just low enough that the sound of the waterfall will drown out his voice in any of the recording devices that Morgan may have placed around the garden.

o o o

"Mr. Addams, do you have anything to report?"

"Unfortunately, I do. It seems that Stowe met with Madam Andriss this morning to discuss the next steps in her treatment."

"Nothing unusual about that."

"Not on the surface, no. But their discussions extended beyond the planned procedure and the methods of payment."

"What exactly did they discuss?"

"While Stowe shied away from specifics, I think it is fair to say that he was interested in Andriss' views of ethics."

"I can't help but feel that you too are shying away from specifics. I have engaged your services for your discretion and for your honest analysis of potential security issues."

"Pardon me, but my services were retained by both you and your partner. I report to him as well as you."

"That is true. You know, we've always been pleased with your work. You have been a valuable part of the Company for years now. Neither Stowe nor I could manage the day-to-day operations without the quiet reassurance that you are standing behind us, watching our backs and heading off our enemies before they can get close enough to harm us. Stowe and I have often discussed our partnership with the thought of making you a more visible member of the Company, the third major shareholder, if you will."

"I had no idea."

"Unfortunately, we decided against such a move. We felt that change would bring a destabilizing force."

"I see. Disappointing, but understandable."

"Only, now I fear that destabilizing forces are already at work in the Company. Normally, I would turn to Stowe for guidance on these matters, but I cannot. You see, I believe that he is feeling doubt and unrest. I worry about what he might do. That is why I have turned to you."

"You believe that Stowe would act against the Company's best interests?"

"I sincerely hope not, but if he were planning to, I would need to know about it."

"I see."

"We should be partners in this. Together we can watch over Stowe as he goes through this hard time, and in doing so, we can watch over the Company."

"And if Stowe is planning to act in a way that could damage the Company?"

"We would stop him. I would allow him to gracefully step down and retire, and I would appoint a new partner—someone I could trust."

"In that case, I believe you may want to know a little more about the nature of Stowe's conversation with Madam Andriss."

CHAPTER TWENTY-FIVE

Coded Games

"Mona, do you like to draw?" asks Miller.

"I guess so," replies Mona.

"Did any of your previous instructors ever ask you to draw anything? Maybe try to recreate a picture or sketch what a building you remember looked like?" Miller smiles helpfully at Mona.

"My first instructor did a little, I guess. But I was always better at describing things. I'm not too good at drawing," admits Mona.

"You know, I was never very good at drawing either," replies Miller reassuringly. "And sometimes it isn't fun to be asked to do something we don't think that we're very good at, is it?"

Mona nods. She is concentrating hard on keeping her facial expressions normal. She wants her responses to sound genuine and unsure. For all the world, this has to appear to be a normal conversation between a student and her new instructor. Mona and Miller have to put on a farce for the recording devices so that they can communicate more easily with one another. Their conversation has to appear mundane, so that they can exchange more important information.

"Maybe we could each draw a picture about something we remember," suggests Miller. "I think that you'll see that you're better at drawing than me. And anyway, I'm more interested in how drawing helps you concentrate on a memory."

"Okay I guess," replies Mona, making sure that she sounds hesitant and nervous. "But you can't laugh at my drawing!"

"That's not fair, Mona," replies Miller. "What if you draw a cow riding a unicycle? I'd find that very funny."

For a brief moment, their charade is almost ruined. Mona pauses. The absurd image of a cow on a unicycle is just the kind of silly thing that Owen would dream up. Mona hadn't expected that from Miller. She feels surprised, sad, and even a little hurt all at once. But before her shock becomes visible on her face, she regains control and smiles.

"I've never seen a cow riding a unicycle," says Mona, forcing laughter into her voice. "So how could I draw a picture of one?"

This is good, thinks Miller. Mona is distancing herself from silly stories and made-up things. The people monitoring the recording will make note of that and conclude that she has gotten over Owen. It's funny that they assume that a child who is so perceptive, a child with such an amazing memory, could forget about her friend so quickly and easily. She is happy to see Mona playing her role so well; it will make the next step easier.

"Alright, no silly pictures then," responds Miller, pulling some coloured pencils and thick white paper from her bag. "How about you draw me your favourite part of the school? Try to add as much detail as you can, but don't worry too much about whether or not your drawing is 'good' or not."

"You have to draw something too," replies Mona. "That's the only way it's fair."

"Alright," says Miller, taking out some paper for herself. "We'll each draw a picture."

The code had been simple, but clever. At their previous session, Mona asked Miller if she'd ever heard of a game called black magic.

"One of the girls taught it to me," explained Mona. "It's easy but you need to have two people who know how to play it and a third who doesn't. One person covers her ears. That's when the person who doesn't know how to play whispers a word to the second person who does know how to play. The two people that know how to play then pretend to read each others' minds. That's the silly part."

"And the point is for the person who covered her ears to guess the word that the person who doesn't know how the game works said, right?" asked Miller, already knowing how the game works.

"Yes," replied Mona. "The one who knows what the word is asks a question like, 'Is it a bus?' and her partner says no. They keep asking questions and saying no, until finally the one who knows the word says something that's black, like 'is it a raven?' That's when the signal to the one who covered her ears that the next thing she gets asked will be the right one."

"It sounds like a fun game to play to trick someone into thinking you have magical powers," replied Miller, wondering what the point of the story was.

"The girls played it on me, but after four turns I figured it out. It's too simple."

"Too simple?" asked Miller.

"If two people need to talk without anyone knowing what they are saying, they'd need a better trick than black magic."

Suddenly Miller understood. Mona knew that the sessions were recorded, and she wanted to have a code so that she could get a message to Miller without alerting anyone else. She was too clever.

Miller didn't know much about codes, but she suspected that Mona already had one in mind, the trick was communicating it without it being obvious.

"It's a shame we can't go visit the garden," said Mona, seemingly changing the subject but making deliberate eye contact with Miller.

This was all important. She needed Miller's help. She couldn't think of another way to get a message to her except with a code. She just had to hope that Miller picked up on the message and was paying attention.

Mona closed her eyes, mimicking the memory exercises she'd been taught.

Miller watched closely, listening for any clues.

"Did you know that bees dance?" asked Mona to the world in general, eyes still shut tight. "I laughed when I first heard that. I didn't think it was true. I wanted it to be true, but I didn't think it was. I hoped that they danced together like people in a chorus line or like the guests at a party. Imagine them all lifting their legs and waggling them back and forth in unison to the hum of their wings. I thought maybe that's where the expression 'the bee's knees' came from."

Mona pauses and waits, hoping that Miller is following.

"In the garden, I used to watch the bees go from flower to flower. I never saw them dance. I had to look up a video in the library. It said that the bees move in figure eights. They also wiggle their bums. The angle of the shape they walk in and the speed of the waggle lets the other bees know the direction and distance to the best flowers. When I sat in the garden, I always wanted to follow the bees back to their hive so that I could watch them dance and see if others came to our garden."

There is a pause. Miller is sure that Mona is asking for directions for a sort of map to find something in the facility beyond the student campus.

"I used to be scared of bees, you know," continued Mona. "But then someone told me I shouldn't be anymore. It's funny how learning about something makes it less scary. Even though bees don't play music or dance for fun, it's nice to know that they can talk to their friends and find each other a long way off.

Miller thinks back to the conversation as she works on her drawing. Like Mona, she is drawing a landscape. Her pupil is hard at work colouring flowers with the coloured pencils. Despite feeling nervous about their subterfuge, Miller can't help but notice the detail that Mona is adding to her drawing. The proportions all look accurate and the colours realistic, despite the lack of fine details. Miller is sure that if you held the picture up at a distance, or unfocused your eyes a little, it would look exactly like the actual garden, right down to the location of the different flowers.

Looking back at her own work, Miller begins to add some lines to map the brickwork of the walls of a church she remembers from her childhood. Her memory is nowhere near that of her students, but it doesn't need to be. She is playing at being a kind instructor who is happy to sit on the floor and draw with her pupil in order to encourage Mona to complete a memory exercise. In reality, she is carefully adding lines and right angles to the rough drawing of the church, roughly mapping the pathway from the exam room in which they sit to the infirmary where Owen was being kept. She is trying to ensure that the number of bricks next to each line corresponds to the approximate distance in meters from one hallway to the other.

The directions in Miller's drawing weren't perfect. Mona would have preferred if they could share a map or speak more plainly about the layout of the building. But two things were clear from the thicker line running through the brickwork of the sketch of the church. First, with this information, Mona could now find her way to Owen. Second, Miller was willing to help.

Mona smiles and hands Miller her drawing.

"This is beautiful, Mona," says Miller. "I can't believe that you were worried that you weren't an artist. Tomorrow, I will ask you about specific details in your drawing and about your garden."

"That sounds fun," replies Mona. Of course, she thinks. The garden! She could map her way to the garden and now with Miller's drawing she could map her way to Owen. Little by little, with Miller's help, she could map out all the pathways from one place to another. It would take time, but she could combine them to build a complete map of the campus and to start to learn how they changed the rooms around.

But will I have enough time? wonders Mona. Will Owen?

o o o

"We need to move forward with Mona's program."

"Respectfully, I disagree," replies Stowe. "Ms. Andriss is away dealing with business matters and won't return until the end of the month. During that time, I suggest we continue to build the girl's competencies and foster her experiences. I want the memories we implant to be the best we've ever harvested."

Stowe wonders if Morgan can hear his nervousness. Does Morgan know that he's stalling for time? He looks at the hawk-like features of his colleague. Nothing in the cold eyes betray that Morgan has any idea that Stowe has lost his nerve, that because of testing Owen's dream, he's had a crisis of conscience.

"I will arrange more sessions in the garden with Mona's new instructor," replies Morgan smoothly.

"Good," responds Stowe, looking far off out the window. "And maybe additional free play with the other children."

"That does not fit with Andriss' profile," cautions Morgan.

"Oh no?" responds Stowe. "Yes of course, you're right. My apologies. I don't know what I was thinking. Still, in my last session with Andriss, she mentioned enjoying walking on the beach at sundown. Perhaps we might arrange such a memory for Mona?"

"I will look into it," replies Morgan standing to leave. "If we are not moving forward with Mona, we should schedule extractions with some of the other students. There is no sense in giving up the lab time."

Stowe looks up and blinks for a moment. What can he say to pause extractions on other students? In trying to save Mona will he condemn someone else?

"I suppose we could hold off with any extractions, if you have a reason for a delay," probes Morgan.

"No," says Stowe, stealing himself. "No reason to delay the procedures. But we will hold off on Mona's extractions." His voice is finally confident again.

"How interesting."

"What is?"

"I cannot recall a single time when you ever referred to a student by name."

Stowe sees himself through Morgan's eyes. He sees the fear and uncertainty that he is trying to hide, and he wonders, does Morgan see it too?

CHAPTER TWENTY-SIX

Knot Gone

H is hands fumble with the rope. He is sure that yesterday he could tie a bowline. He is sure that he has been practicing his knots for weeks. Now his hands don't seem to know what to do.

Nick sits on his bunk and looks down at the length of rope. He makes a small loop with his right hand then takes the end of the rope with his left and threads it through ... but then what? He can remember the books on sailing and knots, but he can't pull back the pages of diagrams or the instructions.

Learning the knots was a frustrating process. They all had funny names and involved complicated diagrams and endless repetition. Luckily, Nick was used to practicing and drilling exercises until they were perfect. Whenever he got frustrated he would do the calming exercises that Miller had taught him. Taking a few deep breaths with his eyes closed, he would rationally examine what was causing his frustration, he would take a moment to identify possible solutions or ways to avoid becoming too annoyed, and only then would he continue.

Looking down at the tangle of rope in his hands, Nick is keenly aware of a new sensation. Despite the difficulty he is having tying a knot, he is not frustrated. Rather, Nick is feeling apprehensive. This is the first time that he has ever forgotten anything that he practiced.

Just like the tangle of rope, Nick's thoughts are an unorganized mess. The feeling of apprehension is growing and making his chest tight. How could he forget something? What's going on? He can hear the blood rushing in his ears like waves on a beach. He drops the rope and starts to pace the length of the boys' dorm. Is he going to be kicked out of school? With all his training, why can't he remember a simple mechanical task? What will Miller say if she finds out?

The thought of his strict instructor helps to focus Nick for a moment. He remembers her direction to help him control his reactions so as not to let emotion get in the way of his memory exercises. He closes his eyes and takes three deep breaths. The sound of pumping blood in his ears dies down. He relaxes a little. He knows that panic will not help. He must concentrate and pull back the memories.

Nick sits down on his bunk again and tries to remember.

The air was cool and smelled of salt and the gentle wet rot of seaweed. He walked with Miller down a long wooden stage that led out into the water. What was it called? Not a stage, not a bridge, because it didn't go anywhere. What was it?

Nick breathes deeply and tries to concentrate on another detail.

Miller introduced him to a man wearing a strange vest. The man laughed and helped Nick put on a similar vest, pulling straps until it was tight. Then they got in a small boat. The cool air picked up some of the water and covered their faces in mist as it filled the sail and pulled them forward.

Nick smiles. Now that he is starting to isolate the memory, he can feel the sense of unease abating.

With the wind kicking around them, the small boat began to pick up speed. It was exhilarating! One side of the boat began to lift out of the water with the speed and power of the wind. It felt like they were about to fly away. After a few minutes, the man turned to Nick and said, "Do you want to steer her?"

Nick's eyes snap open. He is sitting on his bed, his palms sweaty.

He cannot remember what happened next. He has no recollection of steering the boat or the rest of the day on the water. The only thing he can remember after the man handed him the tiller is falling asleep next to Miller on the bus back to the school.

Nick breathes deeply and tries to run through his memory exercises, to pull back more of the day on the water. But the more he tries, the more it feels like trying to remember a dream after you wake up. There are fragments here and there, but little by little it fades away, until the little boat is lost in the mist entirely and all that is left is Nick sitting on his bunk, trying to remember how to tie a knot.

o o o

"You seem pleased with the memory that you extracted today," says Addams.

"I am," replies Morgan. "I am even more pleased to have been able to apply some of the new innovations we've been working on to the case of this student. I had hoped for more than a memory, for a full experience, and I believe that is what we extracted today."

"The boy is recovering in the infirmary, but seemed a little confused after the process."

"Some disorientation is normal. It may be a little more pronounced with this new twist on the procedure."

"Do you know if the effects are long-lasting?"

"Are you concerned about the student?" asks Morgan, wary about the need for a partner who is focused on the Company, not the individual students.

"Not at all," replies Addams with a certainty that puts Morgan's mind at ease. "My only concern would be to ensure that if the effects were more long term, we put protocols in place to keep the other students from interacting with this one, Nickolas I believe is his name. We could, for example, tell them that Nick was promoted to a new Pod."

"A clever idea," admits Morgan with a smile. "Not only does it shield the others, but it could motivate them. But what would we do with Nick if he doesn't recover?" Morgan already knows the right answer, but needs to confirm that Addams is ready to be a new head of their firm.

"I would hope that Nick will recover so that we could perform additional extractions. However, if that is not the case, then it seems to me that there are already many children on the streets. What's one more?"

CHAPTER TWENTY-SEVEN

What You Sow

There is a fine powdery mist blowing through the city. Harriet pulls a scarf over her hair and adjusts her sunglasses and face mask before stepping out into the street.

Normally, she would avoid going outside on days like today. The official reports broadcast on the news say that the dust "does not pose a significant health risk and is in no way linked to fallout or the grey cough." Still, the news anchors always caution citizens to remember their masks and to wash their hands after being outdoors.

It seems like the dust storms have been more frequent recently. Harriet can only remember four or five last year, but already this year there have been seven. Each time the dust comes rolling in from the east on a hot wind. Each time the news broadcasts that there is nothing to worry about. Each time Amelia would tell her that the hospital recorded a higher number of deaths related to breathing issues.

"They say it's not fallout, but it's fallout," explains Amelia as they walk together to Harriet's second meeting with Amelia's friends. "Only it's not old fallout from the war years ago. It's recent, from bombs that are being dropped on the Eastern Bloc."

"There haven't been any reports about aggression from the Eastern Bloc," replies Harriet. She is still trying to wrap her head around having a sister who is an active member of an anti-government resistance group.

"They don't report on it directly. That's not their style," responds Amelia. "But if you watch the commodity prices, you'll notice that the cost of rice has gone up steadily. That points to difficult trade negotiations. Next, the ministry of the interior started to run a campaign encouraging everyone to invest in wheat and barley. Around the same time, there were rumours that a foreign power was planning an attack on our southern farmland. Nothing happened, but it put a strong focus on local production of food and a distrust of anything coming from the outside."

"So, they were setting the stage for public opinion to turn against one of our biggest and most important trading partners?"

"You're catching on fast," smiles Amelia. "They were also setting up a narrative that would allow them to blame the food shortages and rationing on the Eastern Bloc. That way, by the time the news does come out that we've been bombing them, the majority of the public will back our dear old Chancellor for standing up to the bullies who want to hurt our crops and starve our citizens. We've got to protect our farmers after all."

They walk on in silence, Harriet a little in awe and disbelief at the conclusions her sister is drawing. She's never really liked the Chancellor, but Harriet finds it hard to imagine that a government would create such elaborate fictions just to keep its own people on side. Then again, the Company told plenty of lies to keep her and her fellow instructors working away while they tore into the brains of the children they were claiming to raise and educate. Maybe Amelia's theories about the government weren't so farfetched after all?

As they turn the corner, Harriet sees an oddly dressed man in the small public square just outside the church where they are meeting Amelia's friends. The man is not wearing a mask and his hair is matted with dust and sweat. The grey of the dust on his skin and clothes makes him look like a grotesque statue come to life.

Harriet watches him stumble about as a group of street kids take turns running forward and pretending to kick him. Eventually, one gets brave enough to actually land a blow, which sends the man raving and turning in all directions, as the other children howl with laughter.

It's an ugly sight, but not unfamiliar. The children that grow up on the street are often tough and given to cruel games, exacting their limited power on those few in lesser positions than themselves.

Amelia pulls on Harriet's arm to keep her moving. They both know that even if they are able to scare the children off, chances are they will just return as soon as she and Amelia move on.

They pass the man, giving him a wide berth, and continue on to the church. Harriet can't help but feel that there is something wrong with the scene she'd just witnessed, beside the obvious cruelty of the street kids. Suddenly, it hits her and she whips around, startling Amelia.

"Leave him alone!" screams Harriet at the kids who are laughing and dancing just outside the man's reach, like prize fighters facing a punch-drunk opponent. "Get away from him!"

A few of the kids take flight, but one or two of the braver ones stay to continue their torment, happy to have two targets now.

Harriet descends on them threatening to hit them with her bag. The larger of the children jumps back and runs a quick circle around the man, putting him in between her and Harriet.

"Watch'ya gonna do lady?" taunts the child. "Him grim-bum, you too-slow." She chants in a sing-song voice.

"Just leave him alone," cries Harriet, half yelling, half pleading. "He's a friend of mine."

"Some friend!" laughs one of the other children. "You make kissy-kissy with a grim-bum?" They all laugh at this.

All the while the man is looking around confused, as if he doesn't understand where he is or who the people around him are. Tears leave clean tracks on his dusty face. His lips are so badly cracked that they are almost bleeding, the red sore areas contrasting brightly against his dust-grey skin. Harriet chokes back tears seeing Sam this way.

She is so distracted by the state of her friend that Harriet doesn't see the rock being thrown. It hits her painfully in the shoulder and as she cries out, the children begin laughing louder. The few that had run away are returning now and Harriet is starting to feel worried not only for Sam, but for herself as well. That's when Amelia steps into the fray.

The older girl that had been leading the torment is dealt a swift stinging blow to the shin, dropping her to the ground. Her scream startles the other children who stop their cruel game to see what has happened.

Harriet looks over too and sees Amelia with a handful of the leader's hair in her fist. The girl is looking much younger and less threatening now as she pleads from her knees to be let go.

"When I let go, you run," Amelia says in a voice like iron. "You all run or I will make you wish you had! And if I ever see you around here again, tormenting poor confused men, I will have the authorities tear down that rats' nest on Leed Street that you all call home."

Even the most brazen of the children blanch at the sudden revelation that this woman knows where they sleep. When Amelia releases their leader, they all scatter like mice.

"Are you okay?" asks Amelia now that the excitement is over. But Harriet doesn't listen, she just rushes forward to the dust-covered man.

"Sam, Sam, are you okay?" asks Harriet. "What happened to you?"

"They cut out years," replies Sam staring past Harriet at nothing in particular.

"Sam, what do you mean?" asks Harriet.

"I'm not him ... they cut me ... I've ... I used to but now I can't," mumbles Sam, shuffling back away from Harriet.

"Just wait," pleads Harriet. "Sam, we'll get you help. You can come with us." She reaches and grabs Sam's coat to stop him from retreating.

Without warning, Sam makes a wild swing, catching Harriet in the face with the back of his hand. The blow isn't particularly hard, but it is sudden and shocking enough to knock Harriet back. Freed from her grip, the dusty man that was once Sam runs into an alleyway.

It takes Harriet quite some time to calm down. Amelia fusses over her at the apartment, insisting that she drink something hot and hold a cold cloth to her face.

Harriet's cheek is an angry red and Amelia says that there will likely be an ugly bruise. But the real damage from the punch was that it came from Sam. Sam who had always been kind and gentle. Sam, who used to love to make her laugh. Sam, who only a short time ago, she had imagined touching her face to kiss her after a date.

Harriet did not even recognize the man she saw today.

"They cut out years," she says to herself as Amelia takes the cloth and replaces it with a fresh cold one. "They cut out years."

"What does that mean?" asks Amelia.

"It means that they performed an extraction on him," explains Harriet. "It means that they did to him what they are planning to do to Mona and the other students."

"That's horrible!" gasps Amelia. "I had no idea what the effects ... I mean you told me that you thought it could hurt them but that?"

"I know," replies Harriet. "We need to get Mona out now."

"But how are we going to do that?" asks Amelia. "My friends tell me that they can get her safely out of the city without the authorities knowing, but they can't get her out of the Company's compound."

Harriet drops her head to the table.

"I was hoping that we could ask someone inside to help us," she says. "But now I've lost him too."

o o o

Stowe is used to using his clipboard to type all his messages. His hands can move quickly over the screen to craft letters to clients, instructions to staff, or even memos to the Chancellor's office.

He is out of practice writing with a pen and paper.

The advantage of paper is that there is only one copy of the message and it can be burned.

Stowe carefully crafts his first letter. This one is to Andriss. It will not be an issue to get the letter into her hands without it being seen by an intermediary. Both Stowe and Andriss employ solid, dependable people—people who are both trustworthy and too fearful to betray their employers, for good reason. The second letter will be more difficult. He will have to be careful in ensuring that it is delivered and that there is no way that anyone can find out.

He sighs and begins to carefully form his letters.

Dear Andriss,

I am not accustomed to asking for help, but I fear that I must ask for yours in an important matter. I do not feel that it is safe to provide too many details at this time (that can wait for our next meeting), but suffice it to say that I now have a much better understanding of the difficult decision that you faced with your sister.

I am not being hyperbolic when I tell you that I face a similar situation. On the one hand, I can choose to save myself and my firm. On the other, I can save a life.

I am ashamed to say that until recently the decision would have been easy for me. I have certainly made similar decisions in the past and, as you may surmise, my firm has grown and prospered.
Something has changed. Something in me has changed. I have grown to appreciate another point of view. As a result of this quite painful realization, my perspective has been altered. I may even say that I am altered.

I can no longer do what is expected of me, nor can I let others make the same decisions in my absence. But there are forces within the Company that will not simply allow me to change course.

Without your help and guidance, a young girl will likely die. This will happen whether I act to oppose it or not. I am not certain how to stop what feels inevitable. I am not certain how to undo the mechanisms that I put in place to cause this situation. I only know that I must try and that my best chance of success requires your help.

Sincerely,
Thomas Stowe

Stowe carefully folds the letter and seals it in an envelope. He then removes the piece of paper under his original and burns it to ensure that no one could reproduce the letter from the impression his pen made on the backing sheet.

"Now to write to Harriet."

CHAPTER TWENTY-EIGHT

Spoiled Plans

Mona frowns. Her map isn't right. She's mapped direct paths from the examination room to more than a dozen locations around the larger campus compound. She knows how to get to Owen, how to get to the garden, how to get to the cafeteria where the instructors eat, even how to get to the subway that takes the Company employees home in the evening. But her map doesn't make sense—too many lines overlap and cross over each other.

She closes her eyes and imagines a blank piece of paper. *You are sitting in the exam room*, she tells herself. *A red dot appears on the clean white paper. If you leave the exam room and go right down the curved hallway you can take the path to the garden.* In her mind, a blue line extends from the red dot and twists and turns as it moves across the paper to a large green square representing the garden.

Mona frowns again. It doesn't make sense. Miller told her that going right out of the exam room also leads to where the scanning equipment is kept. It took some time communicating back and forth in their code, but eventually Mona was able to get enough details from Miller to know that the hallways weren't the same. She would have thought that Miller was purposely trying to trick her if she hadn't run out of the exam room that day to find herself in a locker room.

Sitting with her eyes closed, Mona fills the white piece of paper with lines, each leading somewhere important, somewhere she may need to go. The lines spider out of the central point—the examination room. As they intersect and overlap, Mona becomes aware that there are hubs all over the building where something is shifting. Mostly these hubs are small rooms, like the exam room, but sometimes they are stairwells or long curved hallways where you can't see one end from the other. Someone or something is cunningly changing the structure of the building by rotating or moving these spaces so that they lead you somewhere else.

It isn't fair, thinks Mona. She was finally feeling like she had a reliable map of the building, but now she's figured out that someone is twelve steps ahead of her and has built in a mechanism to confuse even the instructors. If she ever did escape, Mona would find herself running down the hallway to the train, only to end up running into a diagnostic room or a security station. Worse still, based on everything she'd learned from Miller, Mona is sure that there is no path through the building that does not go through at least two of the hub points.

The only silver lining Mona can think of is that the hubs must have to shift very gradually. Mona has sat in the exam room hundreds of times and has never felt the room move in any way.

No that's not right, she thinks. When Harriet first took her out of the exam room, she felt that odd sensation, an unseen force pushing on her stomach. It was subtle but it was there. *If they can move the rooms*, she thinks, *they must move very slowly*. That means it takes time to shift the building around and change the pathways. If she was able to move quickly, she might be able to get through two or three hubs before they could shift the ones in front of her. That might be enough to get to the subway. Maybe.

Mona opens her eyes. She could get out. She would have to move quickly. She would have to be sure of which hallway she would be stepping into outside of the exam room to know the best route to take. She would have to run. She would have to hope that no instructors or guards were around. There are a lot of risks, far too many to control, but she could get out.

Mona can feel the spark of hope in her stomach. She imagines it like the light from a firefly. It twinkles in the darkness, inviting more and more twinkling lights to join it, until the dark space inside her is filled with moving light.

"I can do this," she whispers to herself. "I can get to the subway that takes the instructors out of the main building." A smile flashes across her face, only to fade just as quickly.

What about Owen? Mona walks through the map in her mind. To get from the room to where Miller thinks they are keeping Owen means going deeper into the compound before heading to the subway platform. Mona counts three hubs that she would have to go through to get to Owen. Then she would have to go back through them and at least two more to get to the train. Even if she could get to Owen and somehow get him to run with her to the train, the guards would have at least eight chances to stop her or send her running down a maze that they controlled.

It isn't fair. Mona can feel a stinging in her nose as she tries to hold back tears. It isn't fair. They've won before she can even try.

She rolls over in bed. It is just before six. In a few minutes the morning bell will ring and she and the other students will get out of bed and file down to the student cafeteria for breakfast. After breakfast, it's time to shower and dress in the school uniform. Then classes, a break for morning chores, lunch, more classes, chores, and individual time with the instructors. Later in the afternoon most students will have free time while Mona, Stephanie, and the girl in the other pod continue to work with their instructors. Nick no longer has extra time with his instructor. His work has been slipping. With Owen gone, Nick is suddenly and surprisingly the new plomp in her pod.

Mona sits up. How did that happen? Nick was the best student. Mona even thought that he might be better than her. He was certainly better than Stephanie and he was miles ahead of everyone else. Now suddenly he was forgetful and slow.

Nick wasn't acting like Owen used to. Owen was always fun and silly. He was a plomp because he didn't take anything seriously, because he would daydream and make up stories instead of doing his lessons or practising his exercises. Nick was different. He was clearly trying, but always seemed lost in a fog. He would have moments of brilliance but would slide back just as quickly.

It had only started to happen in the past few days, just after Nick got back from a field trip outside of the school. Everyone had been so jealous and so eager to hear about what happened. No one could remember when another student got to actually leave the campus. Nick returned late at night and slept in the infirmary so as not to disturb the other boys in his pod. The next morning, everyone crowded around him at breakfast. Even Mona tried to get close enough to hear his stories.

Nick looked embarrassed. "It took a long time to get there." He said. "It was cool and foggy and the air smelled funny. Then I think I fell asleep or something. The next thing I remember, one of the instructors was waking me up telling me it was time to head back to the school."

This was tragically disappointing for everyone. Nick, a top student, fell asleep during the adventure of a lifetime.

Seeing her chance to further advance in everyone's eyes, Stephanie laughed. "You're worse than Owen!" she said. "If you're not careful, they'll send you home too."

Nick just looked hurt and ashamed.

"Come on, let's not sit next to the plomp," finished Stephanie, adding insult to injury as she led a group of students off.

But Owen wasn't sent home, thinks Mona. *They performed extractions on him and they must have done the same thing to Nick.* If she could talk to him, she might be able to figure out how to get out of the compound by some other way apart from the train. She thinks about the code that she carefully folded up and gave to Miller a few sessions after Miller drew her first hidden map. Since that time, they'd used the code to communicate more complex questions and answers, hiding the symbols in drawings or notes.

She could write another for Nick and he could destroy it once he had it memorized. Then they could pass notes.

Mona quietly stands and moves over to the small desk in the dorm, meant for writing letters home (although almost no students have family to write to). She pulls out some paper and begins transferring the simple code with its lines and squiggles. If bees could communicate by wiggling a little and pointing in a direction, then so could she.

She starts by using a ruler to make a table four by thirteen. Then in the first and third column, she writes out the alphabet. Carefully, in the second and fourth column, she draws the symbols that correspond to each letter: a raised bump and a line facing right for A, two descending bumps and a line facing left for B. Each letter gets a symbol, the simpler symbols for the more common letters like E, R, S, and T, the less common letters like J, X, and Z have slightly more complex symbols.

A	⌒	J	⅔	S	⸮
B	⌄w	K	⅔	T	↳
C	⌒	L	⸹	U	⅔
D	⅔	M	⌄⌄r	V	⌒
E	⸹	N	⌄	W	⌒
F	⸍	O	⌄	X	⅋
G	⌒m	P	⸹	Y	↰
H	⸺	Q	⸹	Z	⸮
I	⌄	R	⸹		

All in all, the code is simple and easy to follow. Miller says that she still needs to use the key from time to time, but Mona can easily remember the whole thing.

Mona stops and tears up the paper. It's too risky. Miller can hide the key, but they would find it on Nick eventually. Mona can't trust that he can memorize it anymore, so she can't risk giving it to him.

"I'll just have to find somewhere to talk to him," she says to herself.

The bell rings and the other girls get up and rub their eyes. Together they file down to breakfast.

o o o

"I need you to arrange a meeting for me."

"Of course, sir, are you inviting Ms. Andriss back to the Company to continue her treatment?"

"Ms. Andriss has other business to attend to for the moment," replies Stowe, looking up from his desk. He is not sure he can trust Addams. The sudden mention of Andriss has him on edge. Why would Addams mention her name? Has Morgan been asking about her?

Addams looks expectedly at his employer.

"I want to meet with Mona's instructor. The new one," explains Stowe. "I think it is time that we prep Mona for an extraction."

"Will Morgan be participating in this meeting?" inquires Addams.

"Not at this time," replies Stowe, noting the mention of his partner. "No, this will only be an initial meeting to discuss the memory program that I wish to run with Mona. Andriss has some specific requests and I want to ensure that Mona's instructor is up to speed so that she can be ready to coach Mona through the experiences if needed."

"Morgan may be interested in hearing about your plans, it could help with the extractions …"

"I will brief Morgan on the plan later," interrupts Stowe. He is now sure that Addams is Morgan's creature. His own list of allies is running short and Andriss has not yet responded to his letter.

"Very well, I will set up the meeting," responds Addams casually. "Is there anything else?"

"No, that will be all," replies Stowe

As Addams leaves, Stowe pulls up his file on the clipboard. From here he can access all of Addams' communications within the company. A quick scan reveals nothing untoward. Actually, it reveals nothing much at all. *That's surprising*, thinks Stowe. It is almost as if someone has cleaned the system to ensure that no damning communications could be found.

"So, you're on to me, Morgan," says Stowe to no one in general. "You know I'm up to something. Well fair enough. I'm on to you too."

CHAPTER TWENTY-NINE
Cultivating Sunshine

H arriet sips her tea. For a brief moment, the warm aroma and gentle sweetness distracts her completely from her surroundings. It is real tea. Real tea with real honey and real lemon. She wasn't even sure how she took her tea when it was offered to her. Ms. Andriss, feeling the pregnant pause as the server stared expectantly at Harriet, smiled and instructed that they would both take honey and lemon. Now Harriet can't imagine having tea any other way.

It tastes comforting and nourishing. The warmth coming from more than just the hot water. Harriet touches the tip of her tongue to her lips and lets the taste of honey linger a moment.

"I find it calming, don't you?" interjects Andriss.

"Yes, very," replies Harriet.

"The lemon is said to be good for your throat too. A nice touch in this dusty weather I find."

Harriet is acutely aware of the abnormality of her current situation. She is sitting across from one of the richest women in the world. A few days ago, she saw one of her best friends rant and rave like a maniac. Only a few days before that she found out her sister was part of some secret, underground resistance movement. It was only a few weeks ago that she was gainfully employed with the Company, on an upward trajectory. Now she was unemployed, staying with her sister, trying to figure out how she could save one of her former students.

Then Andriss called. Or more accurately, one of Andriss' associates waited for Amelia and Harriet outside their building and subtly handed her a letter. It said:

Dear Harriet,

Why would you trust me? I have nothing that can reassure you or convince you of my intentions. I will not try to persuade you to help—either you will, or you won't. Regardless of your decision, I plan to proceed.

We must save Mona.

I cannot get her out of the facility alone. Even if I could, where would she go? I need help. I need the help of someone Mona can trust ... someone I can trust to take care of her and make sure she is safe.

Stowe

That was it. That was all it said.

Amelia wanted to take it to the media, to use it as proof of the damage that the Company was doing.

"This will shine light on all of them," she said. "Not just the Company, but any firm that deals in memory manipulation."

"I'm not so sure that's a good idea," responded Harriet. "The Company is well connected. They could spin this into a story about a disgruntled former employee. I could end up even more of a pariah than I am already."

"That's true, I guess," conceded Amelia. "But you can't trust that snake!"

"I don't see how I have a choice. Besides, if it is a trick what do I have to lose? If it's genuine, then how can I pass it up?"

That was it. That was all it took.

Now Harriet is drinking tea across from a woman so infamous that it is rumoured that she has a private back channel to the Chancellor—her own hotline to change government policy or have a tariff lifted if it would help her business.

"I'm glad you came," says Andriss, putting down her tea. "I need you to help make sense of a letter I got from a … friend."

"Why me?" asks Harriet.

"Because he sent you a letter too, albeit through me," explains Andriss.

"Stowe isn't my friend," says Harriet coolly.

"I did not say that he was. No, from what I understand, you must consider him to be a singularly evil man."

Harriet waits.

"He is not evil," continues Andriss. "Not in the true sense of the word. He has done some terrible things or allowed terrible things to happen— of that I have no doubt—but he is not himself an evil man."

"I wouldn't be so sure," replies Harriet. She is uncomfortable here in this room. Andriss holds all the cards. Harriet came here for help and now she is listening to this intimidating woman apologize for a man that Harriet knows to be unfeeling and apathetic.

"Do you know what 'contrition' means?" Andriss asks. "Don't answer. You may know the definition, but I doubt that you truly know what it is to feel contrite."

Harriet is about to protest but something tells her to hold her tongue.

"On the surface to be contrite is to feel remorse or apologetic. I have no doubt that a young woman such as yourself has had to apologize at some point in her lifetime. You may have also felt truly sorry for something you've done or not done," Andriss pauses to give Harriet a searching look.

Harriet looks down at her hands and thinks of Sam. She didn't push hard enough to find out what was wrong when they were at the facility together, and she didn't run after him to help him after she saw him on the street.

Harriet can feel the weight of Andriss' gaze. Even with her eyes looking down, she can feel the older woman measure and assess her.

"Maybe you do know a little about contrition after all," continues Andriss. "I may have been wrong."

Harriet is oddly heartened by this victory and manages a weak smile. She is surprised to look up and see Andriss smiling back at her.

"I must apologize," says Andriss, not unkindly. "I am so used to dealing with old arrogant men or young ambitious ones that I have almost forgotten how to have a pleasant conversation. I am too used to measuring my opponent and breaking them down. I have cracked titans as easily as a stick over my knee. But of course, you are not my enemy. You are my guest. Will you be so kind as to let me start again?"

Harriet nods and sips her tea, trying to remember how the warmth of it calmed her nerves before.

"Thank you. You are kind," smiles Andriss. "We have both seen a different side of Stowe. I do not blame you for how you must perceive him. He is a hard man. He has had his fair share of enemies, but very few are left now. That is a sign of his intelligence and his ruthlessness. You may see him as a monster, but I have known too many monsters to reduce him to that.

"A few days ago, I received two letters from Mr. Stowe. The first was addressed to me. The second to a person I had never met or even heard of—you. I read my letter and considered reading yours as well. But something told me that our mutual friend wanted you to read it first and that after we should meet. So here you are."

"What did your letter say?" asks Harriet.

"It said that without my help a young girl will die," replies Andriss.

"Did it say that Stowe is one of the people who is allowing this to happen?" Harriet shoots back. Her body is tense as she struggles to control her outrage. "Did it say that he's done this sort of thing before, that he's profited from it?"

"Yes," responds Andriss calmly. "Maybe not as succinctly as you have just expressed it, but yes, the letter did imply that through his actions Stowe has caused harm to come to many children all for the profit and growth of the Company."

"Then how can you say he isn't evil?" replied Harriet, almost shouting.

"Do you know what contrition truly means?" asks Andriss. She fixes her gaze back on Harriet. Under the intense stare, Harriet feels the self-assurance brought on by her anger waning. She sits back in her seat.

"To be contrite is to feel regret or grief for past sins. Another word is 'penitence,' when someone is so ashamed of their former actions that they seek to atone for them," explains Andriss.

"And Stowe is contrite? Is he a penitent man?" asks Harriet in disbelief. "I believe so."

"If you believe he is, then what do you need from me?" asks Harriet. "You have money and resources, he has infinite access to the Company's database and facility, what can I do?"

"To start with, I need you to tell me everything you know," explains Andriss. "Dear Stowe may be feeling contrite, but I need to understand what is truly happening at the Company to know if his remorse is genuine or if he is merely having the all-too-clichéd crisis of conscience that destroys so many good business minds."

"How can you say that?" Harriet gasps. "They're hurting children. They're cutting out sections of their minds and leaving them broken beyond repair."

"No hyperbole," warns Andriss. "No exaggeration. I don't condone sweat shops or child labour, but since the war, such things are often regrettably necessary."

"This is no sweat shop," responds Harriet. She searches her mind for a way to explain the gravity of the situation. "What if your life were all darkness and misery? What if you were haunted by painful memories from the war or from your life after the war?"

Harriet pauses and waits for a warning from Andriss not to be so dramatic. Instead, her companion is strangely quiet. Her body is still and her eyes unfocused.

"Imagine your pain like a fog, like the dust clouds that grey-out the city, covering and smothering everything, shutting out all colour and light," Harriet pauses. She can almost see the grey creep up Andriss' face. "Now what if I could sell you sunshine?" she asks. "What if I had a warm light that could cut through the dust and find a patch of dirt that still had some seed of hope in it?"

Harriet remembers the first time Mona described the warm sweetness of honey. She remembers laughing as Owen and Mona chased lightning bugs around the garden. She remembers how tears came to her eyes when Mona's fever broke and she woke up with a smile.

"That's what they are selling," continues Harriet. "They are cutting memories out of children to give them to rich people like you who want more plenty, more goodness, more happy days, more joy …" she trails off.

Andriss is crying softly. "They're cultivating sunshine," she says.

CHAPTER THIRTY

Falling Short

M ona is terrified. She waited too long. She wanted to plan too much. Now she is trapped. A strong hand on her shoulder leads her down a long hallway. There are no windows, no meeting rooms, just plain blank walls. Behind her, Miller frets in the examination room. In front of her, lies a door to the diagnostic laboratories. They are going to scan her and perform an extraction.

She wants to run, but her legs feel weak. She wants to run, but the hand on her shoulder would tighten and hold her in place. She wants to run, but that would give away that she knew what was about to happen.

Mona closes her eyes and lets the hand guide her. She needs to stay calm, so she practices her memory exercises. She breathes in and out, slowing her heart rate and trying to calm her nerves. She imagines a white wall in front of her. She traces out the lines leading from the examination room to the other areas of the facility. She needs to know where she is in relation to the other landmarks that Miller has identified. She needs to know how many hubs lie between her and possible escape. She needs to know where to go the second she can run.

The hand on her shoulder gently pulls her to a stop. They are standing in front of the door. Five seconds pass in silence before the door opens.

Behind the door there is a severe looking man in a light grey suit. His jacket is off and hung on the chair behind him and the sleeves of his crisp white shirt are rolled up. His bright blue eyes lock with Mona's for a moment before looking past her to the guard.

"You can leave us now," commands the man. The guard obediently turns and walks back down the corridor.

Mona is left alone with this man. She looks around to see a table, not unlike the doctor's table in the school's infirmary. The room also contains standard looking medical equipment and supplies. The major difference between this room and the exam room in the infirmary is a large piece of machinery above the exam table. It looms over the table. Mona is sure that it is the machine with which they perform the extractions.

"Would you please come this way?" asks the man gesturing toward the equipment in the centre of the room.

"No," replies Mona.

The man smiles, as if laughing at a private joke. Then he sits down on the table himself and pulls a metal loop around his head.

"You're going to try to convince me that there is nothing to be afraid of in this room," says Mona. "You're going to do that thing that adults do. You're going to show me that the machine doesn't hurt by pretending to use it on yourself. You'll try to convince me not to be afraid so that I'll get up there and let you pull things out of my head. But it's not going to work. I know you did that to Owen and I won't let you do it to me too."

The man's smile fades at the mention of Owen's name. Suddenly he looks weaker.

"I am going to do no such thing," he says after a pause. "I'm going to get you to perform a scan on me. There will need to be diagnostic data in the computer at the end of the session or Morgan will be suspicious. It will take too long to run any analysis to figure out that the scan isn't of you. By the time they figure it out, you'll be long gone."

"What are you saying?" asks Mona, more confused than scared now.

"Mona, I'm saying that I am going to help you escape," replies the man. "Not just me, but Harriet too."

"Who are you?"

"My name is Thomas," replies Stowe. "I am one of the bosses here at the Company. My partner Morgan and I created all this. We made the machines that perform the extractions. We figured out that children can be trained to remember finite details of happy experiences. We perfected the process of harvesting memories. We made billions. Now I am going to dismantle all that we built. I am going to put an end to the Company. And I am going to start by getting you out of here."

"Why me?" ask Mona. "If you're the boss, couldn't you just let everyone go and shut down the Company?"

"It's not quite that easy, I'm afraid," explains Stowe. "My partner Morgan won't just let me shut things down. We've worked too long to be where we are and we have ... had ... aspirations of even greater things—Morgan still does. That's why I have to make my moves carefully. I have to start by getting information into the right hands. I can't trust just anybody, but I think I can trust you."

"You don't even know me."

"No but I've watched you, and more importantly, Owen knew you. He trusted you and loved you and laughed with you ..."

Mona listens as Thomas' voice dies down. His blue eyes become wet with tears and he looks away from her. He looks hurt and alone, oddly desperate to reach out to someone. It reminds Mona of the first time she spoke to Owen, when he asked to eat lunch with her. Strangely, she feels sad for Thomas.

"Do you know that bees dance to communicate?" she asks, not knowing what else to say.

"I do, actually," replies Thomas, looking up at her again. "It's how they share information about where to find the best flowers."

"Owen always laughed at the thought of bees dancing in their hive," smiles Mona. "How did you know him? Was he the one who told you about the bees?"

"In a manner of speaking," replies Thomas Stowe. "I was the one to test the memory that we extracted from Owen."

There it is: the confession. It floats in the air between them. Neither know what to say next. Stowe waits for Mona to speak, too afraid to break the silence. Mona chokes back tears, too angry to form words.

"It's your fault," she says at last.

"Yes," he replies.

"All of it."

"All of it," he admits.

"Why should I help you?" she says. "Even if you say you're going to get me out of here, why should I help you? You hurt Owen. You probably just want to hurt me too."

"I can see why you would say that," replies Stowe. "I've had to ask a lot of people for help recently. People who have no business trusting me. People for who helping me might mean hurting or endangering themselves. I didn't have much to convince them and I don't have much to help convince you either. You don't trust me. I understand that. But maybe you'll trust Harriet."

Stowe picks his electronic clipboard up from the exam table and hands it to Mona. Displayed on the screen is a still image of Harriet.

"Click on it," instructs Stowe.

With a tap, the image comes to life and suddenly Harriet is speaking to Mona.

"Mona, they tell me that they'll get you this message. It's me, Harriet. Mona, are you okay? Oh, I hope you're okay. Listen, I don't think there's much time. They are going to perform an extraction on you. It could kill you or leave you brain-dead. I have friends who say that they can get you and me out of the city if we can get you out of the compound. I know that this is probably all very scary, but you need to be brave. Stowe is going to help. He's not a bad guy ... well maybe he is, or he was ... I don't know. I just know that we can't do this without him. I believe that he wants to help. I've spoken to his friend on the outside and she says that he is sorry for everything that he's done and wants to help make it right.

I want to believe that's true. I need to believe it so that I can see you and know that you're safe. Listen to his plan. Please, Mona, listen to him."

"Not exactly a ringing endorsement, is it?" asks Stowe. "But it's an honest one."

"Say I do believe you," replies Mona. "What's your plan?"

"It's pretty simple actually," explains Stowe. "In a few days, I've arranged for you to go on a field trip to a beach. The idea is to give you a wonderful memory of a day on warm sand with an ocean breeze. Blissful and carefree. It would be one of the many memories that we would harvest from you for Andriss, the friend Harriet referenced. Once you're outside of the facility, we will arrange for you to go with some of Andriss' people. She will get you to Harriet and then it's better that I not know where you go. Most likely, Harriet and her friends will get you out of the city and away from Morgan's sphere of influence. In the meantime, I will resign. Losing a student will be the perfect reason for me to step down. I will then bring information about the Company to the public light. Within a month, we will be under investigation. Within a year, we will be shut down. Even the Chancellor can't publicly condone using children the way we do."

"What happens to the rest of the students?" asks Mona.

"I will work with Andriss to see that they are taken care of," replies Stowe. "I have substantial savings and Andriss makes my small fortune look pitiful. Between us, we will ensure that the students will be safe."

"What happens to you?"

"I'm not sure. But honestly, it doesn't overly concern me. Perhaps I will be the scapegoat for all of this. Lord knows that I deserve it. Perhaps they will let me off with a fine or some minor punishment; too many members of the parliament have been clients to dare to string me up. They'll be afraid of who I might implicate. Regardless, my future is not my primary concern right now."

"What about Owen?"

"He is safe right now," replies Stowe. "I give you my word that by the time all of this is over, Owen will be in the best of care and if he ever gets better, we will get word to you somehow."

"What do I need to do?" asks Mona.

"First," says Stowe, smiling. "Let me teach you how to use this machine. We need a scan on file. Next, I want to show you some of my files."

"Why?" asks Mona.

"Mona, the best way of staying one step ahead of your enemies is to let them think they are one step ahead of you," Stowe's blue eyes shine with renewed enthusiasm.

"I don't understand," replies Mona.

"It's a little complicated," explains Stowe. "But right now, Morgan and Addams, our assistant, think they know my next move and I think I know theirs. The best way to ensure success is to have a backup plan just in case they actually are clever enough to be one step ahead of me, just in case they actually do know my next move."

"How will showing me your files help? I can't do anything."

"Mona, how unlike you to forget something," laughs Stowe. "You are the best student we've ever had. If I show you the files, I can smuggle them out with you. Even if they burn my notes and erase my electronic imprint in the Company, I can get the truth out with you. All you'll have to do is remember it."

"Okay, I'll do it," replies Mona. "But only if you tell me about the hubs."

"What hubs?" asks Stowe.

"The hubs where you can change which rooms lead where in the building. The hubs like the one outside the instructors' examination room, or in the stairwell to the east of these diagnostic labs. How do they work?"

Stowe looks genuinely surprised. "Well, it seems you are the best student in more than one way," he replies. "Okay, it's a deal. I'll tell you what you need to know."

o o o

Addams watches as Stowe carefully removes the crown from his head. Clever move to ensure that a scan is on file so that the analysts wouldn't flag the session for Morgan to review. Stowe had thought of nearly everything. Fortunately, Morgan had anticipated such a move and had instructed Addams to bug the diagnostic labs a few days ago. Stowe might have access to the security recordings and the access records, but Addams' bugged recordings were held on a completely separate, autonomous system.

Addams runs his finger along the screen to scan through the recording faster. Morgan will be interested in the full contents of the conversation, but for now Addams just wants to identify any red flags. Stowe taking Mona's place under the crown was the first red flag; a few minutes further along the recording, Addams discovers the second: Stowe pulls out his clipboard and invites Mona to sit next to him. Together they spend the next ten minutes going through a variety of files. Unfortunately, Addams doesn't have a bug placed anywhere in the room to capture what is on the clipboard screen, but it's easy enough to guess based on the snatches of their conversation. Stowe is showing Mona a complete layout of the facility. Worse still, he is showing her confidential student files—evidence that the Company's practices have a significant mortality rate.

Addams closes the file and sends it to Morgan under an urgent alert. He doesn't need explicit instruction to know what to do next. He has to find Stowe.

Addams shuts down the recording before finishing it and opens the security log. The system recorded that both Mona and Stowe left the diagnostic lab about twenty minutes ago, but Stowe returned through the same door less than a minute later. It does not show any further activity. Stowe is still there.

Addams removes his tie and changes out of his suit. His actions are smooth and fast, like those of a well-trained soldier. He throws his clothes on the floor of his closet and removes a hanger containing a black version of the uniform that the security staff wear. The fabric of the uniform is stiff and coarse but is both shock and puncture resistant. Addams then unlocks his desk drawer and removes a medium sized box. He unlocks this too and quickly pockets the small firearm inside. He does not expect Stowe to put up a fight—what would be the point—but Addams has dealt with enough desperate men to know that it is always better to be safe than sorry. Also, despite the difference in their age, Stowe has twenty pounds on Addams, so why take the risk?

o o o

Stowe is surprised to see Addams when the laboratory door opens. The diagnostic computer creates a barrier between them. It might give Stowe enough time to turn and run for the door that Mona left through, but he knows that Addams would have surely placed a security lock down on the lab. The only way out is through Addams.

"You've been spying on me," says Stowe calmly.

"Under Morgan's instructions," replies Addams.

"Obviously. I figured that the two of you would catch on to me eventually. I was pretty sure that you knew I was up to something. I just thought that I'd have more time."

"Disappointed?"

"Only in myself."

Addams makes a move toward Stowe. In response, Stowe mimes reaching for a weapon just out of Addams' view.

"Got something behind the workstation?" asks Addams, placing a hand on his hip.

"You weren't the only one with enough forethought to bring a weapon," lies Stowe. He can see the lump of a pistol on Addams' hip. It can only be a small caliber, probably a twenty-two. Still, Stowe is familiar with Addams' record; he knows that Addams could draw and fire a deadly shot before he could get past him. He looks down at the imaginary weapon that he is pretending to hold. All that is in his hand is the memory file from the extraction that he performed on himself after Mona left. He locks eyes with Addams and slides the file behind the computer screen. So much for a contingency plan.

"What were you doing in here so long?" asks Addams. "You had enough time to get back to your office or to leave the facility entirely."

"I was sabotaging the equipment," says Stowe, wishing that it were true. "I've planted a bug in the system. None of the extraction systems will work. It'll take weeks to reset them."

"Giving you time to save Mona and the rest," responds Addams.

"Precisely. Now I suggest that you let me leave. There's no need for violence." Stowe mimes picking up the imaginary weapon and sliding it behind his back.

Addams clears his throat and glances past Stowe. "Which door are you going to leave through?" he asks.

"I'm not picky," replies Stowe, taking a step back. "If you'd be kind enough to unlock the door behind me, I can make my way out through the student section."

"I never locked the door," replies Addams smiling.

"You didn't lock me in? I thought you were some sort of a professional?"

"It's not that I didn't want to lock you in," smiles Addams. "It's that I didn't want to lock your partner out."

Too late Stowe realizes why Addams had glanced past him. He feels a sharp pitch in his arm, then his legs go weak.

"Quickly, don't let him fall," instructs Morgan, pulling the syringe from Stowe's shoulder.

"His gun?" asks Addams, moving as swiftly forward.

"He's unarmed," replies Morgan.

Stowe tries to speak but only slurs a few garbled words. Morgan and Addams catch him as his legs begin to buckle and lead him over to the diagnostic table.

"He sabotaged the whole system," says Addams. "He says it will take weeks to repair."

"I doubt it," replies Morgan coolly. "I don't think he understands the system well enough to do that kind of damage."

Morgan looks down at Stowe. Stowe's vision is blurry and his limbs feel too heavy to lift. He wants to get up and run. He wants to get a message to Harriet and Andriss telling them that he's been found out. The plan will have to change. They'll have to adapt. But if he can't get a message to them, how will they know? Harriet and Mona will proceed as planned and walk right into Morgan's arms. Harriet will probably be arrested. Stowe can't bring himself to think of what will happen to Mona. Tears well up in his eyes. He has failed.

Morgan lowers the crown and fits it around Stowe's head.

"What are you doing?" asks Addams.

"Running a system test," replies Morgan.

"You're going to perform an extraction on him?"

"Certainly. If the system is damaged then this is the fastest way to find out. If it is working, then this will allow us to find out what our colleague has been planning."

"You'd have to pull out weeks of memories," warns Addams, his voice rising in surprise.

"Safer to extract a few months," replies Morgan. Then Morgan turns and faces Stowe, addressing him directly. "That way we can be certain that we know the full extent of your betrayal."

"That size of an extraction will ..." Addams trails off.

"It will necessitate a restructuring of the Company to find a replacement for Stowe," responds Morgan. "Now, Thomas, what have you been up to?"

CHAPTER THIRTY-ONE

Mazes

S itting on her bed, Mona is not sure that she can trust Stowe. She turns over the envelope he gave to her in the hall outside the diagnostic lab. He pushed it into her hands without a word. When she went to open it, he put his hand out and stopped her, gesturing that she should hide it instead. Another secret on top of the hundreds she'd seen in his files, not all of which she understands.

Mona looks down at the envelope. Written in neatly printed letters are the words, "In case things go badly." Mona tears the envelope open and tips it over. A security card falls out into her hand. There is no picture on the card. In place of a name, the card reads "cuckoo bee."

Mona smiles. Cuckoo bees are types of bees that infiltrate the hives of other bees. Sometimes they eat the bees' food, other times they lay their eggs in the hive and leave the other bees to feed their larvae. They have to be careful, however, if they are found out, the workers and drones will kill them.

The meaning is clear. With this card, Mona can move around the whole facility. She guesses that she'll probably only be able to move through one or two areas before the card is flagged or security is altered. Still, it should give her what she needs if there is a problem on the way to the field trip.

Mona hides the card again, sliding it into her shoe. She then zips up her sweater and picks up her bag.

Outside the dormitory door, her housemother is waiting to escort her out of the student section to where Stowe will meet her to take her on the field trip.

Mona runs through her calming exercises to slow her breathing and stop her heart from racing. If everything goes well, then tonight she and Harriet will be on a train leaving the city.

Mona's housemother uses her ID card to open one of the doors leading from the student section of the building. They are not going through the exam rooms today, but rather through the entrance that the classroom teachers use to enter and exit the student annex. Mona glances down a long hall to her right, knowing that it leads to the diagnostic area and the laboratories where they perform the extractions. From there, she could pass through one of the hub sections of the building and, with a few more twists and turns, get to either the executive offices or the infirmary. She pauses for a moment and thinks of Owen. The firm hand of her housemother snaps her back to the present and guides her down the corridor.

Mona's housemother pulls out the ID card again and swipes it to open a door to a stairway. Mona knows that this is one of the most complicated hubs in the whole building. The stairway is long and curved, moving in a slow spiral down a number of levels. There are landings at the north, south, east, and west, each with an exit to a different floor of the facility. Above a skylight lets in beautiful natural light.

Mona thinks back to Stowe explaining the design of the stairwell.

"The whole thing can turn," explained Stowe with a note of pride. "We control the rotation to match the speed of the people walking up or down the stairs. This helps mask the fact that the entire room is turning. There are exits to the north, south, east, and west, but also to the northeast, northwest, southeast, and southwest. So, a quarter turn means that the exits off of each landing have completely changed."

"What about the skylight?" asked Mona. "Wouldn't people be able to see that the clouds were rotating or that the shadows from the sun were moving too quickly?"

"You're very clever," replied Stowe. "But we thought of that too. The skylight is a fake. It's a complicated light display that projects an image of what the sky looks like outside. Since it is a fake, we control it and make sure that it stays stable regardless of the orientation of the room."

"So, it looks like there are four exits off of the stairwell, but really there are eight?"

"Actually, there are sixteen," smiled Stowe. "We can rotate the stairwell up and down too. Kind of like a nut turning on a screw. This means we can have exits leading to different levels of the building."

To illustrate his point, Stowe drew an octagon on a piece of paper and turned it so that each side faced a different direction.

"It's a complicated hub," he continued. "We rarely use it."

"Where do each of the sixteen exits lead?" Mona asked.

Stowe smiled and began to explain. Mona had to pay very close attention, so as not to miss any detail.

Holding onto the rail Mona walks down the stairs. Her housemother is still with her. They were going to take the exit at the bottom of the stairs. Mona knows that it leads to a private entrance to the facility, where vehicles could pull up to drop off or pick up elite clients. There she will meet Stowe who is going to take her in a car to Harriet.

Mona is excited but manages to keep her breathing calm. It's so close now. Once she's out she can share everything that Stowe has told her about the Company and then she and Harriet can save Owen and the other students.

Without thinking she takes five or six quick steps, skipping ahead of her housemother and dashing across the first landing.

"Mona, slow down," snaps her housemother.

The words are like a whip and Mona instinctively freezes in her tracks. That's when she feels it. It is almost like a slight pull on the soles of her shoes. The room is being rotated!

Mona's housemother catches her by the arm and continues to escort her down. But Mona knows that they are not going to the private entrance. She can only guess that they are going to a sublevel of the facility—a secure area with few entrances or exits.

She'll be trapped.

Mona's calming exercises aren't working. She can feel panic start to rise in her chest. Either Stowe has betrayed her, or he was found out.

At the bottom of the stairs, Mona's housemother swipes her ID card to open the door. This time nothing happens. The older woman mutters to herself and rubs the card against her skirt removing whatever imaginary dirt is preventing it from working properly.

Mona looks back up the stairs. There are exactly seventeen stairs to the next landing. She could probably get there in less than twenty seconds. That wouldn't be enough time for them to spin the room around, would it?

Just as she is about to make her move, the door opens. Behind it, there is a well-dressed man clearly waiting for them.

"Trouble with your ID card?" says the man smiling.

"Oh Mr. Addams!" replies the housemother. "The funny thing wouldn't work. What a bother."

"No matter," replies Addams cordially. "I am happy to take Mona from here. Why don't you head back to the school? You can check in with security on the way to see if they can fix your card."

"Well, if it's no trouble for you," says Mona's housemother. "I mean, I'm supposed to take the little one the whole way to the car. That's what Mr. Stowe said, and he likes things to happen the way he says for them to happen."

"Honestly, it's no trouble," replies Addams, maintaining his casual air. "Run along, I've got this."

"Alright then, you go with this young gentleman, Mona, and mind that you behave yourself. Mr. Addams is an important man around here. I won't hear of one of my kiddies causing him any trouble."

"She'll be no trouble at all. Will you Mona?" smiles Addams, reaching out for her hand.

Defeated, Mona takes Addams' hand and allows him to lead her down the short corridor that leads off the stairwell. Stowe clearly designed this one to look exactly like the corridor to the lobby and private entrance. Even Mona's housemother didn't notice a difference.

"Where are we going?" asks Mona when she and Addams are alone.

"On your field trip, of course," smiles Addams.

"You don't have to lie," replies Mona. "I know that you're taking me to the sublevels of the facility. So, where exactly are we going? Am I going to be put in a holding cell? Are you going to lock me in the morgue?"

"My my, Stowe did manage to tell you an awful lot of Company secrets, didn't he?" responds Addams, his smile disappearing and his grip on Mona's hand tightening.

"Just one or two, Mr. Addams," shoots back Mona. "Like the fact that you keep the bodies of the students that you killed frozen in the morgue until you can have them incinerated off sight. I doubt many families know that before they agree to send their kids to the school."

Addams simply smiles back, responding, "You'd be surprised. Most families are just grateful to have one less mouth to feed. And the orphanages are happy to turn a blind eye with the money we pay them. Besides, the mortality rate isn't that high. No one misses one or two kids."

"Harriet will miss me," says Mona. "She'll get me out of here."

"Is that so?" asks Addams. "I honestly don't see how."

He opens the next door and pushes Mona ahead of him into the next room.

"Keep moving," he orders. "Morgan is waiting for us."

o o o

"Ms. Miller, isn't it?"

"Most people just call me Miller," responds Miller, not looking up from her meal. She's taken to eating her lunch alone in one of the gardens, rather than in the staff cafeteria. She no longer sits with her fellow instructors, discussing promising students or new memory exercises. Nor does she try to mingle with the directors in hope of getting an in with them. In truth, ever since she'd started working with Mona, she's wanted less and less to do with the Company. Her resignation letter sits sealed in her locker, waiting for the day that she will have the courage to hand it in.

"My name is Andriss. Perhaps you've heard of me?"

"Of course, Madam Andriss," sputters Miller looking up at the woman in front of her.

"Please dear, no need for titles," replies Andriss calmly. "May I sit with you?"

Miller only manages a nod.

"Thank you," responds Andriss, taking a seat. "You know I've enjoyed the many beautiful gardens in this place since I've been a client here."

"I had no idea you were a client," replies Miller, still a little awestruck.

"No, I don't suppose that it is common knowledge. But here I am."

They sit in silence for a while. Finally, Miller gets the courage to speak.

"Is there something I can do for you Madam … Andriss?" she asks.

"Well that depends on a few things Ms. Miller," replies Andriss. "You see, we have a mutual acquaintance. One Ms. Harriet."

Miller is too shocked to respond, so Andriss continues.

"Now Ms. Harriet is of the opinion that you are a dedicated employee, hell-bent on climbing the ranks of the Company. She is not so sure that we can trust you. I, on the other hand, think that we can, partly because ambition and compassion are not mutually exclusive and partly because we have little other choice."

"I don't think I understand," stammers Miller, trying to make sense of how Harriet is connected to Andriss.

"It's fairly simple really. Given the chance, would you choose to advance your career and help make all the people around you rich, or would you choose to save the life of a little girl?"

"Mona," whispers Miller.

"Yes," replies Andriss. "And before you answer, let me tell you about my sister."

CHAPTER THIRTY-TWO

Run

M iller runs.

She left Andriss sitting in the garden, eyes closed, head tilted to the sun. The last thing the formidable woman said was: "You can do the right thing."

So, Miller runs.

She can feel panic rising inside her. Where should she go? Andriss has explained that she had not heard from Stowe, as they had originally planned. That could mean a great deal of things, but one possibility was that the plan was shot, and they had to improvise. Andriss hated the word "plan." So much could go wrong with the plan or with a plan. Now the word "plans," that was a different story. You could have a plan, but only if you also had a backup plan and a contingency plan on top of that. Stowe was the type of man to have a Plan B, maybe even a Plan C; Andriss liked to have more plans than God.

"Imagine all that could go wrong, all the potential issues or roadblocks," explained Andriss. "Then set about solving each problem."

Right, thinks Miller. *I need a plan … or plans.*

She bolts down the hallway to the diagnostic labs. Checking each door to see if a session is in progress. Nothing indicates that an extraction is taking place. So, she continues on to the security desk nearby. Breathless, she pleads with the guard to locate Mr. Stowe. The guard protests until Miller slams her palm down on the metal counter. The combination of the sharp loud crack and the metal in her voice convinces him that he can break the rules this one time.

"Mr. Stowe is in diagnostic lab two, just around the corner," explains the guard. "He's been there all morning."

"Has anyone else been in with him?" asks Miller.

"I only came on shift an hour ago," shrugs the guard. "But I did see Mr. Addams leave from that area."

Without a word, Miller sprints back down the corridor. She finds Stowe sitting in the laboratory. The halo of the crown is still around his head. His shoulders are slumped, and his arms limply hang down between his legs. He looks like a heap of rags slung over a chair.

Miller walks forward slowly.

"Mr. Stowe," she whispers. "It's Miller sir. I … I'm looking for Mona."

Stowe looks up. His slack face contorts. For a moment he seems to concentrate, frowning hard to pull a memory forward. Then his face slumps back, his jaw dropping and eyelids drooping.

There is nothing left of him.

Miller pushes forward. Grabbing Stowe and shaking his heavy, slack arms.

"No, no, no!" she screams. "You can't … they can't have … you have to remember!" She twists and jerks his torso violently, trying to shake him awake, but knowing that it's no use. They've performed a complete extraction. Tabula Rasa, they call it in theory. Miller never believed anyone would be cruel enough to actually do it.

She lets Stowe go and wipes the tears from her eyes. Using her sleeve, she pats the drool from his chin. Then she reaches her hands up to take the crown from his head.

Stowe's strong hands crush Miller's fingers in a vice grip. He springs to his feet and, roaring like an animal, throws her away from him. She flies backward, barely staying on her feet as she crashes painfully into the desk behind her.

For a minute, Miller cannot catch her breath. Her ribs ache and she has to lean heavily on the desktop to keep from buckling to her knees. To her relief, Stowe falls back on the diagnostic table.

Finally, Miller is able to pull in a few ragged breaths. Her side is screaming with pain, causing her to slump further down on the desk. After a few minutes, she is able to pull herself together and open her eyes. There in front of her is a portable memory file. It must have been behind one of the computer screens before Stowe threw her into the desk and dislodged everything.

Miller picks up the small file drive and turns it over. Printed neatly on the side of the file is the name Owen.

She realizes that she has to find Addams. This time, she won't be nearly as patient with the security guard.

o o o

Addams walks Mona down a concrete corridor. They are deep in the sublevels of the facility now. Mona struggles to remember the layout down here. She had paid much more attention to the complex system of hubs in the main levels of the facility, never imagining that she would end up in the nexus of hallways with heating and power systems running overhead to all areas of the facility. She keeps trying to pull up the image of the blueprint Stowe showed her of this level, but fear keeps pushing the memory out of her mind. Despite all her efforts to keep calm, Mona is unable to concentrate sufficiently as she walks toward Morgan and the extraction that will leave her like Owen or worse.

Owen. The sudden thought of him brings tears to her eyes. Not only is she unable to escape, but now she won't be able to save Owen either. All the information that Stowe shared with her, all the ways to bring down the Company. They will die here with her, or else be sucked from her mind along with memories of gardens, fireflies, and her friends.

Mona is as lost and helpless as when she was sick with the fever. Only this time Harriet isn't there to comfort her and help pull her through.

They reach a security door. Addams gently pushes Mona so that her back is against the wall. Then, keeping his eyes on her, he pulls out his security card and swipes it by the lock. An audible click lets him know that the door is open. He then gestures to Mona who pulls the handle and opens the door to the next room.

The door is heavy; Mona has to lean back a little to open it. This forces Addams to step back, giving Mona a split second where she can see into the room, but he cannot. Waiting on the other side of the door, much to Mona's surprise, is Miller. They only have time to exchange a quick glance before Addams pushes Mona through the door. He looks confused for a second and then reaches for the bulge on his hip.

"Run, Mona!" screams Miller, throwing something behind her before barrelling forward, pushing Mona aside and crashing into Addams. The force throws them back into the long corridor.

"Run!" Miller screams again as Addams wrestles her off of him.

Mona runs across the empty foyer and picks up the memory file Miller threw that is still spinning on the tiled floor. She reads Owen's name on it and smiles.

Miller is able to hold Addams down for a moment, but her ribs are burning, and he is wiry and strong. Without thinking, she smashes her forehead against his chin. There is a sickening crunch and for a second, she is able to gain the upper hand. She tries to kneel with her full weight on his arm and chest, pressing him to the floor and keeping his hand well away from his hip.

Addams shakes off the rough hit. He can taste blood in his mouth. For a second, his head swims but then he smiles and regains his composure.

Addams' reptilian smile is unnerving. Miller tries to recoil from him, but he catches her with his free arm and rolls so that they are lying side-by-side. She kicks and struggles, but he is in control now. With swift, deliberate motions, he punches her hard, three times in the ribs.

242

Miller screams and buckles. She is panting and sweating as Addams stands. For a moment, he considers drawing his gun, but then decides not to, opting instead for two more hard kicks to her ribs.

Miller grunts and lies still.

o o o

Memory file in hand, Mona is running. Running to the stairway at the other end of the foyer. Running away from Miller's screams. Running to escape Addams.

She reaches the door to the stairway. Like the door leading into this room, a security card is required to open it. Miller has stopped screaming now.

Mona looks back to see Addams wiping blood from his mouth as he steps through the door leading to the corridor. Miller lies limp on the floor behind him.

"You're trapped, Mona," he says. "All access points from here require clearance. Now why don't you just come with me?"

Addams begins walking quickly toward her. He'll be on her in seconds. Mona turns and kicks her foot up to the security panel.

Nothing happens.

"You can't break it, Mona," taunts Addams, stumbling a little after the blow to his head. "Now just come with me."

Mona kicks her leg up again. This time the security sensor reads the card in her shoe. The door clicks open. She grabs the handle and runs through, pulling the door shut behind her.

Addams' face fills the small rectangle window in the door. Mona keeps her hands on the handle, leaning back to keep the door shut. She strains her muscles, but he is so much stronger than her that he'll easily be able to pull the door open once he swipes his card.

Addams' realizes this too and laughs looking down at Mona as she braces her feet against the wall. He swipes his card.

Nothing happens.

He swipes again, but still nothing. The door stays locked. Cursing he begins punching codes into the security screen.

"What did you do?" he screams. "Who gave you a clearance card?"

Mona lets go of the door and pulls the card out of her shoe. "Cuckoo bee," she whispers. One last gift from Stowe.

She runs up the stairs away from Addams, who begins beating on the glass with the butt of his gun in a vain attempt to get to her.

Mona gets to the top of the stairs and pushes the door open. She is in the section of the facility where extractions are analyzed. All around her are rooms populated by giant computers, humming in the dark. She closes the door and tries swiping her card against the dormant security panel. It comes to life and indicates that the door is now locked.

Mona smiles to herself. Back on the main levels, she now has a good sense of where she is in the facility. To her right, she'll find the cafeteria and the employee area. It may be crowded, but it is the fastest way to the subway that leads to the employee apartments and, ultimately, out of the facility. To her left, she'll find the gardens and the space reserved for patients and clients. There is a way out there too, but she'll definitely be noticed. And straight ahead, the infirmary.

"Owen," she whispers. She starts running.

CHAPTER THIRTY-THREE

New Plan

The corridors that lead to the infirmary are, thankfully, empty. Mona knows that much of this portion of the facility is off limits to instructors and general staff. The computer banks are too important to the Company to have employees wandering around without the proper training or supervision. Stowe and Morgan kept the fact that there was an infirmary, outside of the small infirmary in the student section, secret from even higher-level directors. It's not good business to have it common knowledge that children are harmed in the production and harvesting of memories.

Mona moves cautiously, despite the fact that the corridors are deserted. At each junction, she checks behind her to ensure that she is not being followed. It helps that the lights automatically turn on when she comes to a new hallway and turn off behind her. If anyone is following her, she should be able to see them coming.

Her other advantage, she decides, is that no one knows where she is going. She imagines that Addams and Morgan are putting blocks in place to prevent her from getting out of the facility. Instead, she is travelling deeper into its structure. They probably won't start searching here until they are certain that she can't get out any other way. Time isn't on her side, but at least it's not against her yet. Still, she can't afford to slow down.

Mona stops when she reaches the small lobby leading to the infirmary. Like many areas of the facility, there is a manned security station there to ensure that only authorized personnel enter or leave. The cuckoo bee card would let her through the doors, but the guard would stop her well in advance. She bites her lower lip. So close.

Carefully, Mona pokes her head around the corner. The guard is sitting at his desk, looking down at a magazine or newspaper. He probably doesn't get many people coming this way, she decides. Behind him are the locked doors to the infirmary. Owen is just behind those doors. She could probably crawl past the guard's desk, but first she would need to get close enough to the counter to be shielded from his view. She needs a distraction, something to make him turn and look down the hallway to his right for a few seconds.

Mona sits down and closes her eyes. She needs to remember the layout of this area of the facility. The white sheets are in front of her and one by one she adds the lines that Miller described. Then she overlays the map of the hubs that Stowe showed her. The security desk and entrance to the infirmary sit at a T intersection of hallways. Mona is sitting in a hallway that runs parallel to the top of the T. In her mind, Mona sees the grid of hallways like a letter H on its side. If she walks down that hallway, he'll be able to see her coming. If she crosses the hallway connecting the middle section of the H, the guard will have a clear view of her. But if she could cross the hallway, then she could get to the next intersection, where there is no security station. She could make a noise to distract the guard then run back to where she's sitting, down the hall that makes up the middle of the H, and through the doors. She would only have a few seconds and she'd have to move quickly and quietly.

I can do it, thinks Mona.

It is quiet. The only sound is the gentle shuffle of cheap paper under the guard's fingers. Mona takes off her shoes so that they don't squeak on the floor when she stands up. Then she counts the seconds until the guard turns the next page. Mona is very good at keeping track of time.

When the guard looks down and turns the page of whatever he is reading, Mona makes her move. She treads lightly and silently across the hallway. Her heart is pounding so loud that she is sure he will hear it. Reaching the other side, she holds her breath and waits for a shout or footsteps, but there is nothing. A few moments later she hears the sounds of the cheap sheets of paper gliding over each other again. It worked!

Mona walks down the hall and makes a right. A few steps further and she reaches a T intersection only about fifteen meters from the security desk. She gets ready to run, then slaps the sole of her shoe down hard on the ground. The loud crack breaks the silence and seems to echo down the empty hallway. The next sound is that of a chair being pushed back. Mona is off and running, she makes a left then sprints barefoot the fifteen meters to the hall that leads to the security desk. She can hear the guard's footfalls moving away from her as he goes to investigate the noise. Holding her breath and her shoes, she darts across the hall behind him and opens the door to the infirmary. It locks behind her.

Owen is sitting on his bed when Mona finds him. He looks up and, for a moment, smiles, but it quickly fades. No, he doesn't know her. But there is something familiar about her, he thinks. She isn't the normal lady who comes to check on him. Her dress looks familiar too. He looks down and realizes that it is the same colour and material as his own clothes. Unconsciously, he worries the fabric between his fingers and then touches them to his cheek.

"Owen," says Mona. "Owen, it's me."

He stares blankly back at her. "I'm Owen?" he manages after a while.

"Yes," replies Mona, tears coming to her eyes. "I've missed you, Owen. I've missed laughing with you and playing in the garden."

"That sounds nice ... did we do that?"

"Yes," she whispers.

"I can't remember," says Owen, looking sad and turning away.

"I think you will soon," says Mona. "Come with me. I think I can help you remember."

There is a ghost of a smile on Owen's face, but it grows as what she said begins to sink in. "Really remember?" he asks.

"I think so, but we have to hurry."

Together they walk further down the infirmary hall to a hub that Mona activates. With a few swipes of the screen, she programs the hub to transfer them to the diagnostic labs. Beneath their feet, the floor raises and turns much faster than it would if the hub were in normal use. The sensation is dizzying and Mona nearly falls into Owen, causing both of them to giggle. It almost feels like one of their old games. For a moment, Mona feels happy and safe, but she quickly remembers the need to move quietly.

"Owen, you have to follow close behind me and be quiet until we're in a lab okay?" she explains.

Nodding his head, Owen follows Mona as they skirt around the more populated areas of the diagnostic wing.

Finally, they get into a lab.

Mona has never used the implantation equipment before, but Stowe showed her what to do when she helped him perform his extraction. She lies Owen back on the diagnostic table and applies the numbing cream. Like the extraction, two needles push into the base of his neck. Mona winces in sympathy, but reminds herself that it is a few moments of discomfort against Owen being himself again.

The machine hums to life as Mona uploads the memory file and begins to align it with Owen's scans saved in the database. The memory maps nearly perfectly to Owen's scans almost automatically. It is like fitting the last piece into a puzzle.

The machine hums loudly for a few minutes, pulsing the sounds around the room. Then the needles extract themselves.

"Mona?" says Owen, blinking up into the lights aimed down at the diagnostic table.

"Owen? Are you okay? Can you remember me?" stammers Mona.

"Of course I can," replies Owen with a giggle that brings tears back to Mona's eyes. "Now you're being the silly one."

"How do you feel? Can you run? We need to run to get out of here!" Mona is asking these questions as she pulls the equipment from Owen and drags him to his feet. She isn't sure, but she guesses that an unauthorized use of the lab will be a red flag for Addams. At a guess, she slides the security card through the reader by the main screen. The screen blinks a few times and then gives her the option to erase the data of the last procedure. She taps accept.

"Where are we?" asks Owen, still a little dazed.

"One of the labs," replies Mona. "I'll explain everything later, but right now we have to run. I mean really run."

"Is this a game?" asks Owen.

Mona stares at him for a moment.

"It's not a game?" says Owen. "It's not a game." He repeats these words to himself and seems to concentrate for a moment. "None of this is. Not even the memory exercises they call games." His brow furrows and his eyes scan from side to side as if he is reading something important.

"Yes, yes, that's right," pleads Mona, pulling Owen to the door. "Come on, we have to go!"

"No, you do," replies Owen, shrugging himself free from Mona. His voice is calm and controlled. To Mona, it sounds oddly more mature and self-assured.

"I can remember things that aren't mine to remember," says Owen, as much to himself as to Mona. He frowns and sets his jaw forward a little in concentration. For a moment, Owen's happy round face almost resembles Stowe's stern countenance.

Mona stops trying to pull him. "What do you mean?" she asks.

"I can remember you. But I can also remember watching myself playing in the garden with you. I can remember making you a card with a funny story, but I can also remember making you sick," Owen stops, clearly puzzled. "I don't think I could have made you sick. You're my best friend.

I would never hurt you." His voice is small, almost whimpering. "But I remember hurting you, and planning to hurt you more. I remember hurting lots of students. Did I do those things?"

Mona looks into Owen's pleading eyes. "No," she says. "Stowe and Morgan did those things. You never would, Owen. You're my best friend. You only ever made me happy."

Owen smiles. "I didn't make Stowe happy," he says, still smiling. "My memories ... the experiences he pulled from me made him miserable. They made him doubt himself. They changed him. They made him love you and hate planning to hurt you because I would never hurt you."

"How do you know all that?" asks Mona. "You were in the infirmary the whole time. You couldn't even remember me or our games. You couldn't remember anything until just a minute ago. How do you even know his name?"

"When you implanted a memory in me," says Owen, "there was a memory Stowe extracted from himself. I think in his attempt to give me back the extraction he took from me, in his attempt to return the dreams that he pulled from me, I got some of his memories too."

Mona is suddenly aware that Owen doesn't sound quite like he used to. He is speaking with more confidence, sounding more authoritative, but also less playful, curious, and whimsical. Like Owen mixed with a little Stowe.

"I don't think he meant for me to get his memories of you," continues Owen. "But I think it must be hard to separate all the different fragments in a person's mind when you're performing an extraction. I think that's why they train us with so many exercises."

"So, some of him accidently spilled over into you?" asks Mona.

"No, I'm still me," says Owen. "Only, I have some of Stowe's memories too."

"That could be a good thing," says Mona. "Stowe showed me a lot of information. I think he wanted me to use it to shut down the Company after I escaped. You can help! You can fill in some of the blanks and together we can get the other students out by destroying the Company. Only we have to escape. We have to leave now!"

Owen thinks for a moment. He closes his eyes and takes a deep breath before stepping forward and hugging Mona. He squeezes her hard and leans his head in close to her ear.

"I have to stay," he whispers. "They still think I'm a plomp. They think I'm worse than a plomp, that I'm ruined. They'll ignore me. I can use Stowe's memories to get everyone out from the inside. You use what he told you to attack the Company from the outside."

"But …" whimpers Mona. "You could …"

"I want to go with you," whispers Owen. "But I don't think we can get out of the facility. They're coming for you. But they don't know I'm out too. I can get to Stowe's office and line up the hubs to get you out. Then I can go back to the infirmary without them ever knowing."

"No, we can leave together," says Mona between tears.

"Maybe, but this is the only way to be sure that you get out. If we go together, they will have a much better chance of catching us."

"How will you find us when you and the others get out?" asks Mona, choking back her tears.

"Me? You're the one who found me. You're the one who saved me and gave me back my dreams. You're the clever one. I'm just a plomp." He smiles at her. "You're gonna have to find me."

"I will," says Mona. "As soon as you escape. As soon as the Company is destroyed."

"Promise?" asks Owen, looking at her the same way he did when he first asked to eat lunch with her.

"Of course," she replies, feeling stronger and more resolved.

"Then go."

CHAPTER THIRTY-FOUR

One Escape

Mona runs.

All around her it is dark. The lights are out in the whole facility except those Mona needs to escape. She can hear instructors and security guards cursing as they stumble around.

Owen shut down the lighting so that the only places the lights are on is right in front of Mona, guiding her on the fastest, safest path out. He sits in Stowe's office unlocking and relocking doors, guiding her to safety. He keeps two computer screens on Mona, one looking ahead of her and the other on where she is right now. He keeps another screen on Addams and Morgan, who are in Morgan's office frantically trying to reboot the system and find Mona. They're almost back in, but it won't matter. Mona is too close now. She's almost at the subway. Owen flips the screen to the station. There by the tracks, a woman is waiting. She is standing in the pitch black using her phone as a light. By the light from the screen, Owen can just make out her face. He racks his brain to remember her name. It must be Harriet, he decides after a while.

○ ○ ○

On the platform Harriet is waiting, holding her phone. About an hour ago she received a call from Andriss.

"The plan has changed," Andriss said briskly. "I haven't heard from Stowe and I think something is wrong. I'm going to see what I can do from here, but I don't think there'll be that much. You'd better find a way in here; we might need you."

"I don't have my ID card anymore," replied Harriet. "What can I do?"

"You can stop whining," snapped Andriss. "The girl will die, the least you can do is think on your feet and try something. Better to die trying to save her than live with her death on your conscience." Then the line went dead. Harriet made her way from where she was supposed to meet Stowe to the subway station at her old apartment building. The train didn't run often this time of day, so Harriet snuck onto the track and walked the three kilometers to the facility. Not long after she got to the platform the lights went out and she was standing alone in the darkness.

Harriet feels helpless. She fumbles forward. Using the light of her phone she is able to find the stairs and climb to the facility's entrance, but the door is locked. She sits down on the stairs and leans back against the door.

o o o

Mona runs. The lights slam on and off as she passes each hallway, leaving people momentarily blinded then groping once again in the dark. She reaches the main lobby with its stairway down the subway platform. This is the one place where Owen won't be able to help her. The lights stay on for a few seconds, giving her enough time to mentally map the room. She is on the catwalk that wraps around the second floor of the lobby. Below her are security guards and Company staff, blinking in the sudden bright light. They are spread out around the lobby looking confused.

The lights go off again, leaving a picture in Mona's mind of where everyone was standing. So, long as they don't move too much, she should be able to make her way to the exit and down to the subway.

o o o

The lock on the door clicks open behind Harriet. Did she just imagine the noise, or did it happen? She stands and pulls on the door. The darkness in front of her is deep and immense. Despite not being able to see, Harriet is aware of the vast empty space beyond the door. It is the lobby she knows. Someone has not only turned off all the lights but also used the facilities controls to black out the windows.

Harriet can hear voices in the dark calling out to one another. People are whispering and even laughing as they bump into each other, but most sound worried—this kind of thing is not normal, the Company never loses power, there are too many fail-safes in place. She pulls out her phone and lets the light from the screen reflect off her face.

o o o

It's Harriet, realizes Mona with a sigh of relief. She runs forward in the dark, keeping close to the walls to avoid bumping into anyone. A guard turns on his flashlight and the sudden cone of light makes Mona stop short.

The guard shines his light on Harriet and the exit. "Lights out in the subway too?" he asks.

"I think they're out everywhere," replies Harriet.

"Well, we'd better step outside then," responds the guard. "Follow me, folks." With that he turns to the door and begins guiding the staff outside into the sunshine.

As the doors open and flood the lobby with natural light, Harriet catches a glimpse of Mona hiding behind a column. She smiles and gestures to Mona to hurry while everyone is turned to the doors.

Mona runs forward and grabs Harriet's hand. The two disappear into the subway. Once the door behind them closes, the lights come back on. They stay on as they run to the track.

Harriet jumps down first then helps Mona down. Owen watches as they run into the empty tunnel, away from the Company.

o o o

"I can't help but feel that you had something to do with today's dramatics," says Morgan.

"I'm sure I don't know what you are talking about," replies Andriss. "Now if you'll excuse me, I have an appointment to get to." She stands and walks toward the door of Morgan's office.

"I am well aware of your appointment and so is Mr. Addams," replies Morgan gesturing to the door, which opens revealing Addams. "I'm afraid that the original program that we were planning for you isn't ready. So, we will have to proceed with our backup plan."

Andriss freezes in place. "What back-up plan?" she asks.

"We had been preparing a series of sublime memories for you in one of our top students," explains Morgan.

"Mona," says Andriss, closing her eyes.

"Just so. But recent events mean that those memories are unavailable."

"So, she escaped," smiles Andriss, turning to face Morgan. "It worked. We got her out."

"Yes," replies Morgan. "A loss of a significant investment for us, not to mention the opportunity for you to escape the terrors of your own memories."

"Somehow, I think I'll live," replies Andriss, "and maybe with a bit more happiness than before because of today."

"No doubt you'll live for quite some time," smiles Morgan. "But I cannot speak to your level of happiness with any confidence."

For Andriss the room seems to chill. She is not a woman given to feeling intimidation, but there is something in Morgan's smile that makes her want to run.

"We prepared another candidate for you," continues Morgan. "These memories are less sublime and more ... how did you put it back when you met with my former colleague? Ah yes, 'a sense of terror so great that it inspires awe.' I'm afraid they won't help you escape your demons, but they will help break that iron will of yours and leave you more pliable."

Andriss collapses into her chair. "You made a child go through appalling things just so you could break me?"

"Yes," replies Morgan. "We had three other top candidates apart from Mona. A boy, who broke too easily. A girl Mona's age who may yet serve other uses. And the youngest, a girl named Kadi in the pod below Mona. Kadi was the best candidate as a backup for you. Our second choice, but still a strong student. Would you like to meet her? She's quite remarkable, especially considering all that she's been through."

"All that you put her through, you mean," accuses Andriss through clenched teeth.

"I suppose I did devise the program," admits Morgan nonchalantly. "It was my strongest piece of work actually. Once we realized that we could implant memories so strong our patients would actually be able to relive an experience again and again in their head ... well it was a revelation. Just imagine, we now have an innovative way to map and implant intense feelings of excitement, happiness, joy, or ecstasy. Or fear. Or terror. Or despair. Any number of emotions really."

Andriss lets herself go limp.

"Why don't you come this way?" prompts Addams as he and Morgan lead Andriss out of the room.

EPILOGUE

Harriet can imagine Mona curling up under her arm as they pull out of the city on a train. Harriet will listen as Mona's breathing grows slower and deeper. She will wait until Mona is fully asleep before pulling out her phone and calling Amelia.

"We're on the train," she'll say. "Please thank your friends for helping get us out of the city."

"I will," Amelia will reply. "Look, don't call me again from that phone. Get another one and call me when you two are safe, okay?"

"Okay," will be all Harriet can manage to say back, knowing that she will be leaving her sister behind.

"I love you. Keep each other safe."

"You stay safe too."

They will sign off. She will destroy her phone. That will be it.

Harriet will pull up the news on the screen by her seat. She won't be surprised to see Andriss giving a news conference. The reporter will chime in saying that the head of one of the largest companies in the western hemisphere is stepping down for health reasons. The news will cut back to the main anchors who give platitudes about Andriss' long and successful career.

"From the death of her father during the war until today, Madam

Andriss has been a leader in the business world. It is not clear who will succeed her at this time," the anchor will finish.

"That's right, but speculation is that it will be someone outside her immediate family," the second anchor will add. "Madam Andriss was not only a titan in the business world, but she was also a major force politically. While she didn't run for office herself, there were rumours that she had significant influence as far up as the Chancellor's inner circle."

Harriet will watch as the footage cuts back to the press conference. Andriss will be sitting with members of her family as one of her top executives gives a polite speech about her career.

Harriet will be surprised to see the aged but formidable Andriss looking weaker, almost broken. She will see Andriss slump slightly in her chair as she stares off into space, seemingly unaware of the cheers and applause around her as the speech ends.

The news will switch over to politics, outlining that the situation with the Eastern Bloc is growing worse. The experts brought on by the report will predict that the Chancellor will order tactical strikes in the next few weeks.

"Speaking of the Chancellor," one of the reporters will say. "He has just appointed two more top aides to his inner circle of advisors. Not much is known about Morgan or Addams, except that they are rumoured to have been directly backed by Madam Andriss for this appointment, lending more credence to the rumours of her ties with the Chancellor's office."

Neither Mona nor Harriet know that this news is waiting for them as they crouch down in the backseat of the car that whisks them from the Company's apartment complex to the public train station. The man driving is tight-lipped and stoic, but he's one of Amelia's friends, so they can trust him.

Soon we'll be on the train, thinks Mona. *Soon we will be headed west, away from the city and the Company.*

The sun hangs low in the sky, painting the clouds red and pink against the grey buildings speeding past.

"We'll come back for Owen?" asks Mona.

"We will," replies Harriet. "As soon as we can."

"He'll be alright until then," says Mona. "They still think he's a plomp, but he's the best cuckoo bee of all."

www.ingramcontent.com/pod-product-compliance
Lightning Source LLC
Chambersburg PA
CBHW070552120726
47909CB00007B/2318